The
Heartbreak
Bakery

The Heartbreak Bakery

A. R. CAPETTA

CANDLEWICK PRESS

Copyright © 2021 by A. R. Capetta

First edition 2021

Library of Congress Catalog Card Number pending
ISBN 978-1-5362-1653-0

21 22 23 24 25 26 LBM 10 9 8 7 6 5 4 3 2 1

Printed in Melrose Park, IL, USA

This book was typeset in Warnock Pro.

Candlewick Press
99 Dover Street
Somerville, Massachusetts 02144

www.candlewick.com

A JUNIOR LIBRARY GUILD SELECTION

Cory
all of the love stories are for you

1

The splintered crack of my egg on the counter sounds like an ending. I raise my hand and tip the runny liquid into the bowl, letting the yolk slip out. It's bright, orange, unbroken. It's beautiful, and I want to keep it that way.

Maybe forever.

But I have to whisk it, and with a few turns of my wrist the batter swallows it up. The yolk disappears like it was never there.

I dump the dry ingredients in with the wet, then check my recipe card for the fourth time. Red velvet. My hands know how to do this. Snap the bowl into place on the stand mixer. Stir on the lowest setting until everything barely swirls together. Don't overmix, or the cake comes out stodgy. I flick the switch at the perfect moment, as the last of the dry, crummy bits dissolve into silk. My hands are good at this. Which is helpful, because the rest of me isn't really here.

I slap butter-flour paste into four round cake pans, then pour batter into each one. It folds on top of itself like a ribbon. This part usually feels like I'm finishing off a present, and the people who eat the cake later will be able to taste that it's a gift I made with them in mind. Even if we're strangers. They'll taste it, and they'll know I want them to be happy.

Baking is magic that way.

But I don't feel like giving presents right now. And I'm not really here because I'm still in her bedroom, wrapped in her towel, shivering as she peers at me without her glasses on and says, "Maybe this isn't working."

Like we're a recipe that isn't coming together right.

"Syd, do you have a minute to take muffins to the front?" Marisol calls from across the kitchen.

She's being delicate with me. Marisol isn't delicate with anything, not even meringues. On a normal day she'd let me know how unacceptable it is that I'm four cakes behind when we're about to open. She'd remind me that I'm *so* young, too young to be a full-time baker, even though she's only a few years older than I am. I do the whole routine in my head. Then I throw my red velvet rounds in the oven.

I grab the muffins, warm and waiting. Drop them in pale wicker baskets, inhaling the comforts of triple ginger, oatmeal and peaches with a brown sugar crumb topping, cherry vanilla strewn with dark chocolate. Each smell hits my nose and burrows into the part of my brain that believes things will be all right. But then I get to the savory breakfast muffins, sharp cheddar and smoky bacon and green onion. Those are W's favorites.

I don't know whether I should put one aside for her. I don't know what she wants anymore.

I head to the front, where Vin is standing at the cash register, settling rolls of change into the little nooks. "Hey, Syd darlin.'" His voice is a dark crackle, his southern accent like a drizzle of honey on top of burnt popcorn. Actually, that sounds good. I start a recipe in my head. Anything to avoid thinking about W.

"Need to talk?" Vin asks, without looking up from the quarters.

"What?"

"Seems like you're holding something in," he says. "That's not good for your constitution."

I look around the bakery. The front room is filled with early morning light and nooks where people can have private conversations. Beyond that is the wooden porch painted in thick rainbow stripes, and wrought iron tables set in a lush, wild garden. Upstairs is a wide-open community space lined in vintage couches and bookshelves stuffed with queer literature. Vin and Alec have done everything they could to make this place safe and comfortable for someone like me. Every day since I found it on a lucky wander through South Austin, that's how I've felt. Safe. Comfortable.

But right now the Proud Muffin's magic isn't working. I feel foul.

And Vin can tell just by looking at me.

"Don't worry," I chirp. This isn't my normal voice. Did I leave it behind at W's? How much of me is missing?

"It's my job to worry about all of you," Vin says. He means it, too. He and Alec treat everyone who work for them like the ever-expanding family that seems standard in Texas. I was born in Illinois. I have parents, a sister, a scattering of aunts, and a single awkward cousin. When I told her I was dating W, she said, and I quote, "That's a bad idea, but okay."

"Syd, you still with me?" Vin asks.

I can't let him think that my feelings about W are shaking my ability to get through a shift. I could lose the best job in the world. No matter how nice Vin and Alec are, I'm the youngest person they've taken on as a baker—and it wasn't a picnic to convince them.

Actually, now that I'm thinking about it, every picnic I've been on has felt like a high-stakes situation involving me making lots of food with the likelihood that the entire outing will be ruined by some unforeseen factor.

Convincing them was *exactly* like a picnic.

"I think I'm hungry," I say, and my voice sounds as least halfway mine. "Didn't get a chance to eat this morning. I'm going to grab a Texas Breakfast if that's okay." Those are the peachy oatmeal muffins.

Vin nods sagely. He does everything sagely. He rides a motorcycle and listens to endless history podcasts and works out constantly. His tanned white skin is heavily tattooed, mostly with poetry running in all directions, and even though he's as friendly as Alec, he hides it better—which all adds up to a burly dad vibe. "Take the register for a few minutes, will you? Gemma's coming in, but I need to run to the bank and get change. Y'all keep going through my singles like this is a strip bakery."

Marisol would have laughed at that. I just nod at Vin, completely mature and trustworthy.

Saturday is our second-busiest morning of the week, and the moment Vin opens the doors customers start flying in. The black coffee flock comes first, mostly teachers from the Texas School for the Deaf down the street. You'd think they would sleep in on the weekend, but people get attached to their morning caffeine rituals. I sign the basics back and forth and pour brown liquid into cups. Gemma comes through the front door just in time for the morning muffin rush. She throws her *I'm a Proud Muffin* tank top over a basic black one. Her box braids swing and her track shorts shimmer as she moves at high speed, making sure the espresso machine is always gleaming and ready to go.

"Can you stay up front until Vin gets back?" she asks.

I hesitate for just a second. "Sure." She doesn't need to know how behind I am in the kitchen.

I make myself look busy, keep my head down, but some of our regulars aren't deterred by things like body language and how many cakes I still have to pop out before noon. They're going to make small talk at any cost.

Jessalee, one of our day-old-pastry hunters, pushes through the basket of rejects for the least squished croissant. "Syd! I haven't seen you out here in weeks!"

"Baking, baking, baking," I say.

"Words, words, words!" she responds brightly. She's always writing on the porch.

Jessalee's youngish, but she wears boxy vintage dresses and lace slips, as if her entire life is a rehearsal for being an old lady. Even her hair, which she dyes Easter-egg pastels, has a throwback feel to it. Today it's the color of a blueberry, pieces flying out of her bun as she holds up evidence of victory: a perfectly wrapped almond croissant. "How are you, sweetie?" she asks, flushed with the rare find.

"I'm fine," I say, testing the words on my tongue. They're not as bitter as I thought they would be. Maybe I *am* fine. W and I had a fight. A marathon fight. Our first real one. But couples do that, right?

Maybe this makes us *more* of a couple than we were before.

Jessalee reverently sets the almond croissant on the counter as I ring up her usual latte, which Gemma is already making, head down, looking at anything but Jessalee.

"How is W?" Jessalee asks with the delighted smile of a stranger who knows exactly one personal thing about you.

"W is good," I say. "I think she's great, actually." That was one of the main points in our fight. I think she's great, and she thinks I like having a girlfriend too much to notice that sometimes she isn't.

"That pretty girl of yours coming around today?" Mr. Trujillo asks, nosing in with his large coffee. I pour the thinnest trickle of almond milk into his cup, even though I know he likes more.

I have no idea what W is doing. Where she's going, what piece of her day she's delighted about or dreading. This is the first time in a very long time that I don't know every little detail.

The door swings open. It's Vin with a black zippered bag from the bank down the street. He looks off, like the heat is getting to him. I've never seen that happen before, even when the temperature slides up past 110 degrees, creeping toward the certain doom of 120. "Syd, get to the kitchen," he says. "Give me a special to write on the board, get everyone out here excited."

I give an oversized nod, which turns out to be a good way to keep tears inside someone's face.

"Brownies," I say. "I'm making brownies."

Vin doesn't show any surprise, just chalks Syd's Unexpected Brownies on the specials board and sets the price at two-fifty.

Brownies are simpler than what I usually go for. They require three things: a single bowl, a sturdy spoon, and a dedication to dark chocolate. Brownies are also W's favorite. I'll set one aside and bring it to her later. She'll see it, take a single bite, and everything will melt back to okay.

"Are those red velvets going to be finished soon?" Marisol asks the second I set foot in the kitchen.

"Damn."

I forgot them while I was up front. Marisol pulled the rounds out of the oven for me, but I have to finish off those cakes before I start anything new. Even though they're a little warm to frost, I rush through the steps. Crumb coat first. A thicker layer of cream cheese frosting with the offset spatula, one generous swipe at a time. I pipe a shaky *Happy Anniversary Bob and Barb* and squish a few half-hearted roses along the border. It looks like a lie, like the cake knows that I didn't want Bob and Barb to be happy until I know that W and I can be happy, too.

"Done," I shout.

Then I rattle around the kitchen, gathering what I need for brownies, setting some ingredients in my favorite mixing bowl and nestling the others along my arm. This feels better already. This is baking for *me*, not Bob and Barb or the regulars. This is baking because my hands are twitching and my heart is raw and I need to get out of my head, even if it's just until the timer goes off.

The second I dip my measuring cup into the flour, there's a knock at the back door.

"Harley," Marisol announces while boxing up her cakes. She slides cardboard panels together, sharp and exact.

"Right," I mutter. "Of course."

I always answer the door for Harley.

I settle my brownie makings on one of the long wooden tables and hurry for the back door. For the first time, I wonder if I look like someone who's been fighting with their girlfriend.

How blotchy is my face? How curdled is my expression?

As soon as the door opens, I check the pin on Harley's bag: he.

I look down at my feet. Harley's sneakers dance lightly, back and forth. It feels like we're at a party and my smile forgot to show up.

"Here for deliveries," he finally says, twisting the front lock of his hair. He's always roughing up his reddish-brown curls to revive them after they've been smashed down under a bike helmet. Harley is a single inch taller than me, with brown eyes that I can clock for their exact chocolate content. Sixty percent. Semisweet.

"You're always here for deliveries," I say.

"You don't know," he says with an elaborate shrug. "Someday I might be here for a completely different reason."

On most mornings Harley takes the cardboard boxes out of my arms, talks to me in the alley for two to five minutes while balancing the weight on his bike baskets, and then takes off. Today I haven't brought the boxes to the door, so he follows me inside and I point out where everything is stacked. Then I go back to my brownies, and Harley keeps following. He leans over the baking table as I spread out my ingredients.

"W and I got into an argument," I say without Harley even asking. I've spent hours avoiding the truth, stepping around it. Now I'm pouring sugar and telling the cute bike delivery person.

The weird part is, Harley already knows more than a little

about my relationship with W. Not that I go out of my way to tell him about my personal life, just that it's easy to talk to someone you see for two to five minutes at a time.

"Was it a big fight?" he asks.

I dump the sugar.

"How long did it last?"

I poke at the sugar with my wooden spoon. I won't add it to the batter until the chocolate melts.

"Hours."

"How many?"

"Eight?" That math does not make me feel better. Math has always been on my side in this relationship. W and I have been together for almost four years. We've had zero fights—until yesterday. We've kissed thousands of times. We've been each other's dates at twelve school dances and two weddings. We've named our future kids, then changed the names three times.

"What did you fight about?" Harley asks.

"Nothing. Everything." I can't remember how it started. It kept stretching and taking up more of the night, and by the time I tried to trace the whole thing back to an origin point, it was lost in a haze of held-back tears.

"How did it end?" Harley asks.

"I had to leave for work."

"Huh."

Harley drums his fingers on the wooden tabletop. Long fingers, blunt nails. "*Where* did you fight for eight hours?"

Does that matter? "It started at the Thai place on South First, you know the one with the great patio?" Harley nods. "They have those long tables that you share with other people. They call them community tables, although I've seriously never seen anyone spontaneously become best friends at a restaurant just because they were squished together like that. Anyway, W and I were sort of half fighting over our food and half pretending it wasn't happening so the people on a first date next to us wouldn't notice." I'd felt like a bad representative of coupledom. "W's parents went on a last-minute business trip and my parents thought some of our other friends were there, which they were at the beginning of the night, but by the time we went out to dinner it was just us so we decided to go back to her place—"

"Full parental workaround," he says. "Got it."

"And the fight kept going, but then we . . ." I make a sort of rolling motion with my spoon.

"You spooned."

"We had sex."

Harley's eyes go a little wild, like I really threw him off the scent with the whole spoon thing. "Ohhh."

"I thought everything was better, but it wasn't, and by the time it got really bad, we were in the shower. We stayed there until the water got cold and we had to turn it off, but we weren't done fighting so we just stood there wet *and* cold."

"She broke up with you in the shower?" Harley shaves his voice down to a whisper. "*After* sex?" His current level of eyebrow intensity makes him look so worried that I want to hug him. Then I remember that *I'm* the one with the problem. "Please tell me it wasn't your first time," he adds.

"Fighting?"

Harley squints at me. "No. Your first *tiiiiiime*."

"Oh." I check to make sure nobody else is paying attention, then shake my head. "We didn't *break up*, though. We fought."

Harley blows out a dramatic breath, and Marisol shoots us both a look over her shoulder. Harley and I inch a little closer to each other. "What you described doesn't sound like a fight."

"What does it sound like?"

He winces, looking sincerely uncomfortable with what he's about to say. "Being dumped."

"Oh," I say, grabbing the baking chocolate, hacking into the bar. "Oh. Okay. And you're sure about this, why?"

"Because I've been dumped," Harley says apologetically. "I know what it looks, feels, walks, and talks like."

"Have you ever been told 'maybe this isn't working'?" I ask without looking up from my knifework. "As part of the dumping process?"

"Oh, sure. If you're looking for a list of generic ingredients, that's the flour."

I laugh, but it doesn't sound like laughing; it sounds like chocolate snapping into pieces.

"You're telling me I didn't just get broken up with, I got the grocery store *box mix* equivalent of being broken up with."

"Did you just carve a *W* into that chocolate?" Harley asks.

I look down and there it is: a big, sharp *W*. I don't remember doing that.

Marisol comes over, bumping my hip with hers, putting an arm around my shoulder. "Harley, can you come back after your first round of drop-offs? We got behind on some orders this morning."

"Sure." He flicks a worried glance at me as he backs away. Then he spins and starts loading his arm with cake boxes.

Marisol squeezes me to her side. "Let's bake," she whispers, and I can't tell if this is a threat or a really nice suggestion.

Marisol is one of the best bakers in all of Austin. She's also the Proud Muffin's resident heartthrob. A steady stream of her significant and not-so-significant others hangs around, hoping to see her stride out of the kitchen in her white tank top, dark hair slicked back, arms strong from carrying enormous bricks of butter. Marisol has probably endured a dozen relationships ending while we've worked together, and I've never once seen her break. Maybe I should ask her for advice.

No. No.

I'm not breaking.

W and I aren't broken.

I shrug away from Marisol. She smells like cinnamon and hair wax and it lingers in a weirdly comforting way. "Almost done with the special," I say through a thick, pre-crying throat. "I'll get the rest of the cakes and you do lunch rolls, okay?"

Marisol nods.

Harley peeks around the tower of cake boxes in his arms and gives me a quick, bright "See you tomorrow!"

Tomorrow is Sunday. W and I have a standing date to split an eggs Benedict at Counter Café after my early shift. Then we usually walk down to the Alamo Drafthouse and cram two movies into the hottest part of the day, drinking brown sugar lemonade, kissing every time a character makes a dramatic exit. Her lips tart and sugary. Her hands cold from clutching the glass.

I have brownies to make, but I can't go another minute without knowing. I pull my absolutely-banned-from-the-kitchen phone out of my back pocket.

Did we just break up?

W is quick to respond if she's anywhere near her phone. So when she doesn't, I know she's busy, or she's angry. Either of those is okay. She's cooling off; she'll text me back when she's ready to talk.

I get back to my brownies, whisking the thin batter. Just as I'm about to slide them in the oven, I hear a commotion in the front. This sort of minor celebration happens anytime someone we all know enters the bakery.

I get the sweaty cold sense that I know *exactly* who walked in.

Her lemony voice cuts through everything. That same voice found me at a party in eighth grade, when I was new in Austin and she was newly out. She asked if I wanted to skip the game of spin the bottle and just kiss. I said yes. I waited an excruciating two days until homeroom on Monday and asked her out, and she said yes. By the end of that first date, she asked me if I wanted to skip the part where we weren't sure about each other and just be a couple. I said yes. There's hope in my throat, swelling until I can't breathe around it.

"Is Syd here?" W asks.

Gemma yells, "Syd!" without coming back.

It feels like a long walk from the kitchen to the front counter.

The last time I saw her, she was as wrecked and naked as I was. Now W is wearing a low-cut black T-shirt, her perfectly distressed jeans, and the black cowboy boots with the turquoise details. It's early spring, but her freckles are already out in force. Her lips are a straight line, betraying nothing. I can't see her eyes. Her sunglasses are firmly on, even though she's inside.

I wish I could go back to not knowing the contents of her day.

"I can't believe you had to ask me that," she says, skipping right over any kind of greeting. But W isn't whispering, and I take that as a good sign. Nothing we're saying is a secret. We're two people who love each other, two people who had an argument and are now talking in normal voices.

"Ask . . . what?" Like there's any other question in the world right now.

W looks around as though she's memorizing the Proud Muffin. Like she has to re-create this place from scratch later.

That's when I realize she's leaving.

Everything slows down to syrup.

"We broke up." She pauses, then says it slightly louder. "We're not together, Syd."

She turns away from me, giving Gemma a hug over the counter. They know each other. They're friends. W is friends with everyone, but she's *with* me. At least, she was until a few hours ago. Now she's pointing at the basket filled with savory muffins, the ones that she likes to douse in hot sauce until she can barely taste anything.

"I'll take these to go." She looks right at me and says, "I don't think I'll be back for a while."

Breakup Brownies

~~~~ INGREDIENTS ~~~~

4 oz unsweetened chocolate, broken up (I mean,
it's right there, how did I not see this coming?)

½ cup (1 stick) butter

1 cup granulated sugar

2 large eggs

1 tsp vanilla extract

½ tsp sea salt

2/3 cup all-purpose flour

1 cup dried cherries

Powdered sugar for decorating

~~~~ DIRECTIONS ~~~~

Preheat the oven to 350 degrees. Butter your pan before
starting. This works best in an 8 x 8 pan for a single
batch, though you can double and use a 9 x 13 pan if
you've been left at the altar or something.

Carve the name of your ex into the chocolate.

In a microwave, melt the butter and chocolate in a large bowl in 30-second intervals, stirring between each. If your breakup has driven you to a tiny cabin on a mountaintop or somewhere equally dramatic where there's no microwave, you can do this step in a double boiler, or fake one with a small metal bowl over a simmering pot of water, stirring until the butter and chocolate mixture is smooth.

Let the melted chocolate mixture cool slightly. Whisk in the sugar, then the eggs one at a time, the vanilla, and salt. Toss the cherries lightly in the flour before folding them both in. This coats them so they don't all sink to the bottom when you bake. Stir all the ingredients until the moment when the white disappears and everything becomes the same gooey dark brown: be careful not to overmix.

Pour the batter into the prepared pan, and spread the top until even, remembering when your relationship looked shiny and unbroken just like this. It's a good thing that your fingers are covered in brownie goo or you might be tempted to text your ex again.

Don't.

Bake for 25 to 30 minutes.

Test for doneness with a toothpick, fork, or cake tester. It should come out JUST clean. Let cool slightly. Slice the brownies generously. Cut a heart into a sheet of parchment paper and sift powdered sugar over the cut-out shape on top of each brownie, creating a series of perfect hearts.

Misery loves to look pretty.

2

You know what's not pretty?

Standing in your first gay bar alone, surrounded by sweaty darkness and lasers and the pushy bass of dance music even though no one is dancing.

A handful of Twizzler-thin boys in muscle tees are circled up, laughing at jokes I can't hear. Pretty femmes are grouped together at the bar, pulling up hair and pushing down necklines, touching the skin where each other's crop tops end, while they down the sugary fake cocktails that this place serves for its eighteen-and-over night. I turned seventeen in January, but it's not that hard to get in when your bakery caters events all over the city and you're not actually trying to drink. My neon green "don't give this one alcohol" bracelet feels like a beacon in the sweaty darkness of the oldest gay bar in Austin.

I've never been here before. I'm not even remotely sure that this was a good idea. But I needed to spend my first night without W somewhere other than at home, stretched out on the floor, listening to the banshee wail of her favorite indie bands and thinking about what to bake next.

It felt good to pour my feelings in those brownies and then walk away.

This place isn't what I expected, though. I don't want to break it to anyone, but it looks like a regular bar for straight people and maybe that one closeted uncle. The space is split down the middle: a sports-focused area with the TVs set to football—European, not American—on one side, and an ancient black-painted dance floor on the other. Even the music is mostly straight artists with a little Kesha thrown in for good measure.

I ease into the beat of the first Beyoncé song that comes on, thinking I'll be a magnet for everyone else who needed to be out tonight, everybody young and queer and freshly single, so fresh we can still taste our breakups.

But I'm out here alone, dancing to "Crazy in Love," trying to make it look like this solo act is what I wanted to do. I'm a solid backup dancer, but W is incredible, her body fused to the beat. Now that the spotlight is on me, I keep swiveling things, hoping for some kind of miracle.

The beat changes, the lights get more dramatic, and I

think the main event must be starting. A single twenty-ish guy comes out of a back room wearing a G-string. Some wilted old Madonna starts up, and he struts out onto a platform and starts dancing without a whiff of enthusiasm.

"Let's turn this party up to eleven!" shouts a bouncy DJ voice.

I try to shuffle off the dance floor, but the voice bursts out of the speakers again, coming at me from everywhere. "Don't stop now! We're just heating up!" I freeze abruptly, afraid to get called out again, like I'm being sent to the Big Gay Principal's office. G-string guy notices me and looks down with understanding, even pity.

I try to smile, but my face is broken.

"You okay, honey?" he shouts.

Even this half-hearted, ninety-percent naked dancer feels bad for me.

I run to a dark crevice of the room. I'm ready to call this a horrible time and go home, when my phone vibrates in my pocket. I check it, thinking maybe it's my sister, trying to make up for how unhelpful she was a few hours ago.

It's Marisol. Which is weird. She's never talked to me outside of work.

Harley left a # in case you need to talk to someone

I'm about to thank her and maybe ask if she wants to hang out next weekend, because I can't ever do this again.

Don't text back I'm on a date

I add Harley's number to my phone, saving it with an

exclamation point. *Harley!* Usually I would let it sit in my phone for weeks before I sent an exploratory text, but tonight I'm doing new things. I let my hands take the lead, the way I do when I'm baking. I let them type whatever they want.

Help I'm stranded in a gay disaster

Harley texts back half a song later.

Prepared to rubberneck

In less than twenty minutes, Harley bounds into the bar, smiling so big that it makes up for the smiles I messed up earlier. Those red-brown curls are shining from a recent shower—no sign of helmet hair tonight. As soon as Harley's close enough, I look for the omnipresent bag and Harley's pronoun pin: they.

"Thanks for coming!" I shout over the music.

"I never turn down a gay disaster," they shout back, and I swear it's flirty, and I swear I didn't realize we were flirting until this moment.

We're standing close together. In the dark. In a place I invited them to, right after I told them about my relationship probably ending.

"Are you okay?" Harley asks.

"Today has been a lot," I admit.

"Did you and W talk?" they ask, peering into the laser-strewn darkness like she might be hiding somewhere.

"You were right." My neck feels hot. Not as hot as a stack of ovens in a Texas spring, but close. "She broke up with me."

"So we're going to dance it out?" Harley asks. They're wearing artfully loose jeans, a fitted T-shirt. I feel certain their finger-combed waves of hair would do all kinds of adorable things while they dance.

"Already tried that," I shout. "It's hopeless."

Harley shoves their hands in their pockets and leans forward to make sure the words reach me. "It's not you. This music is stale!"

As if to prove them right, a song comes on that I don't think I've heard since elementary school. It's dully electronic, the lyrics all about heartbreak. About being bulletproof the next time it comes around. The music video glares at us from three different TVs, and I get caught up in how androgynous the singer is, mesmerized by a broad, freckled face and lean body. I used to think I should look like that. I used to be confused every single time I stared at the mirror and what I saw screamed back *girl*.

I'm used to the way I look now, the hips I can't hide no matter what pants I wear, the broad waist and the small feet, the combination of round cheeks and rough jaw. For a long time, I thought my body should be different. Now I'm pretty sure that no particular body would make sense to me all of the time. That's one of the reasons I like dancing, or baking, or anything where I'm inundated by what I'm doing, too busy *feeling* to feel wrong.

"Wait," Harley says, closer to my ear than before, close enough that they don't have to shout. "Something's happening."

The guy in the G-string has a friend now, wearing an equally tiny string and nothing else all the way up to his head. "Is that . . . a baseball cap?"

"A bright purple one," Harley confirms. "Do you think he came straight from a game?"

"Of what?" I ask. "Sexball?"

Harley gives a few shy blinks. They try not to smile. But their dimples are winning.

"I'm in love with this look." I wave at the leather-and-cap combo. "It's like two ingredients that shouldn't work together, but they do."

It's more than that, though. He's dancing. *Really* dancing, with brazen moves and zero self-awareness, to a song nobody's thought about for ten years. He fills up the entire platform, arms wild and lunge-steps shameless. The singer in the video sounds so bored with the idea of becoming bulletproof, eyes sad like they already know it isn't going to work. But this guy dances like he believes it. We hit the chorus, and he does the shopping cart. It's glorious. He's buying *everything*.

"He owns this song!" Harley shouts.

"He *is* this song."

"I'd say we should join him, but I think we have to let him have this one."

"Tonight belongs to Red," I agree.

His enthusiasm must be contagious, though, because Harley and I look at each other and a bolt of energy passes between us. Five minutes ago I felt ready to end the night, but now it seems like it's just starting. Grabbing Harley's hand, I sprint out of the bar before the DJ can yell at us.

Sixth Street is what a bloodstream must look like during a sugar rush. On weekend nights they close it off to cars, because there are too many people out partying. Harley and I try to walk next to each other, but the sidewalk gets choked up. They fall behind, their fingertips still linked with mine. I don't know where we're going, but I'm not giving up. W can break up with me, but she can't make me miserable.

Not unless I let her.

I walk confidently past block after block of restaurants and bars. Above us the sharp teeth of high-rises chew up the sky. Greenery all around us and live music leaking from every doorway keep Austin from feeling like every other inter-changeable city.

Besides, this is just downtown.

We walk south, toward the lake, and even though I can't see it, I can feel it there, a natural barrier separating us from South Austin, where I live, where I work, where most of my life takes place. W lives downtown. She's the reason I came here all the time, browsing at BookPeople while I waited for her to meet me, driving down to Mozart's on the water and sitting under trees wrapped in white string lights while we clutched our hot chocolates in Austin's never-truly-winter weather. I wonder how often I'll cross the bridges now that I know she's not waiting on the other side.

"I picked the last place," I say. "Where should we go now?"

"Wherever you feel better," Harley says.

And maybe just by saying that they've summoned it, but the next window we pass is a popsicle shop. The entire wall facing the street is made of windows. We can see the toppings sorted into a rainbow of options, the menu plastered with sweet, icy suggestions. It might be getting late, but that doesn't mean it's getting any colder. It's definitely still hot enough to want one.

"I don't know this place," Harley says.

"Neither do I. That's what makes it an adventure."

There are new places in Austin all the time. Some days it feels like the city won't stop to catch its breath, like whenever you look up, it's trampled something you love.

Tonight, I'm glad this is here.

Tonight, I need new.

"Do you think the employees wear G-strings?" Harley asks. "You set a high bar for the evening."

I push their shoulder and laugh.

We get coconut dipped in chocolate, and half-dipped strawberry, and pineapple with coconut flakes, and banana with a shaggy coat of sprinkles. One popsicle for each of our hands. Harley bumps the door open with their back, then spins out into the night. I follow, and in the single moment it takes me to catch up, everything that felt complicated in the bar is simple again. I have sweet things and a slight breeze, and someone to share them with.

We walk the last block to the lake. It's down a slope from where we're standing, so we're not on the bank but above the water, looking across the trio of flat bridges that lead to South Austin. It's calmer there, and the lights look warm. I try to pick out the Proud Muffin.

"Want to walk over?" Harley asks.

"Maybe just halfway."

It takes longer than I think it will. We stop and stare out at the dark ripples and get really invested in our popsicles. I want a bite of the strawberry one, so I sort of dive for it, and Harley holds it out.

I lean in and bite. It tastes good, with patches of real strawberry. And then this feels weird, because it's how I would share with W. And then it feels weirder, because her family's condo is only a few blocks from the bridge, and all I can think about is her looking down and seeing me share dessert with Harley the day after we broke up. Technically, it's the same day.

I swallow and retreat a few steps.

"How did you end up in that bar?" Harley asks.

"It's my sister's fault."

"Your sister brought you to a gay bar and then ditched you?"

"Well . . . no."

Harley laughs and then waits, like they did at the bakery. Like they're making room for me to say more.

"My sister Tess is at Northwestern," I say, sticking to my pineapple popsicle. It's good, but not as good as the strawberry. "I didn't want to tell my parents about W yet. They kind of love her. I thought calling my sister would be like . . ."

"A warm-up?" Harley offers.

"When I told her what happened, Tess said that it sounds rough, because I don't really have a life without W."

Harley winces. "I'm glad my siblings are little. They just accidentally pee on me and hit me with foam swords." I imagine Harley surrounded by tiny people, clinging to their arms and legs, demanding snacks.

I have to stop. It's way too sweet.

"I wanted to prove that I could go out and have fun," I say. But when you move somewhere and find an amazing girlfriend right away, all of your memories of that place have the person baked right in. "I just . . . needed somewhere W and I have never been together."

Harley nods, like this makes complete sense.

"Was she your first girlfriend?" they ask.

"Yeah."

We're still close to the intensity of downtown, but here above the water, the night is so quiet.

"And . . . did W call you her girlfriend?"

It takes me a second to see the whole question Harley's asking. "W thought it was funny that I like to bake. Most people think cupcakes and kitchens are girly, but I'll throw on a frilly apron over cut-offs and boots and shave my head like it's no big deal. She called me her *Bold Baker Girl*." I remember the feel of her playing a hand over my freshly shaved scalp, and I shiver, even though the night's as warm as her skin. "After a while, I told her I'm not a girl. At least, not most of the time."

I look down at the lake. It's dark but covered in shine, the city lights trembling on its surface. During the day, the water is a pretty but boring blue, covered in paddleboards and ringed by joggers. Right now, it feels like we're the only ones who know about it. Like it's a huge secret, right in the middle of everything.

"What are you most of the time?" Harley asks.

"Agender."

That word takes a lot to say out loud. I reward myself with the rest of the banana popsicle.

"Got it. And W . . . got that?"

"It didn't seem to bother her." It still took me six months to work up to saying it out loud to a single person, and when W broke up with me, it felt like I lost that moment of bravery as much as I lost her.

Everyone at school knows I'm queer. My family knows. I know how lucky I am that I was never scared to say it out loud. I don't know why it's harder to tell people that I don't feel attached to a specific gender. That some days wearing a femme outfit or acting a masc way feels nice, but neither of those things is *me*.

Harley leans with their back on the stone railing. "I've been thinking." They take their time with the last bite of coconut. "You and W were together for a long time, right? Don't they say that you need to be sad for at least as many months as you dated the person, in years?"

Four miserable months?

I can't feel the way that I felt today for *four months*.

"Who is *they*?" I ask, ready to fight whoever came up with that rule. "Who says that?"

Harley shrugs the casually stubborn shrug of someone who thinks they're right. "People who research relationships. Love scientists?"

"Love isn't science," I push back. "The chemistry matters,

that makes sense, but that's where it starts, not where it ends. Baking is like that. It's not just a predictable set of reactions. It's—"

"It's what?" Harley asks with a quirk of the lips that feels like a dare. They lean one elbow against the railing, cross their boots at the ankle.

I don't talk about this, but then again, I don't talk about *any* of the things I just told Harley. I wouldn't have done it a week ago, and a week from now I might talk myself out of it, but tonight I have this compulsion to tell Harley how I feel about baking, and therefore about love.

"It's magic."

I keep thinking about the brownies I made. How they were more than a simple dessert. They were everything I felt as W broke up with me.

"Magic . . ." Harley echoes. I can't tell if they believe me, if they're not sure, if they're silently judging me.

Then Harley smiles again. It's not the broad grin from when they showed up at the bar. It's the smile of someone who's been let in on a secret. They hold out the last bite of the perfect strawberry popsicle, and I dip my head for it.

I don't care if W's watching from somewhere above us.

This tastes too good to pass up.

A Bad Night

~~~~~ INGREDIENTS ~~~~~

1 breakup, fresh if you can get it

4 popsicles, eaten earlier in a fit of trying to forget her

1 sister who won't text you back
because college is so much fun

46 neighbors at a house party next door, most of
whom seem to be making out near your window

2 assignments you have to finish before Monday because
you spent all your homework time on breaking up

$1/10$ of your normal confidence

A pinch of parental worry

10,000,000,000 frantic phone checks to see if your ex
texted you (she didn't) to say she wants you back (she
doesn't), which you definitely know, and have basically
come to accept, so why are you still checking your phone?

1 possible new crush at the worst possible moment

Heat the world to 94 degrees.

Add the popsicles to your stomach. Let sit.

Get home late and watch your parents react. Mine skulk around in suspicious silence. Your flavors will vary.

Shut yourself in your room, shut your ex out of your mind, shut off your phone.

Definitely do not look to see if she's gone on social media to post anything cryptic, or sad, or—worst-case scenario—sexy.

After you've checked, shower it off. Wrench the water to a dead stop when you remember how much you hate showers now.

Armor yourself in your comfiest pajamas and climb into bed. Realize that the post-sugar misery pounding inside your head is being echoed by the pulse of a party next door.

Shut your window.

Get too sweaty! Turn up the AC!

Get too cold. Open your window to the sweet smell of lemon blossoms and the less sweet sound of people making out in the alley behind your house.

Slip back in time, to every party you spent in the darkest corner, the backyard shadows, the guest room with the door gently shut. Relive every middle-of-the-night wonder, every discovery in the dark, all those times you felt too good for words.

Wonder: *If that doesn't work, what does?*

Think about your new crush. Try to stop immediately, but once you've poured in an ingredient, you can't unpour it. It's in the mix now, swirling around. Think about your new crush's secret smile. Their eagerness to talk.

Their hands.

Decide that since you're not sleeping, you might as well do some homework. Fall asleep with your face in the vagina of a textbook.

Wake up the next day.

No, really.

Your alarm is ringing.

3

Most people think you can't have a bad hair day with a shaved head, but my porcupine of frizz and I are here to tell you they are wrong. Fortunately, there's no one around to see me when I slump into the back door of the Proud Muffin. I flip on the kitchen lights, one row of switches at a time. Oil shines on the wooden worktops. The steel of the great big mixing bowls glows, pristine. Rows of darker cake pans wait to be filled.

The bakery counter is beautiful, the porch is bright, the garden welcomes everyone, and the community room upstairs gives them a big queer hug, but this is the heart of the Proud Muffin. A kitchen that gets wrecked every day, and by morning looks perfect and untouched.

Why doesn't my heart feel like that?

I knot my apron with thick, stupid fingers. I thought I would be better today. I thought this would get easier, not harder.

I check the tags for special orders. Not that many, which is normal for Sundays, just a few basic birthday cakes. I line up everything I need to whip through these and get back on Marisol's good side—whichever of her sharply shaved sides that happens to be today—and show Vin and Alec that I'm not the kind of teenager who can be taken down by something as obvious as a broken heart.

But before I start baking, I check on my brownies.

The counter staff hasn't arrived yet, and I keep the front lights dim. The baked goods that keep for more than a day— the cakes and pies and cobblers—are lined up and mummified in plastic wrap. The plate of brownies is exactly where I left it, barely dented by the customers yesterday afternoon. There were twelve of them. There are ten left. As I unwrap the brownies, the scent of midnight-dark chocolate nudges me to the past, a place where I really don't want to go.

But I'm already back at the first time I made her brownies. We made it through three whole months of dating before I asked if I could bake for her. Somehow that felt more official than saying the word *girlfriend*. Somehow that was a bigger deal than telling my parents I was going on a date and letting them take a thousand pictures like it was prom, even though I was wearing chewed-up jeans and W was trying to hide a tiny halter top under her jacket.

A dozen dates after that first one, I sat her down in my

living room and put on a movie—*Jane Eyre*, the good version with Ruth Wilson—before I went to the kitchen and got to work. W shouted the plot at me.

"Jane's got a little friend who is definitely into her!"

"Oh no, Jane's friend is dead!"

"Jane got older and now her eyebrow game is amazing!"

In between those shouts, she asked for regular baking updates.

"That ruins the magic," I said. Secretly, I was worried that nothing would get baked with W looking at me. Her stare had the power to unbalance everything. It could have distracted me into scorching an entire pan of brownies.

"Is the magic happening now?" she called in a sharp, teasing voice.

I didn't answer. I just kept stirring, my wooden spoon tireless until the melted chocolate was one glossy puddle.

"Now?" she asked.

When I finally brought out a single brownie on a plate, W smiled at me in a way that could have lit up the countryside in a blackout storm. She accepted the plate as if I'd offered her something precious. The brownie had that perfect just-slightly-underbaked ooze in the center, with a crackle on top. It smelled like the best chocolate I could afford, like tart cherries and good life choices.

These brownies smell like that, too, but they're not the same.

The lights snap on—someone's here. Probably Gemma.

I leave a note for the counter staff.

Push the brownies!

These aren't I'm-falling-in-love-with-you brownies. These are it's-over-and-I-don't-know-what-comes-next brownies. It helped to pour that feeling into a container that could hold it. Now I want them gone.

I go back to the kitchen, and I bake and I bake and I bake. I bake her out of my body, I bake her out of my hands.

I bake until my heart is an empty kitchen, ready to be filled with sugar and heat. Ready to get messed up all over again.

When I finally look up from my work, Vin and Alec are both in the kitchen—a rare sight. Vin runs the front in the morning and otherwise lives in the office. Alec takes the afternoon and evening shifts and hosts the events in the community space, talking to everyone who comes through the door, making them feel seen—or safely ignored. For a moment I think my bosses are grabbing late breakfast and coffee together, being cute in a way that might hurt my stomach post-breakup but, ultimately, is good for my health. Whenever I see a queer couple doing even the simplest things, like kissing or holding hands or existing, I swear I get stronger.

But Alec and Vin aren't sharing a café breve, their fingers curled around the same cup. Vin is leaning forward against a worktable, his hearty forearms showing all the way to the elbow, tattooed poetry spilling. Alec, who is tall and trim and has a Professor of Baking look, leans back with his arms crossed. His apron always seems like he unfolded it fresh from the laundry, and under it his slacks and dress shoes are just as sharp. He keeps pinching his nose just below his perfectly round tortoiseshell glasses. Their voices are low but undeniably clipped.

This is not impromptu-breakfast-date body language.

Marisol hits my shoulder with hers on her way across the kitchen. "Grab some eggs for me?"

"What?" I ask. "You have, like, a gross of eggs right—"

Marisol stares at me with the force of a thousand managers.

"Right."

"I'll get the butter," she adds, like this is the continuation of a talk we've been having and not some weird improv we're doing to get away from Vin and Alec, and starts toward the walk-in. Are we giving them space? Are we running away?

I trail behind her, my body flooding with memories of my fight with W. When I pull the latch and close the door, they all crash down. It's bitterly cold in here. As cold as the aftermath of a bad shower.

"Marisol, I can't hang out in a big freezer," I say, shivering.

"Do you have a medical condition?" she asks, bracing one foot against an upturned, empty crate.

"No," I admit.

"Then sit down and pretend you're in Canada."

I pull up another crate and sit with my knees spread wide. I have a good view of my legs mottling with the sudden cold. Marisol goes to work, making sure the cartons of cream are sorted by their expiration dates, acting like that's what she actually came in here to do.

Knowing that Vin and Alec are fighting makes it impossible for me to focus on anything else. It's like seeing your parents fight, but more upsetting because they're *everybody's* parents.

Maybe if we went back out there, they'd stop. "Are we just supposed to stay here until they're done talking?" I ask. "I don't have a timer on the lemon bars, and they have to come out soon."

"Your lemon bars don't exist without Vin and Alec," Marisol says.

She's not wrong. Vin and Alec *are* the Proud Muffin. Alec likes to say that they opened a bakery because gay marriage wasn't legal in Texas ten years ago and they needed a couples' activity—but that joke is just the shiny finish he puts on the truth. Toxically masculine and homophobic kitchens had already exhausted Alec by the time he met Vin, whose early jobs were in advocacy and activism. Plus, he really likes muffins. They put absolutely every dollar and dream they had into opening this place; now dozens of groups meet in the community space. Regular free drop-offs are made to queer-friendly homeless shelters in the area. And the bakery hosts at least one transiversary a week, cake on the house. Marisol had her first when she still worked the front counter—she made her own cake, of course. And when the Defense of Marriage Act was overturned by the Supreme Court, the very next day Vin and Alec had their wedding in the bakery. Sometimes I think

I'm the only person in South Austin who wasn't there, because I was still in Illinois. Vin told me about it the first time I came to the Proud Muffin, when he caught me running my fingers along a particularly wobbly stripe on the rainbow porch and explained that some of the wedding guests painted under the influence of too much sugar and champagne. The afterparty lasted all week, because people kept showing up to celebrate. Queer folks and trans folks and allies, neighbors and family and friends. If the Proud Muffin is an institution, so are Vin and Alec.

Outside of the walk-in, their voices heat like a suddenly jacked-up oven.

Cracking the door, I give myself a stripe to watch. Vin walks into it, scrubbing his hands over his face like he's trying to wash off a layer of frustration. "You're acting like I'm serious about this."

Alec's sigh could lift a boulder—and set it back down on Vin's big toe. "If you weren't, you would have brought it up weeks ago. Instead, you chose to *hoard* this information. Turn it from a harmless oh-a-funny-thing-happened-today into a big old secret."

"Oh, shit," I mutter.

Suddenly, Marisol is behind me, her hand on my back, her head stacked over mine. All these months of trying to act mature enough to impress her, and I've dragged her down to my level.

"When were you going to bring up the fact that you're

being *wooed*?" Alec asks, marching into view. He takes a bite of something that he's holding in one hand, half-wrapped in a napkin.

"It didn't seem important," Vin growls out. "I'm not interested, and I already told you . . ."

Shit.

Shit, shit, shit.

Vin is being *wooed* by somebody? Who *isn't* Alec? People were always trying to flirt with W, but she never really flirted back. "Just because I'm queer and open to dating all sorts of people doesn't mean I'm going to bat my eyelashes at everyone who walks by," she said on several occasions.

I can be more susceptible. I'll drop my voice a full octave if someone gives me a compliment, and fairly regularly I would stare at a cute waitperson or actor or stranger walking their dog in a way that made W lace her arm through mine and say, "Oh, so you noticed Cutie McCutePants."

"Their pants *are* cute," I would admit.

"You can dream about getting into them, but you're coming home to these," she would say, and slap my hands onto her hips. Then we would laugh and kiss until the stranger was forgotten.

No one here is laughing.

But they are eating. Vin picks up something dark, fudgy brown and scarfs half of it in a single stressed-out bite. It matches the brown stripe at the top of Alec's neatly napkin-wrapped treat.

"You okay?" Marisol asks.

"Fine," I grate out.

"Really, Syd? Your skin is about seven different colors and your hair . . . it's like dryer lint. Wow." She flicks a bit of activated fuzz.

I don't care about my hair anymore. Easing the walk-in door open a little bit, I try to confirm something.

Vin and Alec *are* sharing a late-morning treat.

They're both eating my brownies.

When the silence has lasted long enough that Marisol lets me out of the walk-in, my lemon bars aren't just overbaked. They're gummy, charred, fused to the pan. They reek of rotting citrus and sugar that went to the dark side.

She squats to peer into her own ovens, to see how much damage Vin and Alec's fight did. "How do yours look?"

"They're not winning the Big Gay Texas Bakeout," I mutter.

I scrape them out, but before I have time to properly mourn them, I hear a voice from behind me.

"What's the Big Gay Texas Bakeout?"

I spin to find Harley lingering in the doorway of the staff room. I give the pin on Harley's bag a quick check—they—and remind myself that they are, technically, staff. I've just never seen them over there before.

I've also never hung out with Harley outside of work, and I'm not sure what direction it's going to tip us now that we're back in the bakery. Do we act like friends? Do we flirt harder? Do we stay exactly the same?

Can we stay exactly the same?

"The Big Gay Texas Bakeout is a thing I made up," I say, dumping my lemon bar pan in the enormous sink. Actually, W and I invented it together, out of sheer love of Mary Berry and an epic week of binge-watching. "Like *The Great British Bake Off* crossed with a Texas cookout."

"Sounds like fun," Harley says, hooking their thumbs through their belt loops. "When is it happening?"

"Never," I say. "It's not real. When did you get here?"

"About three minutes ago," Harley shrugs. "I knocked, nobody answered."

Did they catch the tail end of Vin and Alec's fight? Did it leave them feeling just as wobbly as I do? Did they flee to the staff room, hiding out the same way Marisol and I did?

"I need to ask Syd something," Harley says, looking at Marisol like we need her permission.

The empress of the kitchen nods.

I walk over and join Harley in the staff room. It's empty besides us, though there are condoms and dental dams and lube samples strewn across the table, leftovers from the safer sex workshop in the community space last night. Harley picks up a dental dam package and starts fiddling with it mindlessly, without seeming to notice what it is.

Which is not awkward. Not at all.

"What's up?" I ask.

"Oh, you know. I just had a request from one of my delivery customers. For a special order. One of yours."

"Really?" I ask.

This is mildly amazing. When people go off the standard cake-and-muffin menu for special orders, they always request one of Marisol's bakes. It's the first time someone's asked specifically for one of mine.

Right when I'm starting to feel more confident about this conversation, I realize that there's no reason that Harley and I are having it alone. They could have easily talked to me about this in front of Marisol. Suddenly I'm looking at the floor. And I'm aware of every inch between Harley's shoes and mine.

I have a recipe for being in a relationship. I spent four years perfecting it. But I don't know how to do this part— where I'm watching Harley like a pot of almost-boiling water, but I'm still thinking about W every five minutes.

"So . . . the request?" I ask.

"It was from the people I brought those brownies to yesterday." So that accounts for the two that were missing this morning. At least *somebody* wanted them. "They really love your olive oil cake." Harley says the words carefully, like they had to commit them to memory. Do they not know what olive oil cake is? How? They've been working here for over a year. "They were hoping you'd make it for a party they're hosting tomorrow. I was going to fill out a special order form, but . . ."

But Vin and Alec were stomping around the kitchen, strewing their personal business everywhere.

"Do they want mascarpone frosting or fruit?" I ask.

Harley tries double finger guns, then seems to think better of it, quickly uncocking them. "Fruit."

"Did they like the brownies?" Now I'm just fishing for compliments. Or trying to keep Harley here for another few minutes. They're bouncing on the balls of their feet like this is already over.

I'm so sick of good things being over.

"Oh, yeah," Harley says. "Big hit. I mean, they both said they loved them before they started—"

"Started what?" I ask, sharp as a sudden tester speared right through the center of a cake.

"Fighting?" Harley says. "Like, a couple fight? It was really awkward. I've never had that happen on a delivery before. Sometimes people are clearly hitting the pause button on a fight and pretending they're okay. Lots of wincing smiles and sour body language. But Rae and Jay seemed fine when I got there, they dug into the brownies like they just couldn't wait, and then an argument fired up, big and dramatic, and I was standing right there waiting for them to sign their receipt." They wrap their arms around themself, still bouncing.

"You okay?" I ask.

"Sure," Harley says. "I should just . . . you know . . . deliveries."

They care about their job nearly as much as I do. They've

told me about it while strapping a dozen cake boxes onto their bike. I should let Harley go. But I can't stop thinking about those brownies.

The ones that have landed in the hands of fighting couples. Twice.

"Come with me for a minute," I say, tugging at the shoulder of Harley's muscle tee. "And leave the dental dam."

They drop it and leap backward. "Why are those in the *break room?*"

We weave around the worktables in the kitchen, ignoring the cake boxes for now. A few more shirt tugs and we make it to the front counter. The barista, D.C., looks up from some kind of elaborate iced mocha.

"Hey, Syd!" D.C. gives me a glowing smile. He's a white guy, about thirty, with overeager slices of silver in his shoulder-length black hair. A few years ago, he left the military and came home to some realizations about himself, starting with pansexuality and ending with great big drag-queen tendencies. He might be a dozen years older than me, but he's the cutest kind of baby queer. And he treats me like a wise and ancient bisexual, which, to be honest, I love.

"Where are the brownies?" I ask, pinpointing the place where they used to be with a stare.

"Oh, we really pushed them," D.C. says with an extra helping of helpfulness. "Like you asked."

He points to the spot right near the counter, where a single brownie sits on a small plate. All of my feelings about W's abrupt ending have been condensed down to this one square.

I pick it up, inspecting it like it might cough up secrets.

It stays fudgy and silent and unhelpful.

"What are you doing?" Harley whispers, so close to my ear that the feeling flicks down my spine.

"Nothing," I say with a low laugh. I'm tired. I barely slept last night. There's nothing to see here.

My brownies are definitely not breaking people up.

I turn to head back to the kitchen, to fill Harley's arms with cake boxes, to scrub away the memories of Vin and Alec arguing all over the kitchen.

"Um, Syd," Harley says. "I see more of your brownies."

They spin me gently and point to the window.

Two teenagers a little younger than I am are sitting at a table in the garden, their hands flying. In front of them, a shared plate of brownies is busted down to crumbs. I recognize these two from the morning coffee rush—they're students from the Texas School for the Deaf. They love iced green tea and making out while they wait for the counter staff to pour them enormous cups of it. Right now, they're nowhere close to making out. Judging by their clipped hand motions, they are not very happy with each other.

"Do you know those two?" I whisper to D.C. "From the endless drink orders?"

"Sure," he whispers back, playing along though he's not entirely sure why. "Kit is the short one and Aadi is the . . . not short one."

He's right, I notice, as Aadi stands up and unfolds to gawkish baby giraffe height. They continue to argue.

"What's going on?" I ask D.C. I don't know if this is part of his military background, but he knows about ten languages, one of which is ASL.

D.C. watches, waits. "I don't think it's right for me to translate some of the more personal teenage relationship details they're flinging around right now, but let's just say they might be done with the public mouth aerobics."

Kit stands up so abruptly that the little table shudders and two iced green teas erupt. Ice chips fly as Aadi stalks away, frustrated, and Kit is left behind to crouch awkwardly and try to sop up the mess with several napkins.

"Hey," Harley says, touching my shoulder with one fingertip. "What just happened?"

When I look over, the light that floods the bakery seems to melt the chocolate in their brown eyes. I'm stirring up the courage to say it. Harley might laugh, or slowly back away. I'm not sure I would blame them. But I have to let the words out, the ones that have been trapped on the end of my tongue since the moment I saw Vin scarfing down a bite of my bittersweet catharsis.

"I think my brownies are breaking people up."

Sunday night, as the sky burns orange and the bats fly down the Colorado River, Harley and I step out of my beat-up car.

We're not on a date.

We're on the weirdest not-date I can imagine.

Harley is still in the same clothes they wore to bike all over Austin: stretchy shorts, an extra-long Proud Muffin muscle tee, short yellow vest, and those fingerless bike gloves that leave their knuckles exposed. I'm covered in muffin batter. I couldn't wait. Not after what I saw at the bakery this morning.

Harley gave me directions to this place, which seems to be a pocket-size theater. It's tucked between two houses on a side street off South Congress. I've probably been within a block of this building a hundred times and never even imagined it could be here. That's one of Austin's glories. It feels organic and surprising in a way that other cities don't. According to Tess, who watches a lot of History Channel and cares about weird things like city planning, it's due to a complete lack of zoning laws. I told her not to take the mystery out of it, and she told me that I'm a terminal romantic. "In case you're wondering, that's four steps past hopeless romantic," she added.

I scoffed and didn't let her pinch a spoonful of the dough I was working on—lavender and lemon shortbread—a true punishment for Tess, who believes that all baked goods are best before they're actually baked.

Harley strolls up the walkway, hands in their back pockets, like this is just a normal day. Like we do this kind of thing all the time. But this is only our second time hanging out in a nonbakery setting.

And it's definitely our first time trying to break up a couple with my baked goods.

The theater is called the Comeback, according to a sign above the door. The windows are papered with signs for shows, mostly local comics and experimental theater groups. Harley waits by the door, but I feel a little stuck. "I still can't believe you're willing to believe me."

"Three couples sounds like more than a coincidence," Harley says. "And Syd . . . you're a force."

I try not to worry too much about whether that's a compliment, focusing instead on the fact that Harley is telling me they really think I might have infused my feelings into my baked goods, which then stirred up the same emotions in other people. W always teased me about the whole magical baking thing, treating it like a cute little play I was putting on for her.

It was never that.

"Do you have the last brownie?" I ask, nodding at Harley's messenger bag. They pull it out and hand it over to me, careful not to disturb the layers of napkin I wrapped it in.

"Time to put your theory into practice," Harley says. "But first we need to find our test subject."

"Wait," I say. "We're going to *feed* it to someone?"

Harley cocks their head, curls flopping slightly. "What did you think I meant when I said we should test it?"

"Eat it ourselves, maybe? Or study it on the molecular level?"

"Neither of us is dating anyone at the moment," Harley says, and I can't help but notice how they folded their single status into that moment before ducking their head shyly. "We need a relationship here, right?"

"But we'd have to break someone up *on purpose*," I say, as horrified as if Harley told me they love white chocolate—which is not chocolate. It's an abomination of sugar and manufacturing leftovers. Fight me.

Harley is almost at the end of the short walkway to the theater before they twist back and say, "Oh, I've got a couple to nominate."

I rush to catch up, following Harley into this tiny dim theater where they apparently know a relationship in need of crumbling. I hold the brownie loosely in my grip—I don't want to squash it, but I don't want to drop it on this grubby lobby carpet, either. I wince at the sour atmosphere, the ghost of crappy beers past. A black velvet curtain with a few bald spots and a weird stain separates us from the theater—classy—and Harley approaches it, peeling it back to watch whatever's happening on the other side.

I take the other end of the curtain, pulling it aside with my non-brownie hand. There's no audience out there, but the stage is occupied by a group of college-ish people wearing jeans and dark T-shirts who are pretending to be drunk dinosaurs.

"We're going to break up an improv troupe?" I ask.

"As much as I'd like that to be our objective, no." Harley nods at the very back of the theater, where a person is folded up in one of the seats, legs dangling out of the sandwiched halves.

"I'm going to need more information," I say. Harley

wouldn't bring me here to break someone they like out of a relationship—right? They wouldn't use my breakup brownies for their own personal gain, would they?

Harley doesn't seem like that kind of person.

Of course, now is the exact moment when I realize that as much as Harley knows about my love life, I know next to nothing about theirs.

"Eve hasn't taken a night off from practice since they started dating two months ago," Harley says. "Her *boyfriend* insists he needs her here for moral support. He says that it's a relationship builder."

"Sounds like a top-notch significant other," I say, sticky with sarcasm. "Which one is he?"

"The velociraptor in the middle," Harley says, pointing out a screeching white man-boy whose hands are curled into claws. "Eve is really great. She helped me get my bearings when we first met."

"What kind of bearings?" I ask, realizing belatedly that these people are all much too old to be high school students. "Wait, are you in *college*?"

Harley quirks one red-brown eyebrow, letting me wait in a dramatic silence that feels distinctly high school. "Yes and no. I've been taking college courses since sophomore year. Anyway, when I started, Eve was dating Robbie, who's amazing, but he transferred. Then Eve went out with Nia, and Nia is also incredible, but that didn't work out. And then Eve got lonely right around finals and hooked up with *him*."

I've never really faced the idea of dating so many people. Thanks to W, I've been locked in all through high school. Now I'm single for the first time in my entire dateable existence. I honestly can't seem to untwine that strange feeling from the dumping itself.

Harley and I walk up to Eve, who unscrunches herself from the seat. She's tall and Asian and scowlingly pretty—at least until she sees Harley and lights up. Then she's glowingly pretty. "Hey," she says, with the wilted voice of someone who hasn't seen the sun in months. She really has been holed up in here.

"Eve," Harley says. "This is Syd."

"We both work at the Proud Muffin," I add quickly. Which saves Harley from having to say if we're coworkers, or friends, or some mysterious third thing.

"That place is so great," she says. "My boyfriend won't eat baked goods. He says the stage lights add ten pounds. And then he laughs like it's a joke, but I know he means it because I made him pancakes once and he just side-eyed them like they were attacking him with calories and then took a single bite to 'make me happy.'" She rolls her eyes.

"Ew," I say under my breath.

A lot of people look shocked when I tell them I work at a bakery and insist that they *could never*, because they would eat everything and get *so fat*. As if, because I'm solidly built, I'm supposed to share their fatphobic fear.

This is horrible, and I tell people so.

Onstage, the velociraptor screeches.

Harley shudders and whispers to me, "Do you think he makes that sound when they . . . you know . . . ?"

"We brought some Proud Muffin straight to you," I say, holding out the brownie like it might save Eve's life. This whole plan started out feeling more than a little morally questionable, but at this point I'm happy to lend her a piece of my heartbreak.

Her dark brown eyes crackle with interest. Her fingers reach out, wiggling.

Eve tucks into the brownie right in front of us, in the breathless way that I've noticed only small kids and college students eat, like they've forgotten food exists until it's right in front of them again. "Uhhhh. Mmmmmm. Oh my fucking god." Eve is having an intense, private moment with this brownie. She stares at it like she's falling in love. She makes sounds that under any other circumstance would make me blush.

"Wow," she says, as she finishes with a sigh.

Harley and I are both staring now, waiting for the aftermath. For the moment when the brownie unleashes its power and her relationship with this terror of a pretty boy ends.

"How are you feeling?" Harley asks, leaning forward slightly.

"Are you starting a rival troupe back there?" improv boy asks in a pushy stage whisper, and several of his teammates give a stale laugh.

"Just visiting a friend," Harley shouts.

"*Bikes!*" he shouts back, and it takes me a second to realize that this is a nickname for Harley. "Do you want to come up here? Show us what you've got? What about your friend?"

"Let's absolutely leave," I say.

"I'm sorry about him," Eve says, with a sudden hand on my wrist. "He can be such a dick."

"What did you say, baby?" her boyfriend asks, squinting against the stage lights.

"Dick!" she says. Then she blows him a kiss.

I think about people who get stuck in relationships that should be over, who let things burn long after they should be tossed in the bin. Did W think I was doing the same thing? Was it obvious to the people around us, to everybody but me?

Suddenly I'm not thinking about our fight but the date before that. And the ten dates before that one. The late-night gingerbread pancakes at Kerbey Lane, the sunrise runs by the lake before we had to split up for days at our respective schools. Those dates look fine from a distance, but up close they were strangely quiet. Our skin would brush and W would look at me like she'd forgotten I was there.

Suddenly I feel a very special kind of dumb, and I'm pushing my way out of the theater, dashing the curtain aside. Harley pounds along behind me. "Wait. We need to see if it works, right?"

"It doesn't matter." Thinking that baking might be some form of magic is as stupid and childish as thinking that W and I would last through high school, that her feelings would never go stale.

"Syd," Harley says, dragging me back to the curtain. "Look."

Eve is standing up in a smooth, determined way that makes it look almost like she's levitating. There's a gleam in her eyes that even the dim house lights can't hide. She starts throwing things at the stage. Everything she can get a hold of. Pens and paperbacks and the napkin from the Proud Muffin, which flutters and falls short.

"What are you doing?"

"Interrupting your precious rehearsal!" she shouts.

"What? Why?"

"Because I'm funnier in my *sleep* than you are onstage!" Eve shouts. "The only thing funny about you is when you try to . . ." and then she lists a few activities that he's apparently hilarious at.

The rest of the troupe applauds Eve.

"This isn't a scene, assholes!" he shrieks, back to his velociraptor voice, *not* on purpose.

Harley and I turn to each other. I'm waiting for them to say that it's not real, to come up with some explanation. Instead, Harley bum-rushes me, and even though they're only a tiny bit taller, they're strong enough to heave me off the floor and spin me once, twice, to pick up speed and make me dizzy.

"You did that," they whisper. "That was *you*."

"It really was."

"There are so many jokes about magic brownies I'm not making right now," Harley says into my shoulder.

I start laughing, but the sound dissolves when I think about Vin and Alec. And Kit and Aadi. And the strangers

Harley delivered my brownies to. Maybe W and I deserve to be over, but I'm not going to spread that misery to anyone else. I refuse to be the cause of more heartbreak.

"I'm going to get them back together," I say, right as Harley sets me down.

"Them?" Harley asks, pointing at the stage, where Eve and her now-ex-boyfriend are standing on chairs, shouting each other's inadequacies.

"Okay, not them. But everyone else who ate my brownies. I'm going to find them and fix it."

Harley's practicality snaps in place so fast that I don't see it coming.

"How?"

Very Sorry Cake

~~~ INGREDIENTS ~~~

FOR THE CAKE

2 cups all-purpose flour

1½ cups sugar

1½ tsp big grain salt (Kosher salt, sea salt, etc.)

½ tsp baking soda

½ tsp baking powder

1⅓ cups extra virgin olive oil

1¼ cups milk (Not skim! Skim is blue water! Don't apologize to people with runny blue water cake!)

3 eggs

1½ tbsp orange zest (That is a lot of zest, but you're very sorry, so it's worth it.)

½ cup fresh juice from actual oranges (Not a carton. Get in there and start crushing pulp and chasing down seeds. Every time you think about cutting a corner, don't. That's not how apologies work. Do the thing, and do it right.)

FOR THE FRUIT SAUCE

2 cups berries (I used blueberries, but this would
be just as good a fuck-up sauce if you used
strawberries or raspberries or blackberries.)

1 to 2 tbsp sugar, depending on how sweet your fruit is

A squeeze or two of fresh lemon

~~~~~~~ **DIRECTIONS** ~~~~~~~

Ready to fix whatever you've done horribly wrong?

Let's go.

Preheat the oven to 350 degrees.

In a medium bowl, mix the flour, sugar, salt, baking soda,
and baking powder. In a large bowl, whisk the olive oil,
milk, eggs, orange zest, and juice.

See how easy that was? Shouldn't we all say we're sorry
with cake?

Fold the dry ingredients into the wet ones, until just barely
mixed. Pour the batter into your greased pans—I use two
9-inch round cake pans and sauce them separately, OR
you can get truly penitent and stack them for a double
layer cake, adding whipped mascarpone in the middle
(quick and dirty recipe: one 8-oz tub mascarpone, 2 to
3 squeezes of lemon, 2 tbsp of your favorite fine sugar;
dump in a bowl and whip together).

Bake according to your pans—start checking at 30 minutes for rounds. The trick here is to wait until you've got a consistently golden-brown top. And of course, your toothpick should come out clean. If it doesn't, you're still working through your shit and you're not actually ready to center anyone else's feelings.

When the cake is truly golden, shining with sincerity—and oil—you're ready to take it out of the oven to cool and make the fruit sauce. On the stovetop, in a small saucepan, cook down 1 cup of fruit. When it reaches half of its original volume, add the second cup of fruit and a little sugar. Right at the end, when it's getting thick and almost TOO sweet, hit it with the lemon, to taste. Test with a spoon: it should leave a thin coating of sauce behind, and the flavor should burst in your mouth, like the words that are ready to come out.

Say them with me as you spoon the fruit over the cake: *I'm very very very very very very very sorry.*

4

I stay up late destroying the kitchen and then get up early to deal with the batter-crusted bowls and beaters. I considered making these cakes at the Proud Muffin yesterday, but only one is for the couple who put in the special order. The extra, equally important cake is for the rest of the relationships I pushed off the edge of a cliff. The ones I'm now dedicated to putting back together, one bite at a time.

Besides, Harley never actually got around to filling out that order slip. We were too busy watching Kit and Aadi's explosive green tea battle.

So I'm off the clock. A rogue baker.

My parents come downstairs in their matching PJs. They order a set for everyone in the family for Christmas each year.

They are very straight, but this might be the straightest thing about them. Neither of them seems surprised by the clamor of dishes and violently tossed kitchen towels. They're used to my middle-of-the-night bakestorms, but this one was different. This time I was intentionally trying to expel feelings from my chest, funnel them down through my fingertips: how much I wish I could take back the sadness I spread to other people, like giving them an emotional flu. The special tang of guilt that comes with subtracting so much queer love from the world.

I have two perfect expanses of golden-brown crumb in front of me, but I can't sauce them. Not yet. I carefully enclose them in my carrying cases—two plastic domes named Sally and Gillian—and scoop the bright-smelling blueberry sauce from its pan into a little container.

Mom and Dad sit down on the couch together, basically on top of each other, an overlap of arms and legs and sleepy smiles. They sip each other's coffees. They talk about Tess, who checked in from college to say she's coming home for spring break at the end of the week. They fake argue and then laugh at themselves. They kiss. A lot. They're like this: adorable when anyone else would settle for mildly cute.

I'm holding a cake in each hand, trying to slide past them unnoticed. It isn't until I catch Mom and Dad staring at me in parental horror that I realize I'm crying. Not barely-there tears I can wave off. Big, hearty drops glaze my face. When I go to wipe them, I make a sticky-throated sound.

Mom leaps over the arm of the couch.

"What's wrong, Kid?" Dad asks. He called me Syd the Kid when I was little. It usually feels like a throwback, but right now I can feel years sliding off me with each gasp of well-salted snot.

Mom slings her arm around me, supporting my weight even though she's tiny. My head almost settles on top of hers at this point. "You okay, sweetie? Things have seemed off the last few days, but I didn't want to push." Of course she noticed. Of course she didn't push. I might seem like the loud, opinionated, stomping type, but the people who know me know that I can be quiet about my feelings, box them up and save them for later. Like cake you put away until it goes so stale that you don't even bother tasting it.

"Come on, Syd. If you don't tell us what's wrong, we have to start guessing," Dad says.

"That *is* the rule," Mom warns.

"Last time you guessed I was secretly pregnant with W's baby," I say with a laugh that turns on me and almost becomes a sob.

Dad finishes Mom's coffee—she always dusts hers with cinnamon—and shrugs. "Science can do wonders."

"Is this a cake problem?" Mom asks.

"Syd gets tragic when her cakes don't come out right," Dad confirms.

Something in me rears its ugly, perfectionist head. "There's nothing wrong with the cake. The cake is blameless."

Glee sneaks onto Mom's face. "Does that mean we can taste it?"

"Well played." She didn't want to ask for any if I was upset about it. Now it's fair game.

A little taste test can't hurt—right? Even if these cakes serve a practical purpose, I want to know they're delicious before I thrust them at complete strangers. If anything, these people deserve an *extra* delicious cake for what I put them through. Besides, my parents aren't fighting. For them, maybe the cake will just be cake. I snap Sally back open and cut into one of the amber moons, then add a small spoonful of sauce to each piece. I'm stingier than usual—I need most of this cake for the lovelorn. My parents don't seem to care about the portion size. Dad has his head down, his face almost touching his little sliver. Mom is intent on individually spearing every blueberry.

"What do you think?" I ask, unable to keep hope from staining my voice like the blueberry sauce now stains Mom's lips.

"I have to apologize to all of your other cakes, but this might be my new favorite," Mom says conclusively.

Without looking up from his cake, Dad sighs. "I'm sorry to ask again, but you know I have to. It's my job."

"Your job is designing websites," I remind him.

"What's up?" he asks, undeterred. "You're not sleeping, Syd. You haven't taken a single bite of this absurdly good cake. Something is wrong."

I can't tell them about the brownies. Having one person who believes me—one person who understands—seems like pushing the universe to its limits. So, I settle for telling them the other wrong thing.

"W and I broke up."

They don't gasp and demand details. They don't lie and say they never liked W—which wouldn't work, anyway. I know they love her. W and I had a running list of jokes about how they wanted to absorb her into our family by osmosis, why wait for marriage?

"I'm sorry that happened." Mom chews slowly. "Really, really, truly sorry."

Dad takes a bite that is basically the rest of his cake, and adds, "I don't know how to even *say* how sorry I am."

"Because you miss W?" I ask. "Because you thought I was enough to keep her around?" I can't look at them. More tears will fly out of my face. I walk through the living room into the kitchen and stare out the window at the lemon trees.

Mom follows me in and puts the plates in the sink. As soon as her hands are free, they go to work. She's always gesturing when she's upset. When it gets really bad, she squeezes and squeezes, like she's trying to juice her fingers.

She's juicing right now.

"Oh, Syd. I'm sorry you would ever think that."

My heart sets firmly as I snap the cake case closed again. It looks like the magic is working.

* * *

Harley waits for me behind the bakery, one sneaker kicked up against the wall, arms held out to toast in the sun.

I check the pin—he—and push one of my cake cases into his hands. It's my day off, and Harley had to make deliveries for a few hours, but we agreed to meet after I was done with school. When I told Harley that I really was determined to find the rest of the couples, he seemed equally determined to help.

"I'm going to assume the cake that just leapt into my arms is for Operation Get Back Together."

"Gillian likes you," I say, hugging Sally to my side. "Then again, Gillian likes masc types."

"You name your cakes? And give them crushes?" Harley settles the plastic dome in the rear basket of his bike with this careful precision that absolutely requires me to stare at his hands. "And . . . Gillian?"

"I don't name the cakes, just the cases," I say. "And yes, Gillian. From *Practical Magic*."

"The witch movie." Harley nods, one hand cupped at the back of his neck. It's a hot-weather thing, a Texas thing, a *cowboy* thing. I've only ever seen Harley in stamped-flat sneakers, but suddenly I'm wondering if he owns cowboy boots. W has three pairs—a fancy pair, a dirtbag pair, and a down-home-farmgirl, I-will-leap-on-the-nearest-horse-and-outride-you pair. Knowing what Harley's cowboy boots look like is an instant goal.

"So where are we starting?" Harley asks.

"Well, I just left a slice in Vin and Alec's office." They share a tiny room where they do paperwork together. Put a baked good in, and it's bound to disappear. That's part of how I won this job—strategic cake drops.

It worked once. It'll work again.

Now it's off to deal with the other messes I've made. "Let's take my car," I say. "It's faster."

"It's too hot for cars," Harley says, unsticking his tank top from his chest as evidence, peeling it away from his binder.

"It's too hot for everything," I say, suddenly feeling all the places where my own clothes adhere. "You're unfairly blaming cars."

"When's the last time you were on a bike?" Harley asks.

I think my way backward. "Ladybird Lake. I was thirteen. I had just learned to make biscotti and I had a bunch in my pocket, but the dogs thought they were biscuits and I got rushed by about a hundred puppies."

"Sounds like a nightmare," Harley says, barely keeping a straight face.

"It was!" I say, pushing his shoulder. "Tess had to walk my bike all the way home."

"Doesn't *biscotti* literally mean 'biscuit'?" Harley asks. "Those puppies were on to something."

My hackles go straight up. "Biscotti are *delicious*. Biscotti are a *revelation*."

Harley gives his long nose a scrunch. "Biscotti are croutons that people put in their coffee. Coffee croutons." He looks roughly as satisfied with this description as I am horrified.

"We should get going," I say. "Every minute we spend

arguing about this clearly superior baked good is a minute that a couple spends broken up." I start walking toward the parking lot, toward my car, toward sanity.

"Okay," Harley says, catching my wrist, which makes me catch my breath, and then we're standing there in a stopped moment. He starts time again with a slow smile. "Biscotti are wonders and puppies are evil, but *you're* unfairly blaming bikes." He puts one hand over his heart like he's personally vouching for all bikes, everywhere. "I promise, my handlebars are a good time."

I can't tell which of us blushes faster or harder, since I can't see my own face.

I scoff. "I bet you say that to all the . . ."

"Agender cupcakes?" Harley finishes.

Oh.

I like that.

"Maybe we can bike next time." That will give me an opportunity to mentally work up to it. Today we have a cake to deliver, and there's no time for Harley to watch me have an existential crisis on wheels.

"All right," Harley drawls, like he can be infinitely patient about this situation. Then he triple-locks his bike.

I load Sally and Gillian into the back seat. The Very Sorry Cake looks just as good as it did this morning, despite the heat. I should be proud—but all I can feel is a nervous rattle where my pride used to be.

I expect Harley to give me an address to toss into my phone's GPS. Instead, he calmly feeds me directions. We head south on Manchaca, cross under all of the major highways, and keep going.

A few twists later, we turn onto a sudden driveway, and it leads deep into a property that's covered in the crooked glory of live oak trees and the deep green of cedar. The grass is patchy, but the wildflowers make up for it, spicing the ground yellow and red and blue. I pull to a stop on the rocky circular drive. This place is a hidden slice of Austin, nearly impossible to imagine when you're standing on Sixth Street.

"It's pretty great out here," I say softly.

"I know," Harley says proudly, like somehow this is his place, too.

I grab the cake cases and check that the blueberry sauce didn't explode in transit.

Harley and I approach the front door of a house that sits near the center of the property. It's fawn-colored, like it wants nothing more than to blend in with the deer staring at us from a stand of trees.

"Do you think they can smell the cake?" I whisper.

"I don't think deer are into cake," Harley whispers back.

"What do you know about deer palates?"

"Syd." Harley touches my shoulder. "This is not going to be like the puppies."

I give Harley very big, very unconvinced eyes.

"Okay, so the people who live here," Harley rattles off quickly and quietly, making me lean in close. "Rae and Jay. Rae is she/her, Jay uses all pronouns. They're event planners, hence the amazing property. They use the buildings and tents out back for parties, weddings, business stuff . . . Um, they met when Jay hired Rae to do the electrical wiring, I think? They have two kids, who are both—"

"Kids?" I shift the cake case in my arms, even though it was perfectly secure before. But something inside of me feels off-balance. It didn't even occur to me that those brownies could capsize whole families.

My parents might look sitcom-level happy now, but they had a hard time when I was younger. Mostly money related. Back in Illinois, we could only afford the kind of apartment with black spiderweb cracks at the tops of the walls. I would catch them looking at bills and bank statements online, tense and muttering. They had a blowout when I was in second grade when Tess asked for a puppy and Mom thought it would be good for the family, but Dad said we couldn't afford it. There was an entire year where they fought constantly, and I remember days when Dad didn't come home, when Mom wasn't a hundred percent sure where he was staying. She'd smooth over the worries of not knowing, tucking me and Tess next to her on the couch and letting us watch movies with her late into the night. By the time we moved to Austin, things had already gotten so much better. But what if they hadn't made it? What if something came along at the wrong moment and pushed them until they broke?

Harley must notice the sudden cloud cover on my face. He taps my elbow. "Hey. Syd. It's okay. You're going to make things better."

I take a breath that tastes like every mistake I've ever

made. Like burnt cake and bitter fights with my sister, like Monday morning at school after I've been up late baking and not studying for a test, like W's last kiss.

I'm ready to do this. Ready to *un*do this.

"There's something I need to ask," Harley says right after I knock. "What pronouns do you want me to use? For you?"

"Oh. Um." This is not a two second conversation for me. This is a twist-in-the-bed-all-night decision.

By the time the door opens, I still haven't said an actual word.

"Harley!" the person who opens the door exclaims.

"Jay!" Harley exclaims right back.

Jay is tall and stocky and bearded, wearing a utility skirt and sandals that might be homemade. They give off a soft glow of happiness. I wonder if they look at everyone this way, or if Harley has earned a special level of brightness.

Jay is the kind of person who invites us right in even though I'm a complete stranger. Everything in the house is thoughtful and beautiful and looks like it's been created just for this place. Linen couches dip gracefully into the corners of the living room while toy chests for the kids sit under the windows along the back wall, creating window seats. Cedar cabinets with mother-of-pearl handles line a gorgeous kitchen.

My brain immediately starts baking things in there. I'm going to be useless for a few minutes.

"This is Syd," Harley says. "A baker from the Proud Muffin."

I marvel at how easily Harley sidesteps my pronouns— the way I've been avoiding them in my head for years.

"Hi," I say. "Your kitchen . . ."

Jay's laughter at my reverence is quick and kind. "Rae designed it herself."

Jay gives a quick look at a closed door. At least they're not so broken up that Rae is already gone. Then again, Jay and Rae run a business together. They're raising kids. Sometimes breaking up isn't as easy as kicking a person out of a cold shower.

"Sorry, I'd usually ask you to stay for tea, but we've got a party out back. A kids' birthday. I should head back out there soon!" The positivity in Jay's words isn't quite reaching her actual voice.

"Where should I put this?" I ask, holding out the cake like the pitiful offering that it probably is.

"Just set it in the kitchen," Jay says. "I'll let Rae know. I know it's a random Tuesday and we're not really celebrating anything official, but it's her favorite. That's why I wanted to order it in the first place . . ." His enthusiasm trips over itself, his words stumbling to a stop.

"Oh." I want to be with a person who orders my favorite cake just because it's Tuesday. That might be my new working definition of love.

W loves special occasions, but sometimes I felt like the days between those disappeared. She thought I was trying too hard to make every day special, and I thought she refused to see that any day *could* be special.

"Let me get my wallet . . ." Jay says, heading for the bedroom.

"This one's on the house!" I say, a little too loudly. "For being such great customers."

"Hmmm." Jay's eyebrows are clearly aware of how unorthodox all this is. "You're sure about that? Let me at least give you a tip . . ."

I nod with a nervous bobble. I probably shouldn't take any kind of payment—but I need them to believe that this is their official special order and not just some cake I made at home. Vin and Alec could have my apron for this. I've been so worried that I'm not a good enough baker, but maybe there are other ways to mess up my dream job.

Bigger ways.

Jay can't quite beat back a smile. "All right, let me take some to Rae. She really does love this cake."

I set the case down on the kitchen island. The counters are lined with animal-shaped sugar cookies and handmade birthday decorations. When I've found a clear spot, I lift the bell of the case and release a rich wave of citrus. Jay makes a show of swooning, and I can't say that I disagree.

Harley looks suspiciously normal.

I cut a generous piece of cake. Harley draws a little plate down from the cabinets. We work as a team, Harley hunting for a fork as I center the slice and top it with a hearty spoonful of blueberry sauce.

"For two very special customers," I say, handing over the plate. I want to add more, but I can't tell him that I've unbalanced his life because of my own heartbreak. I can't admit that I need him to stay in love.

Everything I want to say is in the cake.

I have to trust that.

Jay knocks, and the door opens. I hold my breath, ready for the yelling, for an argument to be picked up. But Jay just musters a watery smile and steps in. Somehow the silence in that room is worse than any fight.

The door closes gently.

I quickly get to looking around the house to learn more about the people whose collective life I ruined.

The house doesn't bear any obvious signs of a breakup: no hasty boxes, no torn-apart rooms, no book collections divvied up. But then I notice the nails evenly spaced on the cream walls.

"They took down all their pictures," I say.

I've taken down at least a hundred photos of me and W in the last few days. In eighth and ninth grade, I was a little obsessed with collaging. Later I created homemade frames for anything that felt special. The one where I'm sitting on W's lap with her head peeking around my shoulder, which looks extra cute because I'm bigger than she is. The homecoming photos where we both wore tiaras and made the actual homecoming queen so pissed that she photobombed every single one of our couple's shots. The most recent one: both of us walking down South Congress, our backs to the camera, all of Austin laid out before us. I've been studying that one. Was she not holding my hand as hard as I was holding hers?

I head back to the kitchen, back to Harley, but my head is flooded with W.

I keep finding us on my walls, in my drawers. Do I keep some of these memories? How do I pick? Is it healthier to get rid of them all? Can you actually burn photos like they do in movies, or will that release some kind of noxious chemical? Do I stash them somewhere, so I'll find them in ten years and laugh about my first love? Why does that idea—that I could fully let go of her—feel even worse than losing her?

I don't even notice my fork stabbing into the cake, but now my mouth is full. A hard lump of truth bobs up my throat. Over the sound of my own chewing, I announce, "I'm sorry I keep talking about my ex."

"That's okay," Harley says, cleaning off the cake knife. "It's good to talk. At least, it feels good to me. I guess that's one side effect of all the therapy."

"I go to therapy, too!" I don't know why that feels like such a vital thing to have in common. Maybe because I know some queer people who mildly scorn therapy. It makes utter sense that having a bad therapist, especially as a queer person, can be catastrophic. But my therapist is kind of the best.

Harley and I exchange the exploding fist bump of two people who are taking care of their mental health.

"Do you want some?" I ask.

We shouldn't be eating Rae and Jay's cake, but it's not like this is a normal special order. And I can't help it. I want to feed Harley. Maybe I'm predictable, but the second I start to care about someone, I need to give them sweets.

Harley shakes his head, though, and I can't blame him. He probably doesn't want to spend the next half an hour apologizing for anything and everything. But this cake isn't letting up on me, so it looks like we're stuck in this apology cycle. "I'm sorry I don't know very much about your love life. Or general life. I'm sorry I don't know way more about you."

The conversation in the other room picks up, and even though it's made fuzzy by the wall between us, it suddenly feels like we're in the middle of a private moment. "Come on," Harley says. "Let's go for a walk."

We leave the house by the kitchen door, emerging into a new part of the property scattered with rustic wooden buildings and dreamy tents. Several of them seem to be staging areas for the main event: a party unfolding in the distance. Kids are running, leaping, shouting. Parents are clumped around the edges, taking videos and pictures. I see more than one visibly queer parenting unit.

This place is a little too perfect. Which makes me wonder how hard Rae and Jay had to fight for it.

"You're thinking about the cake again," Harley said. "Whether or not it's working."

"Of course I am." My head swivels back to the house.

Harley uses one knuckle to swivel it back. I feel the trace of that touch after he pulls his hand away. I'm left staring into his face, smooth skin with just a trace of sweat, and those melting-chocolate eyes. "I'm right here, and you want to know more about me." His lips tug into a smirk. "Right?"

"Have you always lived in Austin?" I ask as we pass a ring of perfect sitting stumps with a chandelier hanging high above. It's like something from a daydream, just hanging there among the live oaks, and I wonder what it looks like all lit up at night.

I settle onto one of the stumps, and Harley leaps onto another. "*That's* what you're dying to know?" he asks, spinning around on one foot.

I shrug. "The places we live are part of us. Like ingredients."

"And you want to know my recipe?" Harley asks, hopping from stump to stump.

"I'm not answering that."

"Why not?"

"You make it sound so . . . salacious," I grit out. As I talk to Harley, my voice drops deeper and deeper. I like it. I like feeling every one of these words as they leave my throat. "Recipes are wholesome as fuck."

"Right, you're the most wholesome person I've ever met." Harley winks.

Before I can come up with some kind of retort, he's on to the next thing, banter at full blast. "I was born in this little town down by the Louisiana border, but my mom and sibs and I moved to Austin after my parents split up. I was . . . twelve?"

"Do you still see your dad?" I ask.

"Not on purpose."

I let the anger in those words sizzle out before I keep going. "How old were you when you came out?"

"Which time?" Harley asks, sounding instantly weary.

And even though I asked the question, I know what Harley's getting at—coming out isn't a one-and-done thing. Even if you have only one identity factor to deal with, it's not that simple. And if you have more than one? Well. "Does it bother you when people act like it's just this one moment?" I ask. "This day . . ."

"With a parade?" Harley asks.

"And a great big cake."

"You didn't make a coming-out cake?" Harley asks, mock shocked.

"I think it's the only time in my life I *didn't* bake."

Harley laughs, just a snort really, and a bunch of kids bust right through our conversation. They don't seem to care that we're crashing their party. As soon as they've cleared the stumps, Harley starts talking again. "I guess I was never in the closet about being trans. My mom saw it when I was pretty little, and so did my dad, but he was too busy being shitty to really care. The big surprise, for my mom at least, came in middle school when she started talking about all the cute girls in my class and just couldn't stop. I definitely had to announce that I'm not straight. Or any kind of binary." He picks at the peeling bark of the stump. It feels like there's more, so I leave space—the same way Harley's been leaving it for me. "I haven't really talked to many people about being demisexual."

Harley's eyes flick up, studying me as I take that one in.

"So you have to feel a connection with someone before you feel . . ."

"Like giving a handlebar ride?" he fills in.

"Sexy feelings?" I finish at the same moment.

We laugh so hard that Harley loses his footing and falls off his stump. He sprawls out on the grass, looking up at me. His smile softens, and the wild humor leaves his eyes a little bit at a time, until they're calm and confident.

I wonder, again, how long we've been flirting. Did everyone at the bakery notice except for me? Did Marisol's eyes roll 360 degrees in her head whenever I opened the door for Harley? Did Gemma and the counter staff take bets on whether we'd be the new bakery romance? Was I on auto-flirt back when we started? Did I not let myself see how much I liked Harley because I was dating W?

Well, I'm not with W anymore.

For the first time, it hits me in a good way—like the open blue skies when I tilt my chin up.

"Syd?" Harley asks.

I want to stay here, in this moment where the flirting deepens and the flavor changes. But there's more that I need to say, and this stupid magical cake is pushing me to say it. "I'm sorry I didn't answer when you asked for my pronouns. It makes me feel like I'm hiding something, but—"

"You haven't figured it out yet? That's okay." Harley is being so kind about this. No—not just kind. He actually understands what I'm saying. But the next part feels like it wouldn't make sense to anyone but me.

"I don't feel like *any* pronouns fit," I say, so low the words are nearly invisible. "Or any of them fits more than the others. And when I think about all the people whose lives are changed by the right words, people who have to fight for them every day, I feel like I should apologize because my pronouns are *No, thanks.*"

Harley nods. But I can't leave it at that.

"Sometimes I come up with these little recipes . . . like, gender recipes. For how I want to look or feel that day." I might be an agender cupcake, but I have to live in a world where most things have been flavored with gender. Even when I was little, I mixed and played and had fun with those flavors. I showed up to second-grade picture day in a pink skirt with neon yellow suspenders and a blue plaid tie. I made it through most of eighth grade in big unlaced work boots, black tights, and overall shorts. And then there's my baking uniform: guys' baggy jeans, a binder or sports bra under a fitted T-shirt, and a bright sunny apron.

"Gender recipes," Harley echoes. "That's very Syd of you."

I feel myself burn with a blush. The bad kind. The scorching, humiliated kind. I've never told anybody about this stuff before. This isn't for public consumption. This is the secret way that I get through the day.

"I'm sorry, it's ridiculous, I know."

Harley is looking at me with hard, serious eyes. The lingering blueberry sauce is tart on my tongue. It pushes me to apologize, over and over. I fight the feeling down, like acid at the back of my throat, because I shouldn't have to be sorry for who I am—right?

Harley sits up and puts a hand on my shoulder. It starts out as a friendly touch, and then his fingers lift, and they slide, so it's just his fingertips on my collarbone, traveling all the way to my chest, right above my heart.

I can't breathe, but I also don't feel like I need to.

My heart is working fine. I can feel it through my skin, my clothes. I can hear it over the sound of my own voice. "What was that for?"

"It's not ridiculous," Harley says. "It's true."

"So every time I tell the truth you're going to do . . . that?" I look down at my collarbone.

Jay runs out of the back door. Rae—it must be Rae—is right beside her. She's short and white and muscled, with a buzz cut and hands that swing with purpose. Jay is hugging Rae to her side, that soft glow of happiness back.

Their mouths are both blissfully blue. If I needed evidence that they ate the cake, there it is, right on their faces.

"We wanted to thank you," Rae said. "Both of us."

"Did you like the cake?" I want to ask so many more questions. What they each apologized for. What made them break up in the first place—and what convinced them to get back together.

"It was just what we needed," Jay says.

That should make me happy, but for some reason it sets up a buzz of fear in the back of my brain. Rae and Jay special ordered this cake. They basically told me what they needed when they requested it. What about the other couples I broke up?

How do I know what *they* need?

"Now, if you don't mind, we're pretty sure our kids have crashed that birthday party," Rae adds.

Jay looks at the tent, wary and amused. "We should go rescue everyone else from our offspring."

"They're terrifying."

"They're *adorably* terrifying."

"We should head back, too," I say. I want to check in on Vin and Alec and make sure their slices worked as well as these did. Besides, we have three more couples and one rogue brownie-buyer out there.

The sky is settling into dusk, strips of orange and pink layering in natural beauty as string lights come on in every tent and wrapped around the bodies of the live oaks. Harley and I head back to the kitchen to pick up Gillian. The cake case is sitting where we left it.

"Her top is off," I say.

"You do know how that sounds, right?" Harley asks.

I spin around, grabbing Harley's wrist. "Where did the rest of the cake go?"

Harley looks, too, but no amount of looking will bring back a cake that isn't here. "Someone must have thought it was for the party."

We quickstep outside—and that's when I see that Sally is missing from my car and the door is wide open. I didn't even think to lock it. We're on private property, and I've never had someone steal a baked good right out of my back seat before. But I've never been carrying around magical cake, either.

I run to the tent, swarming with kids in the aftermath of

birthday treats. There's a fairly traditional white cake decorated with fondant animals—don't get me started on the evils of fondant—but it's mostly been ignored. Instead crumbs of olive oil cake are on every little plate, fruit sauce scattered everywhere, the mouths of thirty kids stained an incriminating blue.

They've eaten it all.

Jay is kneeling in front of a little kid who looks exactly like a Jay-Rae combo. Their little fists are clenched tight. "I'm sorry I took that cake but also NOT SORRY."

Other kids are chirping, too.

"I played with your birthday gift before I wrapped it! Sorry! Sorry!"

"I'm sorry I ate twelve cookies and I got *siiiiiiiick*."

One of them is keeled over, lying on their side, apologizing to the grass for stepping on it so much.

"I believe that's the birthday kiddo," Harley says, pointing to a tipped-over crown.

"We should probably leave," I say.

Harley and I sprint all the way back to my car.

The next morning I show up to work early, hoping to catch Vin doing his weekly scheduling and drinking tiny cups of espresso. I need to be sure that he's post-apology and back together with Alec.

What I don't expect is an ambush. When I walk in,

Marisol's hands are deep in a bowl of streusel, but her eyes are pointed at the door. She's got her darkest brown lip color on, with a defined lip liner. It's her date-night look, but that makes no sense. It's five in the morning. There's this hard set to her face, like she's determined to tell me something.

"You know that cake you left in Vin and Alec's office?" she asks.

"Oh. Uh. Yeah?" They hated it. They took one look and threw it in the trash. They took one bite of it and fired me.

Marisol pinches off little bits of the streusel and sprinkles them over muffin cups. "I'm sorry to say this, but it was excellent."

"You *ate it*?"

No. No. No.

The kids at the birthday party destroyed the rest of the Very Sorry Cake. I don't have any more for Vin and Alec. And I heard their fight. They had things to apologize for.

"I know the cake wasn't there for me, and it sucks that I ate it anyway." The magic must have lingered, because I've never heard Marisol admit that she did something wrong. Not even that one time when she wrote down a special order incorrectly and someone got a cake that said *Be Mated* instead of *Belated*. She maintains that Gemma yelled out a drink order as she was writing it down.

"Vin and Alec were out of the bakery for a meeting yesterday, the whole day." Before I can fire up my worries about what kind of meeting could keep them both out of the Proud Muffin all day, Marisol pushes on. "I went in the office to drop off the manager's paperwork. When I saw that cake, I couldn't walk away from it. Like when you meet a person and it's so clear you're supposed to know them. They know something true, something that you already know deep down. Like part of you is locked up inside of them."

"Wow," I whisper. I think that's the most lyrical and involved I've ever heard Marisol get in a conversation.

I also think she just described how baking magic works.

That means that Marisol was drawn to the cake for a reason. And if she's going to steal the apology that was meant for Vin and Alec, at the very least I want to know who she was apologizing *to*.

"What did you do after you ate it?" I ask, trying to be casual as I throw on my apron and flour my hands.

"What do you think I did?" Marisol scoffs. "I baked my arms off." The way she looks down at the bowl, I know there's more to it. She's not lying, because Marisol also never lies, but she acts like this when she thinks I'm too young or inexperienced to handle a full-on truth. Which means she's holding something back.

It makes me think of W. How it took me six full months to be honest with her.

It makes me think of Harley. How I've been telling Harley who I am, without even blinking.

Today's Gender

~~~~~ **INGREDIENTS** ~~~~~

FOR THE LOOK

1 pair of black denim shorts

1 Amy's Ice Creams *Local, Not Lo-Cal* T-shirt

2 rolled sleeves

1 pair of rainbow suspenders, bought at Pride,
even though W thought they were ridiculous

1 pair of knee-high athletic socks

2 slightly falling-apart dad sneakers

1 pair of round, metal-rimmed sunglasses

1 shaved head

FOR THE INSPIRATION

Sweet tea

Drag king casual

Kristen Stewart on vacation

FOR THE ATTITUDE

2 parts swagger

2 parts glitter

A pinch of gritty sweetness

DIRECTIONS

Mix everything together. Check it all in the mirror.

Bake in the 1000-degree oven known as high school. Watch everyone around you burn with concern about classes you've already checked out of, friendships you never bothered making, relationships that will end the second the last bell of the school year rings.

Don't watch as people give you looks, confused by both your presence in the halls and your ever-shifting presentation. Mix in reminders that all of this is fleeting, until you nearly overwhelm the taste of being left out.

Walk around with your head high, your socks higher.

Tomorrow, change your ingredients as needed.

5

It's a relief to get back to the Proud Muffin after a full day at school and a few hours of homework at the library. My parents let me work out a special arrangement with Vin and Alec and the school counselor to arrange my schedule around baking shifts, as long as I maintain a B average or better. Most days I split, with baking in the morning and a few classes in the afternoon. And I get a gym waiver because baking for eight hours is more physically intense than playing half-hearted volleyball and learning country-western line dances.

When I pull in, I claim the last parking space. The lot is churning with hot, sweaty people. Dozens of them. It might not be my shift, but I have a great excuse to spend time at the

Proud Muffin: community night. I breeze in through the front door, trying not to look like I have any ulterior motives. I'm here to socialize and listen to a local band. I'm definitely not going to wait until everyone else is distracted and then search through the receipts in the POS system for the rest of the people who bought my brownies.

"Hey, Syd!" Gemma shouts from behind the counter, through the frenzy of drink orders. Her hands are moving so fast you can barely track them. Ten shots of espresso seem to be pulling at once. "You came!"

I feel the sudden contours of my frown. "I'm here every Thursday night."

And then I realize—Gemma is surprised because I'm not at home, crying over W. Honestly, I'm a little surprised, too. I guess there's nothing to get you over a breakup like having to resurrect other peoples' love lives.

"You okay?" Gemma asks over the scratch of frothing milk. She's looking at me with a special blend of pity and understanding. But what, exactly, does she understand? What has W told her about our breakup?

Does she miss anything about me? Is she absurdly, exhaustedly glad to be done? Am I just some sad, overbaked significant other who crumbled while she did the harsh but necessary thing?

"I'm staying busy," I say. "What about . . ." I almost ask about W, then swerve at the last second. "What about you?"

"Oh, you know," she says. "Work." Gemma swivels and sets out two drinks on the counter. "Lone Star lattes!" she shouts in a high-pitched voice. Both drinks are topped with foam in the shape of Texas with a star-shaped silver sprinkle dropped in just the right spot to represent our fair capital city. When most of the baristas do this, Texas is barely a state-shaped blob. Gemma's an artist. An actual one—she's had her own shows in art spaces around the city, and she's saving up money to rent a studio.

"Monday should be a big reunion because so many people are coming back for spring break," she says, burying her attention in new orders. "W wants to come. I hope that's okay?"

There are actually two weekly community nights, one for QTPOC. Alec and Gemma lead those, Marisol brings in her favorite home bakes, and all queer and trans people of color who work at the bakery have the Monday night shift open in case they want to attend. For obvious being-white reasons, I've never been there.

I remember the first time W went, though. Back in autumn, when the sky was smoky gray, I dropped her off right outside. She gave me a nervous strapped-in-the-car kiss and then almost floated into the bakery.

W's dad is Tejano. She has fairly light skin, and most white people who meet W assume she's totally white. It was the only part of her identity that I ever saw her talk about with less than perfect certainty. I wanted to help—but for obvious being-white reasons, I couldn't really give any advice.

So I listened.

And I told her about Monday nights at the bakery, just in case.

Eventually she started going. I'm glad she's still going. As much as I hate that we ended abruptly and I was left standing in the cold—literally with freezing droplets all over my body—I hate the idea of her losing this place.

I hate the idea of *anyone* losing it.

"Yeah. You can tell W . . ." My throat narrows unexpectedly as I picture her on her massive, over-pillowed bed, leaning back, chewing on her thumbnail as she checks her phone. "Tell her of course it's okay," I say as Gemma finishes off a monstrous mocha with a shake of cayenne and a flotilla of chocolate shavings.

Gemma nods, her eyes on the drink, braids whipping as she turns to both sides of the counter and cries, "Smokin' hot mocha!"

It's too busy to check the POS system now. I'll have to wait until everyone's upstairs and the orders have died down. I leave Gemma to finish the drinks and join the crowd of people funneling up the narrow stairs at the back of the bakery.

I spend so much time in the kitchen that sometimes I forget about the special alchemy of the community space. The walls are lined with original art, including Gemma's recent photo series *The Hills Are Alive and (Sometimes) We Live There*, where she took a bunch of rural Texas queers, including some who live in the city now, and shot them in their original landscapes: skimming their fingers over wildflowers, flying around on horses, turning porch swings into everyday thrones.

The outfits in this room are an art form in themselves.

Whole eras of American culture have been deconstructed, ripped apart, and torn wider until there's room for us. Imagination is splashed across bodies; I'm surrounded by a swirl of color, texture, the negative space of bare skin. Then there's the place itself. It's the best living room you can imagine, crossed with the coziest stage in a nineties coffee shop, raised to the power of a queer lending library. A band called the Deep Eddies, dressed in candy colors and razor lines, are plugging in their equipment.

I find myself looking around with purpose. Just in case W's here. Just in case Harley's here. My heart grates against my ribs. What if they're *both* here?

All around the room, people are making the most of this formless time before the party really starts, finding friends or hastily making new ones. I notice a few well-established groups who have smaller meetings here throughout the week: local two-spirit folks by the snack table, a group of UT drag queens in burnt orange dresses, the bisexual brujas lining the back wall, the Shakespeare queers with their voices ringing above the rest of the crowd.

I notice—I always notice—that there's no real agender contingent.

Mini-crowds glue themselves together quickly. But there are just as many folks milling around, intent on doing their own thing, or moving between groups with a sparkling, fizzy fluidity. Most of the people here range from their late teens to early forties, but there are a few middle schoolers looking around at all of this with big eyes and infinite wonder, a group of white-hairs in the corner talking shit about someone named Jan, and a seventy-ish newcomer wearing a they/them pin, a cowboy hat, and a smile as bright as a Texas sunrise.

Onstage, Vin and Alec wait for us all to quiet down. Or rather, Alec waits, and Vin waves wildly at all of us.

That's the other reason I needed to be here. It's a chance to observe Vin and Alec. They *look* like they could be back together. But any good baker knows that how something looks on the plate is only part of the story.

Alec clears his throat once, which does more than all of Vin's hand-flinging. Leaning down into the mic, shoulders bunched, Alec gives the intro. "All right, y'all. Welcome to community night at the Proud Muffin. Make new friends. Find yourself some family. Flirt, sure, but nothing that you wouldn't do in your prude auntie's house happens in this room. Pronoun stickers are by the door. Remember: nobody owes you their labels. And do not police each other's identities or we will kick you out into that humid, heteronormative night. Okay?"

"Okay," a few people chorus. Someone raises a thumb high.

"And cobbler is half-price all night," Vin adds in a natural boom, no microphone required.

"I was supposed to say that, remember?" Alec asks, teeth locked tight, the mic picking up the hard edge of his words.

Most people have already turned away. Most people don't notice.

I push my way forward.

Alec flits around, helping the band. Vin leans on one side of the stage, watching everyone, arms crossed and face in the hardball stage, as clumped and unmoving as dense caramel. They're definitely not back together. They need my help—and I don't know what to bake next. I could try the same cake again, but what if a simple *sorry* isn't enough for these two? What comes after the apology? Make-it-right rugelach? Show-you've-changed churros?

"Why are you staring at Vin like that?" Marisol asks, bumping into me with her hip as a way of saying hello. "He's our dad. Stop."

"Vin's only ten years older than you," I point out.

"Okay, he's our *grandpa*."

I give a grudging nod. Marisol's right. Queer culture—and the way people treat us—shifts so rapidly that two years can easily feel like twenty. Our generations are different. It's a known fact.

"I was not staring at Vin," I say. "I mean, I was staring at his face, but I wasn't enjoying it on a hormonal level."

I can't look directly at Marisol, though. We bake next to each other all the time, and it's not like she's ever anything but gorgeous, but she really goes all out on community night. Tonight, she's got dusky red lipstick on, applied with the confident hand of someone who can pipe a hundred rosettes in under a minute. Her jeans ride low on her hips, the generous scoop of her tank top showing off her sculpted brown shoulders and the upper curve of her breasts. I remember the day she came back to work after top surgery. It was the only time I've seen Marisol approaching giddy.

"I can't stop thinking about that cake you made." She slaps me on the back. Twice. "Perfect crumb."

"Really?" It feels like we just leveled up in our kitchen relationship. There are so many different kinds of relationships, and I'm suddenly glad that I didn't break this one up. I'm also truly proud that she loved the cake—even if it was originally meant for Vin and Alec.

"It was exactly what I needed." Marisol's face tightens with determination and she angles away into the crowd, as if she's looking for someone. Did my cake help her make up with one of her exes, maybe? Did it mend a broken friendship? I track her until she's lost in the churn of people. As much as I want to know what she's up to—and if it has anything to do with that slice of Very Sorry Cake—there are other mysteries to solve.

Like who bought the rest of my brownies.

As the music starts, I edge back down the stairs. There are a few strays hanging out at the tables, but no one is sitting at the bakery counter. Gemma must have taken a break to go up and listen to the band, because the only employee left behind the counter is Lex—a relatively new hire. She's gently butch and nosebleed tall. Wherever she goes there seems to be a dog-eared book nearby. She wears blocky black glasses that stand out against her amber-brown skin. I know that she's Dominican and the only other person at the Proud Muffin who was mostly raised in a northern state. Upstate New York, in her case. We've bonded a little about being the only people here who weren't born knowing what "bless your heart" actually means or knowing about Frito Pie. And I've got to hand it to her—she keeps the flannel look alive despite the desperate heat. Her brown-and-gold curls are pulled up in a careless style that shows off ear tattoos, little black moons that run in matching curves.

"Just going to ring myself up for a drink," I say.

Lex gives me a little nod and goes back to reading. I have about a minute before she realizes I've been on the computer too long, or a customer barges up and places an order. Or worse: one of the managers notices me fiddling around in the POS and starts to ask questions.

I haven't used this system in a year, since moving on from my counter duties, but my fingers are hardwired to remember the menus. I work my way through, only backtracking a few times, until I find the function that lets me print all the receipts for the two days when the brownies were sold. I wait until Lex's back is fully turned, the music upstairs extra loud, and I hit *print*. A long tongue of paper spits out of the register.

Lex turns back just as I shove it in my pocket. Her eyes go wide, magnified by the glasses.

"You need help with something?" she asks.

"No," I say. "I've got it under control."

I duck into the back, to the employee bathroom. I lock the door, take out a pen, and start circling every time I see *SO*, for special order. Then I check the price column. There were three different special orders in play on those days, but only the brownies were two-fifty. I look for spots where they were sold, mostly in five-dollar pairs.

There were twelve brownies when this started.

Two went to Vin and Alec.

One I gave to Eve.

Jay ordered two by phone on the day I put them out—easy enough to spot.

Kit and Aadi, the iced green tea enthusiasts, bought two around noon the next day, which I can see in the time stamp.

That leaves two credit card purchases made at the front register. One by Martin Thomas, one by Araceli Jimenez. They each bought two brownies, which equates to two more couples that I have to find and fix.

It takes me a while to spot the final purchase.

A mystery customer bought *one* brownie and paid in cash.

I leave the employee bathroom, washing my hands first. It's a habit. And it gives me time to think about where I've seen one of those names before.

The kitchen is dead—all of the day's baking is wrapped up by four in the afternoon—but there's always the possibility that Vin or Alec are lurking around the offices. So I keep it as stealthy as I can.

I head toward the counter where we keep our cake binder filled with standard baking instructions and cake order forms. I flip to the section for recurring customers. Araceli

Jimenez and Verónica De León have a standing order for a cake on February 12. It must be their anniversary, because the requested text is "Araceli and Verónica have been swimming for (X) years." This year it was twelve.

I recognized Araceli's name because I was the one who made the cake this year. It's made to look like Barton Springs, with the two figures piped into different places on the cake each year. There's a recent photo for reference: two people in their late twenties, thirty at the most, sitting on the edge of the springs with their feet in the water. They're both femme, fat, beautiful. I remember mixing the frosting colors for both of their bathing suits—a red retro pin-up one-piece with white trim for Araceli and a flower-print bikini for Verónica. They're smiling, but not at the camera. At each other.

Twelve years.

They've been together since they were my age, and now they're not. Marisol said she was drawn to my cake, so maybe they were drawn to the brownies. Maybe there was a reason. Still, it's my fault the brownies were there in the first place.

It's like I pushed Araceli and Verónica in the deep end.

It's like I dropped their anniversary cake on their toes and then shrugged.

I didn't *mean* to, but that doesn't really matter. Accidents happen in the bakery all the time, and you don't just walk away or pretend it never happened. You fix it. You make another, better cake. Because everything we create matters to someone. It can change their day, their mood.

Sometimes, their life.

I go back upstairs, feeling more determined than ever. And that's when I catch sight of Harley in the corner, talking to D.C.

A pronoun sticker shines on Harley's chest. They. We're both off on Thursdays, which means we're not wearing our work clothes, we're out of our comfortable ruts. Harley is wearing a pair of surprisingly tight charcoal jeans, a whisper-thin white T-shirt, and—oh help—a black leather vest hanging open over their chest. Their hair looks even looser and softer than usual. I swear, my fingers start moving toward Harley's curls involuntarily.

D.C. nods emphatically at something Harley said. The two of them are radiating cuteness. I don't deserve someone being cute in my general vicinity right now. Not after I broke up Araceli and Verónica.

Not after I broke up all of them.

Harley's attention snags on the fact that I'm watching, and they turn without my saying a word. The lead singer of the Deep Eddies whispers a countdown into the mic. A new song starts with a crinkle of static and a body-flooding rush of guitar.

Harley's smile cracks open on the downbeat.

I want this entire night to be about *them*. But across the room, I catch sight of Alec. As much as I want to talk to Harley, I keep getting sidetracked by the mess I made during my breakup. Cleanup on aisle Syd.

Alec works his way through the crowd, talking to all of the people who call the Proud Muffin their social haven, their safe space, their second home. He looks happy to see everyone, but under that delight, he also looks exhausted. His clothes have an unprecedented wrinkle, like he's been too busy arguing to iron. His smile is stiff as fondant—seriously, that stuff is the worst—and Vin trails behind him, cracking a joke here and there. They're not together, but they're going through the same old motions.

I rush up to Harley, past all of the dancing bodies. There's no stopping me. I can't see the whole plan yet, but it's starting to take shape. This is how it feels when I know I need to bake, when there's a shimmering need for something sweet.

"I have to go," I shout over the music. "Do you want to come with?"

"Where?" Harley asks.

"I need supplies."

If anyone talks about shopping for food in Austin, they'll probably spout whole sonnets about Whole Foods. The original location, on North Lamar. It's the Disneyland of grocery stores. And listen, I love sneaking in there on the dog-breath days of summer to buy coconut gelato and eat it as I walk around in the AC.

But nobody I know can actually afford to *shop* there.

Harley and I are at HEB, strolling down the aisles, filling a cart with basics because I'm not sure what direction I'm going with this recipe. The answer itches at the corners of my brain.

I don't know how to scratch my own brain, though, so I keep grabbing flour and baking powder and trying to be patient with this magic.

"Grab a cookie sheet, okay?" I ask, pointing, and Harley doubles back for one as I keep rolling forward.

"I didn't know they have pans here," Harley says, hugging it to their chest, treating the shiny silver sheet like treasure. "Wait, don't you own cookie sheets?"

"Of course," I say.

"You destroy them with the sheer force of your baking, don't you."

"Maybe grab two. And a whisk."

This store looks bare-bones, but it has everything a person needs. That's the magic of HEB. The aisles are wide, the store well-lit. The music over the speakers is probably the only source of canned pop in the whole city, which feels strangely rebellious.

"What else?" Harley asks, bouncing lightly to a Selena Gomez song.

When I told them I was baking tonight, they fell into step right next to me, followed me out to the parking lot. There seemed to be no question about whether or not we would leave together.

I get this sudden feeling that everyone in the store, if they bothered to look at us, would see a couple.

I think about putting my arm around Harley, drawing them close and letting my face rest where their curls meet the curve of their neck. There are freckles there, a cinnamon dusting that I've never noticed. I imagine kissing that spot, pressing my lips there. Tasting. Is Harley's skin salted from biking around, or sweet with powder, or both? Would they sigh into the feeling, or buzz with excitement? Or both?

Harley notices me looking, and their face goes through a transformation, a soft twist to their features. It feels like they're asking what I'm up to. It feels like they're perfectly aware of what I'm up to, and they want me to know that they know. I suddenly feel so warm I could melt chocolate without a double boiler.

This is what I need to bake.

This feeling.

Newness, excitement, a dash of surprise. This is what I can give Araceli and Verónica. They've had the same anniversary cake for twelve years; they need something just as delicious, but different.

I'm still not entirely sure what Vin and Alec need, but this is something they deserve.

"What's your favorite dessert?" I ask, stopping the cart in its squeaky tracks.

"What?" Harley asks.

"Your favorite," I say. "Or, if that's too hard, top five." Because when you start to care about someone, when they're taking up all of your thoughts in a new and wonderful and terrifying way, you bake what they like. It's not one of *my* favorite bakes I need to dig up but one of Harley's.

They look up at the ceiling, then down at the gray-streaked floor. "I . . . um . . . chocolate chip cookies are okay?"

"*Chocolate chip cookies are okay?*" I hold up both hands. I stop everything. "You don't like baked goods, do you?"

"That is correct." Harley squints one eye closed and waits, like I'm about to pass sentence and they can't watch.

"You work at a bakery," I reason.

"Right, and if I loved every good that was baked, I would stop my bike and eat people's birthday cakes under a bridge and then where would we be?"

"Why a bridge?" I ask. "Besides, I bake all day and I don't eat everything."

"They don't give you complete lack of supervision and a getaway vehicle," Harley points out.

My initial shock has burned off. The truth is, I've been willfully overlooking this for a while. Harley hasn't shown any interest in the baked goods at the Proud Muffin. If anything, they've shown anti-interest.

I clack my fingers against the bar of the shopping cart.

"You like savory food, right?" I ask.

They nod.

"Salt and heat?"

They nod and nod.

"Nothing too sweet."

They shiver like we just took a hard left into a horror movie.

"Okay," I say, and kick the squeaky cart into rolling again.

"You're acting suspiciously fine," Harley says as they jog to catch up with my newly invigorated march through the store.

"You don't have to like every baked good," I say as I swipe

a bag of candied ginger off the shelf. "I'm just going to system-atically figure out the ones you *do* like."

"That sounds intense!" Harley calls out as I take a sharp turn at the end of the aisle.

I add a few more ingredients to our cart, all of which Harley finds inscrutable. They give up trying to guess what I'm making and focus on lip-syncing to the Carly Rae Jepsen song over the speakers.

The parking lot is coated in darkness. I balance the bags on my arms, feeling strong and capable and hopeful about Harley falling in love—at the very least with the scones I'm going to make.

Halfway to my house, I get a text. I glance down when we hit a red light.

"Shit. My sister is home."

Her last class before spring break was early this morning. I thought she had another driving day before she made it to Austin. She must have powered through and gotten back early.

"Does she not let you bake?" Harley asks, clearly confused.

"It's just, the house will be crowded and Tess will be tired but my parents will want to do family stuff and . . ."

And besides needing to get magic to the rest of these couples, I really want there to be flirt-baking tonight. Bake-flirting? Either way, it's never going to happen if my house is overrun with family members.

Harley looks out the open window, slides their elbow out into the night. "You know, I do have a kitchen."

And just like that, we're headed to Harley's.

They live on a green street tucked behind St. Ed's. There's a single spot in the driveway, and Harley tells me to pull in.

"Is your mom not here?" I ask.

"She works late a few nights a week and my little sibs are with a family friend."

Without another word, something shifts. We both know we're going to have the entire house to ourselves. We both *want* a place where we're not surrounded by coworkers or Proud Muffin customers or broken-up couples. As much as I love community night, leaving suddenly feels like the best idea I ever had.

When we're parked, I pick up grocery bags from the trunk. Harley gets out of the passenger seat, leans back with a foot kicked up against the car, arms crossed loosely over their chest. Their chin tips up when I look at them, smile as brazen as the last bit of daylight in the sky. I don't know if I'm going to kiss them tonight, but I'm going to let myself think about it every time I look at their lips.

Baking involves a lot of that.

Harley grabs the other half of the grocery bags and ushers me inside. There's an exploratory feeling; I move through the space like I'm discovering a new civilization instead of visiting a house a mile away from my own.

There's a carpet of toys underfoot, coral and blue walls covered in family photographs and kids' artwork, sometimes directly *on* the walls. And I'm not talking a few uninvited scribbles. Trees reach up from the wooden floorboards nearly to the ceiling in some places. A row of birds is perched behind the couch. A storm cloud pelts the welcome mat with inky black rain.

"Here's the kitchen," they say, pulling me toward a little open square lined with butcher-block countertops.

I ask for a mixing bowl, measuring cups, a knife, and a box grater.

"We have those!" Harley says, pulling them down from various cupboards painted with stars and moons. "What else?"

"That's it," I say. "Nothing fancy."

I believe, to the depths of my cupcake heart, that whatever magic there is in baking doesn't come from fancy equipment. It doesn't shut anyone out because they can't afford a $500 stand mixer.

I pour out a cup of flour. Harley watches my hands. We fall into a new kind of quiet together. In my last year of dating W, silences were tentative, breakable, spun sugar. Harley has been leaving comfortable gaps for me to fill with my thoughts, and I've been trying to do the same. But this is different. We've been trading banter for days, and now we're letting our bodies catch up.

We move around each other in circles, giving each other plenty of room. Then our patterns tighten, our looks sharpen, our margins grow smaller until we're side by side, arms pressed together. Our shoulders jostling for no reason. My hip jutting out to find theirs in the half-dark.

"What next?" Harley asks, and I honestly don't know if they're talking about the recipe anymore.

"Now I cut the butter in," I say.

"Do you need the knife?" Harley asks, and looks befuddled when I laugh.

I plunge my hands into the bowl. I usually do this part with a pastry blender, but this time I rely on my fingertips, not just because I don't think Harley has a pastry blender—two knives work almost as well—but also because I want to feel everything.

My fingers sink in, down to the knuckles. When the butter is a scattering of silky little pieces that I know will melt just so as they bake, I scatter the candied ginger on the countertop and use the knife to chop it into little yellow flecks that glitter with crystals. I lift one that looks particularly tempting, the cut side a raw amber.

"What are you doing?" Harley asks.

"Tasting as I go." Another thing that I firmly believe in. "We should taste *everything* as we go."

I drop the piece of ginger on my tongue. It releases a wave of sugared heat.

"Can I have one?" Harley asks. Their eyes are somehow both serious and dancing. I place the ginger on their tongue.

They pull away—bold to shy in one move. "What next?"

"Lemons," I say, barely able to get the word out.

They hand me one lemon, then another, and all I can think when their fingertips leave is that we're mixing ourselves together. That's what happens when skin presses skin.

We think of ourselves as solid and separate, but we're not. We trade and swap tiny pieces of ourselves all the time.

The only person I've ever touched like this is W. But I'm a little bit different now that I've touched Harley.

I'm a little bit new.

"Your evil plan to get me interested in sweets is working," Harley says half an hour later, "because those smell really good."

After I pull the scones out of the oven, we move to the couch. A white plate ringed with little yellow suns and blessed with scones sits between us on the coffee table. The toasted, buttery goodness of the smell is unrelenting.

"Which do you want?" I ask, holding the plate up to eye level, watching Harley over the craggy mound of treats.

"This feels like a trick. What happens if I pick the wrong one?"

"There is no wrong one. Just the best one for you."

"So it's a salty Rorschach test." Harley folds a leg up on the couch. "In that case, I want the nubby one with the darkest bottom." One of the notable things about this recipe is the sugar crystals on the candied ginger leaking down to create a dark, caramelized base, a ginger syrup sealing in all the goodness.

"Interesting choice," I say, framing my chin with my fingers as I pretend to calculate something important about Harley's personality.

But really, I'm a mess, waiting for them to try it.

I'm glad that they haven't been eating my bakes this whole time, though, because there's something about being here. Seeing Harley's fingers wrap around the scone, their eyes and hands taking it in before their lips make a move.

They take their first-ever bite of something I made.

They chew.

Slowly.

"Syd," Harley says, tapping my arm in quick Morse-code flutters. "Syd. Syd. *Syyyyyyd.*"

Everyone reacts to deliciousness differently. No one is very subtle about it. I live for that lack of restraint. Some, like Eve, swear passionately while others, like Alec, give each bite molecular attention. People sigh, stutter, lick their lips, groan in public, relentlessly chase down crumbs. Vin has been known to start singing in Italian. If a bake is really top notch, Marisol shakes her head like she's confused at how decent the world can be. W laughs like she can't believe it. More than once, I've shed a few tears.

Harley is the first one to say my name. In fact, they say it another half dozen times, and my body soaks it up like a cool breeze—with a slight tremble. I like how *Syd* sounds in their mouth, along with the last few crumbs.

Because that scone is *gone.*

We're somehow closer together than we were when

Harley started eating. Edging toward the middle cushion, shoes off, our calves only a few inches away from each other. I wonder what it would feel like if my bare leg made contact with Harley's.

And then Harley puts out a hand and grabs my calf. I'm suddenly aware of the fact that I haven't shaved my legs in a month. Then again, Harley doesn't shave theirs ever. "Syd. That was like lemon and ginger had sex in a swimming pool of butter."

I blink, a little startled. That's the first time I've heard Harley reference sex in anything other than a shy, oblique sort of way. It was bold and sudden, and I find myself giggling like a middle schooler at the back of the bus.

They lean in so close that I can see a crystal of sugar shining at the corner of their lips. I touch it with a fingertip, picking up the tiny grain. Harley touches my mouth back—to be fair, I guess. Then they lean in and put their lips to the same spot.

Not quite on my lips. Not quite a kiss.

"I'm doing this because of the scone, right?" they whisper.

"The scone can't make you do anything," I say. "It can only . . . inspire you."

Harley makes a tiny sound. It's like half excitement, half hiccup. It's the cutest thing I've ever heard.

Maybe I do deserve this much cuteness in my life. Maybe we all do.

"Do you want another?" I ask, dancing the plate in their

direction, unable to hold back now that I know Harley likes them.

"No," Harley says staunchly, moving their hand off my leg. That was our first real prolonged contact, and I feel the loss right away. "These children of unprotected lemon-ginger sex have other destinies."

I groan and boo. But Harley's right—these scones aren't for us.

"So how do we deliver these to all the people you still need to get back together?" Harley asks.

"Well, these are for two in particular. Araceli and Verónica." And Vin and Alec. Everything is for them, because they gave me everything I have. "I've been thinking about the delivery process. Taking the baked goods straight to the couples might work in some cases, like Rae and Jay. But for others it would be really hard to dig up addresses, and really shady if we just showed up with unsolicited sweets. Besides, the brownies went out four days ago. Do we really have time to track down everyone and hand-deliver bakes to each couple? What if they start to waft away from each other and no amount of butter can bring them back together?"

I've never thought about it before, but timing is as big a factor in relationships as it is in baking. Which cakes fall and which ones rise. Which people choose each other at particular moments and whether those moments turn into something longer. Something that lasts. The same thing goes for breakups. Couples can get back together months or years or even decades after breaking up, but those feel like the exceptions. There's an expiration date on most people deciding they should work it out.

I wonder if W and I have slid past that day already.

"So we're on a tight magical schedule." Harley leans in, conspiratorial now instead of flirtatious. But it still makes my heart bang like a spoon against the side of a metal bowl. "What now?"

"It's time to bring the broken-up to us." Marisol had hinted at the idea, but Harley talking about the smell of the scones made me feel certain. "Have you ever come home and realized there was something good cooking, maybe an onion softening on the stove or spice thickening the air?"

I wait for Harley's slow, certain nod. Harley can drawl a nod—I have no idea how, but they can.

"Has it ever drawn you across the house, tugged at you, until you could barely think about anything else?"

"Sure," Harley says, like this is the simple math of food.

"We're going to Barton Springs tomorrow," I say, "and we're bringing the scones with us."

Shiny New Scones

~~~~ INGREDIENTS ~~~~

2¼ cups all-purpose flour

¼ cup granulated sugar

3 tsp baking powder

½ tsp salt

¾ cup (1½ sticks) butter

1 to 2 lemons' worth of zest

1 cup candied ginger, finely chopped

¾ cup full-fat coconut milk (the kind that comes in
a can, NOT the kind that comes in a carton)

1 egg (super optional)

~~~~ DIRECTIONS ~~~~

Coconut milk is the real magic in this recipe. It's just as
rich as cream, but it's got more flavor. It keeps the scones
equally good the second, third, and fourth day. This isn't
a short-lived delight.

This is going to last.

Line a baking sheet with parchment paper.

Preheat the oven to 400 degrees.

Mix the flour, sugar, baking powder, and salt in a bowl.

Take out your butter—it should be just-from-the-fridge cold. Cut it into small squares and cut into the flour mixture.

Realize you probably should have added the zest earlier, but you've been distracted by the presence of a cute baking partner. Realize that everything is going to turn out delicious either way.

Zest those lemons. Stir the zest and candied ginger into the dough. Take a beat to breathe in that unbeatable citrus-spice combo.

If your coconut milk has separated, whisk until it's smooth. Make a little well in the center of your bowl and pour it in. Mix until just combined: the dough might feel a little shaggy or crumbly and that's okay. You don't want a wet dough, but you can add another tablespoon or two of coconut milk if it won't stick together.

Shape the scones any way you like. I know that some people are really into wedges. I like to make big, rustic scones, molding them with my hands into large pucks— seven or eight for a batch this size—then watch as each one becomes its own unique, craggy shape in the oven, like a mountain that you can only conquer by eating it.

If you want an egg wash to make the tops of the scones shiny, crack an egg, whisk in a tablespoon of water, and brush the tops of the scones. But honestly, they're already going to be perfect.

Bake for 12 to 20 minutes depending on the size of your scones, longer for larger ones. When they're done, the tops and bottoms should be golden brown and everything between should be golden, and when you taste it, golden rays should burst out of you.

Serve while you are still glowing.

6

Staying out late on Tess's first night home leaves an after-taste of guilt. I scrape myself out of bed before dawn the next morning and make my sister's favorite breakfast. Ricotta pancakes with fresh blackberries and a side of crispy bacon, everything doused in syrup. She comes downstairs and eats a record-breaking *eight* while our parents sleep through the alarm upstairs. Which further verifies my theory that nobody is feeding college students.

I get a flash of myself in the future. I'm camped out in a shared kitchen, flipping pancakes for a crowd of pajama-clad strangers. It's a little exciting, and a little sad because it's the first time I've pictured college without W in the frame. And a little gross because: dorm kitchen.

I've daydreamed about going straight from high school graduation into an apprenticeship. It's the old-school system that professional bakers used to work their way up to positions like head pastry chef or bakery owner. It's what Alec did, and he's offered, more than once, to connect me with his old friends in California, Tuscany, Paris. But staying here and sticking with UT means that I can work at the Proud Muffin.

Most bakers work for years or decades—to develop skills, yes, but also to find a kitchen where they fit. I don't want to walk away from a place where I already do. It feels like dropping a winning lotto ticket on the ground and scratching another one, just to see what happens. Besides, there's nothing that I could learn in Paris that Alec and Marisol can't teach me right here.

"I have to get going," I say, rushing a bite of pancake through my syrup.

"Baking?" Tess asks.

I make a vague *yes* noise. Taking my scones to Barton Springs in the hopes of luring a couple there so I can magically repair their relationship falls under the general category of *baking*.

First, I have to get through a whole day of school, though. Harley is going to meet me after last bell, which seemed like a practical plan when we first made it and now feels increasingly bizarre. I'm still getting used to seeing Harley in the various places that constitute my life.

"I wish you could stay until Mom and Dad actually get out of bed. They're still cuddling," she grumbles in the direction of the coffee maker. Apparently, living up north requires hot coffee. I've never seen her drink it before.

"Cuddling is not a crime," I say.

"Of course not, but I'm only here for a week. Don't you think they can put off some of the regularly scheduled PDA?" She misses the filter with her measuring spoon; coffee grounds skitter away like tiny creatures whose sole purpose is finding a corner no broom can reach.

"It's not public if they do it in their bedroo—"

Tess holds up a stop-that-right-now hand. "You don't still want to be like them, do you?"

"What do you mean?" I ask.

With a mashing of buttons, Tess manages to start the coffee maker. It pees slowly into the pot. "Come on, Syd. You've always wanted a relationship like theirs, with cartoon hearts above your head at all times."

I sit back down abruptly. So abruptly that my plate clatters and syrup flies up, flecking me all over.

I've never thought I had anything in common with my parents, not when it comes to what we care about in romance. They're so straight, so powdered-sugar sweet. But it's possible Tess is right. Since we moved to Austin, Mom and Dad have put a huge amount of time into their relationship. I'm shocked and impressed by how much they genuinely like each other. They give each other compliments all the time. They never stop finding tiny, absurd things to celebrate. They snort-laugh at each other's jokes. They call it snorkeling.

I put my head down on the table. "Stop saying insightful things, it's earrrrrly."

Tess has been home for less than a day and I've already snapped back into being the frustrating, whiny sidekick to her older-and-wiser-sister act. It's not a conscious decision. It's like making a recipe you've baked your way through a thousand times before; at some point, the grooves in your brain take over and you do it without thinking.

"Do you want some?" she asks, brandishing a mug at me.

"Coffee's a liar," I mutter, pouring a glass of ruby-clear cranberry juice instead.

"What are you talking about? Have you been drinking too much of this stuff at the bakery to stay awake? Is this what happens when you try to work a full-time job *and* finish high school at once?"

"My job is not the problem," I insist. "Coffee smells one way and tastes another. That's dishonest."

Tess's sudden attack on my baking ambitions feels out of place. She's always been the first, last, and loudest to support me. But maybe it's starting to wear on her that I've known what I want to do since I was in fifth grade, and she's just starting to figure it out.

Tess loads three more pancakes on her plate, then draws chaotic syrup shapes over them.

"You have a meal plan at school, right?"

"Yeah, but nobody does this like you," she says.

And it doesn't matter how much we argue. When she says

that, the compliment goes straight to my heart.

We're chewing in silence when it occurs to me that I could have imbued these pancakes with some kind of feeling. I think back: the only thing I remember churning around as I whisked the batter was guilt.

Tess melts into the couch with a sigh. "I should have been here when W stomped on your ventricles."

I shrug. "What's done is done."

Unless, of course, it was done by my brownies. Then it's getting *un*done.

Tess looks at me sideways from her place in the folds of the couch. "You're not as sad as I thought you'd be."

"That's good, right?"

Tess pulls her hair into a hasty bun. She has the exact same hair as I did, when I had hair. Soft and swishy and light brown. Forty percent, milk chocolate. I honestly don't remember what it was like until I see hers, and then I get this funny feeling, like I've put my own hair on top of her head for safekeeping.

"Mom and Dad weren't giving me details, but they were clearly worried that you were doing secret moping. They thought you and W would last forever, that you were destined and all that. They were completely unprepared. I've always known it would be my job to take care of you if and when the breakup occurred. That's why I came home as fast as humanly possible. But you weren't even here. If you were out chasing after W, I'm going to feel personally responsible."

Waves of guilt rise up in quick, nauseating succession.

I shouldn't have been at Harley's last night.

I shouldn't be able to move on this fast.

I shouldn't have ignored my sister when I see Harley literally every day.

"Wait. Go back. You didn't think W and I were meant to be together?"

"I don't think anyone's *meant* to be together. I think people choose to be together, and you were choosing W hard and often. I just wasn't sure if she was choosing you back in the same way."

"You neglected to mention *any* of that when we were dating."

"I know." She impales another piece of pancake, then just stares at it. "Most people don't listen when I give relationship advice. It doesn't mean I'm not brilliant." Tess has never really dated anyone. In high school, she was always too busy being on the honor roll and consuming the entire YA room in the library downtown and playing every sport.

"Anyway, I don't think the breakup trashed you completely," she concludes.

"Thanks?"

"You look good, sis." She pops the speared pancake into her mouth.

I wince at the word. It doesn't hurt, exactly. More like the sting of lemon on a cut that I forgot about.

"How's college?" I ask, rolling up a pancake like a scroll and dragging one end through the syrup. "You choose a major yet?"

"Ask me a less boring and yet somehow completely stressful question," she says, balancing her coffee cup on the kangaroo pouch of her Northwestern University sweatshirt. Tess raced back to the Midwest the second she graduated from high school. Besides finding the heat here personally offensive, she's always been more connected to the place where we were born. I'm only a few years younger, but I don't have that same sense of being *from* Illinois.

Of course, some Texans think you're not *from* Texas unless your grandfather's horse's grandfather was born here.

"Do you like the dorms?" I ask. "Are they cozy?"

She scrunches her nose.

"Make out with any co-eds yet?"

She scrunches her whole face.

I feel bad that I could never help Tess with her love life. Even if W and I didn't last forever, at least we had some happiness first. Maybe now that Tess is swimming in a whole new dating pool, things will change.

"Listen, everybody said I was over high school boys, and I'd find someone great in college, but that's not why I'm there. I wish people would stop bringing it up. You're even worse than Mom and Dad. It's practically Victorian. Next you're going to break out the marmalade and start talking about marriage prospects."

"I put marmalade on pancakes *one time*," I say, spearing a final bite self-righteously. "It wasn't even bad! And excuse me for being excited that I might be allowed to marry someone I love someday," I add in a cakey mumble.

Tess puffs air out, her stomach deflating, coffee cup sinking. "Ugh. Yeah. Sorry."

She knows that I've had nightmares—that I've literally dreamed I was walking down the aisle only to have someone shout out, mid-ceremony, that the DOMA ruling had been overturned. It gets a lot weirder from there. Usually I run in slow motion as my wedding outfit, a pair of white silk overalls, frays to pieces. My blurry spouse-to-be gets upset and takes it out on the cake. Which I made, of course, a ten-tier strawberry shortcake—*real* shortcake, which doesn't stack well. The cake falls apart spectacularly, and the redacted love of my life leaves, but I'm not allowed to stop the party because everyone else is having so much fun. Then there's an upsetting dance break: the nightmare version of the spontaneous musical number in a rom-com. At the end of the reception, most people take the wedding gifts back, but someone leaves me a baby giraffe, because even though I'm not married they can't return it to the zoo.

I grab my backpack and scowl at my sister for reminding me of this. It's not fun to admit, but maybe I'm a little obsessed with love because I'm afraid that, at any moment, it could be snatched away.

The school parking lot is inundated with Friday afternoon madness. Harley has to swim upstream to get to me. "This does not look like your scene," they say, handing over the plastic container of scones in individual paper bags. They look like party favors, but instead of goodie bags, they're breakup bags. I immediately smuggle them into my trunk.

"What? Illicit scone drops? I do these all the time."

Harley looks around again. "I only check in at my high school once a week at this point. Being here is kind of weird. It's making me nostalgic for a thing I never did. There should be an obscure German word for that."

This is probably part of why I've always felt so comfortable around Harley. Neither of us went through the Standard All-Inclusive American Teen Experience. It's something I'm sure I felt before I fully knew why.

"I still can't believe you're halfway through college," I admit. It makes me feel a little behind on real life, as if I exist in an alternate dimension where only baked goods and broken hearts matter.

"I still can't believe you made magical scones in my kitchen last night," Harley counters. "But I know you did, because I came very close to eating them all and inventing some kind of lie about a magical mugging."

We get into my car. The drive down to Barton Springs feels like it takes only a few heartbeats.

I get an impossible parking spot, right in the shade, and as much as I'd love to linger here with Harley and do really, really standard teenage things, we both leap out of the car, ready to field test our scones.

"Sorry. No food allowed past this point."

The sweaty person running the Barton Springs ticket

shack looks genuinely apologetic. And did I mention sweaty? Ordinarily I would offer them a scone, but these are reserved for the lovelorn.

"Oh. Right."

"We're not going to swim?" Harley asks me, looking a little lorn, too. They must really like swimming.

"We'll go in as soon as Verónica and Araceli have their scones," I promise.

Fortunately, the south entrance to Barton Springs is basically a big open field where people park their cars, with little kids running around flinging droplets in every direction, people on dates icing each other with generous amounts of sunblock. It's the perfect place for a picnic. I open the scones and settle them on an impromptu picnic blanket, also known as my shirt. Then I take off my shorts.

"Um, you're wearing a bikini," Harley says.

"Um, yes?"

"It looks good," Harley says with what sounds like a very dry mouth. And then they immediately add, "It looks like you."

"Oh. Good. *Genderless bathing suit* isn't really an option that most stores carry, so shopping sucked." I try to keep my tone fluffy, but the truth is that my mom took me on an increasingly frantic mall trip that turned into an entire week of depression on my part, and apology pizza on hers. She thought I was going through a teen girl there's-too-much-pressure-on-my-body phase. She tried so hard to help. I would just stand and stare at myself in the dressing room mirrors and I wouldn't show her any of the options. I *couldn't*.

It wasn't that I hated the suits, or even that I hated how my body looked in the suits. I just couldn't say *yes*. That word got farther and farther away from me; *yes* was there and real and life-size, and then I was hurtling away from it until I was in outer space, and there was no oxygen left, and it was cold, and I wasn't supposed to be alive. Not in that kind of environment, at least.

"My sister found this for me," I say. "She's good at online shopping."

She also knows me really well. Tess might not always be aware of queer culture, or the way my life is different from hers, but, occasionally, she saves the day just by being my sister. She remembered that I've always liked my midriff area. She knows that I don't want my chest to feel like it's about to pop out of whatever I'm wearing, hence the high-necked halter top. The bottoms are boy shorts, which I'm basically wearing every day under my clothes. And then there are the colors—royal blue with rainbow racing stripes up the side— which was just Tess daring me not to love them.

"What did you think I'd be wearing?" I ask, letting the question spill, even though it might lead to a mess.

"A one-piece, maybe?" Harley tries. "Like those sporty suits."

"That sounds good in theory."

There were so many things that I wanted to wear, things that sounded good in theory. But for the most part, they were designed to look good on very thin, "properly" androgynous people. I gave up on them a long time ago and decided to

126

patchwork together other styles. When it worked, it was fun. Sometimes it felt like I was putting the weight of my entire identity on a few flimsy bits of fabric, though. Some days I could barely get dressed at all. Some days I stared at my closet like it owed me answers instead of jeans.

"What about you?" I ask.

"You mean my suit? It's pretty basic, I guess."

I sit back, wanting a good angle for the big reveal. Harley watches what I'm doing with a growing smirk.

"Are you waiting for me to strip, Syd?"

"Absolutely, yes." My cheeks broil.

"I have to get changed when we go inside," Harley says, patting their messenger bag. "My suit's in here."

So we stretch out and talk, letting the smell of the scones waft away. I'm not sure how long the magic will take to spread to Araceli and Verónica, wherever they are.

The good news is that even after days of spending constant time together, our conversation hasn't run dry. When I'm halfway into a monologue about how the word *y'all* is a gender-neutral national treasure, Vin marches up to us. I was hoping he and Alec might show up, confirming my hypothesis about the power of these scones.

Of course, in my head, I wasn't picturing his bathing suit. Or his chest hair.

"Syd. Harley. You're here."

"And you're . . . in zebra stripes," I say crisply.

He looks down at himself like he forgot. "These are fashion."

"Are they, though?" Harley mutters.

"I heard I missed out on your olive oil cake," Vin says, pretending Harley didn't just speak. Vin *is* possibly the biggest fan of my bakes that include Italian ingredients, which is one of the reasons I assumed the Very Sorry Cake would call out to him. He's a hundred percent Italian, though he would say it's more; our people are skilled at exaggerating. I'm three-quarters: Mom's side and half of Dad's. Together, Vin and I developed a gianduja muffin for the bakery that would make someone who loves jarred Nutella weep, and spent hours bonding over the very specific joys of baking with Italian cheeses.

"Sorry about the cake," I say, thinking of the miniscule monsters at Rae and Jay's who ate my backup round. "I do have scones, though!" I hold them up, shaking the plastic container ever so slightly. I have a flashback to Girl Scouts, pushing boxes of Thin Mints at everyone I knew while silently critiquing their cardboard crumb. Girl Scouts was tough, for a variety of reasons. The girls in my troop didn't know what to do with me, I didn't know why I felt so out of place, and in the end, I only sold six boxes of Samoas to my mom. Samoas are actually pretty good.

"Good, good," Vin says, echoing my thoughts as he turns over one of my scones. "Beautiful color."

"They're just scones," I say, suddenly embarrassed to be offering Vin something so simple. I've always felt like I should impress my bosses by pushing for ever-fancier bakes with wildly elaborate presentation. But the truth is, both he and Alec love food in a way that completely lacks snobbery. Alec knows how to construct the world's most complicated tiered cakes and tarted-up tarts, but when they opened their own place, Vin and Alec agreed on homestyle baking, where the emphasis is always on how it tastes and how it makes you feel over how it looks in a display case. It's one of the things that makes the Proud Muffin feel so much like a big family reunion. We've got good, simple food, rampant gossip, endless fighting, fierce love.

"Just scones," Vin scoffs.

He takes one and makes quick work of it. I can feel Harley reach for my fingers, squeeze. We're waiting for the magic— for the moment when his manner shifts, his smile sparks, and he wants Alec in a whole new way.

"Hmmm." Vin chews, thoughtful, but with a lid closed tight over whatever those thoughts actually are. His darkly stubbled chin travels up and down, up and down as his chewing slows.

Harley's fingers are like a tourniquet around mine, keeping most of the fear in. I need this to work. It's going to work.

"Thanks, Syd," he says. "Harley." He nods. "Well, I came to get in a swim before I get back to some paperwork, so . . ."

He turns to leave.

"Don't you want one to take to Alec?" I ask, my voice sounding like the horrible croak of a grackle, the long-beaked nightmare birds that haunt the power lines in Austin and attack any stray bit of food.

"Oh." Vin angles back to me, looking a little surprised, trying not to show it. "Actually we're both so busy that I don't think I'll see him until tomorrow. And you know scones. They dry out so fast . . ."

"Not mine!" I say. "Coconut milk."

"Ah." Vin nods appreciatively. "Some folks are hell-bent on heavy cream, but I see how that could work." We don't sell scones at the bakery, to keep the spotlight on muffins. Normally I would argue him into letting me try them as a special. Today all I care about is seeing him back together with Alec, the way they're meant to be.

Maybe my sister doesn't believe in that sort of thing. But I do.

Vin nods at us one more time and heads toward the pool.

"Can we go swimming now?" Harley asks.

"Did you see that?" I ask. "He has no idea where Alec even is. They're presenting a united front at the bakery, but . . ."

I watch Vin's retreat carefully. Are the zebra shorts a sign? A way for him to state that he's single and free to make bold, questionable choices? Those shorts could mean nothing, or everything.

"Well, the scones seem to be working, so Alec should be here soon. What kind of bathing suit do you think he wears?" Harley asks, bouncing in a cross-legged position. "Tweed? Corduroy? *Houndstooth?*"

We take bets, but as it turns out about ten minutes later, neither of us is right.

Alec is wearing a Speedo.

Harley and I are so mesmerized by the sudden sight of

our boss striding into Barton Springs wearing a single band of fabric, unless you include his flip-flops. Which I don't. It's like when I saw my fourth-period teacher out on Sixth Street in her low-cut party shirt, but times a million.

"Ummmmm. Can I be the first to say that Alec can get it?" Harley whispers.

"Oh." I emergency-tap their arm. "What if he's here *getting it*?"

"Looking for someone new?" Harley asks, face crinkling like old cling wrap. "No. No. Even if they're broken up, they've been together for a really long time. They're *Vin* and *Alec*. Neither of them would be on to the next guy so fast."

I restrain myself from mentioning that W and I have been broken up for the same amount of time, and yet I'm sitting here with Harley, on a tiny picnic blanket that is also my discarded clothing.

My head goes back to the walk-in freezer, watching through a crack in the door. I've tried so hard not to think about that argument, but . . .

"I heard Alec say that Vin was 'being wooed.'" Something inside of me curls up at the memory. "I don't know the details, but it sounded serious."

"I guess that changes things. Maybe Alec feels like he should be . . . out there? Looking? Even moving on?" The consequences play out on Harley's face. Vin and Alec's relationship really could be snapping under the weight of lies and new love interests. And that could spell doom for the Proud

Muffin. For all of us. "We have to get Alec the scone. Now."

I'm not sure if we should, though. If Vin really does have feelings for someone else, Alec deserves a clean breakup, right? But if Alec didn't want to fall back in love with Vin, he wouldn't be here. *Right?*

Just like making macarons, this plan looked neat and pretty in my head, but it's kind of a disaster in real life.

When I look up, Alec is already passing the entrance.

We run after him, sliding to a halt when a voice snaps out *"Stop"* from the little wooden shack. The sweaty ticket giver was nice the first time. Now they just look disgruntled. "No. Food. Inside."

Harley and I back away, our hands up like we're common criminals.

As soon as we're out of sight around the side of the little shack, I turn to Harley. "We have to smuggle this in," I whisper, pushing it at them. "You're the one with pockets."

"The attendant is already on to us. If I put it in my pockets, they'll see, you know, a bulge."

"It's not supposed to be on the side like that, is it?" I ask, pretending to know even less than I do. "My penis education has been, uh, lacking."

Harley folds in half, laughing. When they come back up, they say, "Traditionally it goes in the front."

"Well, your shorts are still the roomiest thing we've got . . ."

"I'm not packing with a scone!" Harley whisper-shouts, and now we're both on the grass, completely collapsed with laughter. Then Harley rolls over and look at me with a smile that feels quieter, thoughtful.

"What?" I ask.

"I just like that I can make that joke with you and feel completely comfortable. You know?"

I do. I really, really do.

"Okay," I say, rolling up to sitting. "I think we're going to need a different strategy."

I pull the top of my suit forward and shove the scone in. The paper bag crinkles and scratches on the way down, but the vaguely round scone lodges in the center of my chest—and the halter makes the whole thing look more or less smooth.

Tess really did pick the perfect bathing suit.

"I'll stay here and make sure Verónica and Araceli get theirs," Harley calls out as I head back to the entrance for a third time.

"Thanks," I say, giving Harley a backward thumbs-up. Normally I wouldn't outsource any part of this.

But I trust them.

And I have to fix things with Alec, before this gets any worse.

I've lived in Austin for five years, but Barton Springs still looks like the enchanted heart of a city where it's always summer.

The water is the first thing that grabs your attention, the

same way it grabs the light. It's not a stinging chlorinated color but a gemlike blue green. The bottom is natural, mossy and slick with stones, the sides rimmed with concrete. That might take away the charm for some people, but to me it seems like the perfect, polite southern nod to the city's balance: living, breathing green rubbing right up against brick and glass.

I like all the nearby springs—Deep Eddy is more like a swimming pool, and if you have a car, you can drive half an hour out of the city to Krause Springs, where you will find not only rope swings, icy full-body refreshment, and a thick slice of country quiet but also a butterfly garden with wind chimes as big as your entire body, if you're into that sort of thing. But Barton Springs is the first place I ever went swimming in Austin, and it's the one I love most.

It's also enormous: the length of at least three regular pools, and wide enough that I can't hold my breath when I swim underwater from side to side, though W can. Which means that when I spot Alec on the other side, I scurry as fast as I can without running, which will get me kicked out faster than illicit snacks. People from all over the city and the suburbs and visitors to Austin throng on all sides, actually cool enough to coexist.

When I reach Alec, he's reading a big tome hoisted high, basically a shield against social interaction. It's Rose Levy Beranbaum's *Baking Bible.* Of course, he's the one person at Barton Springs reading a cookbook end to end, like a novel. He's dog-earing every recipe he likes, which appears to be every recipe in the book. Alec is doing the exact opposite of flirting with strangers, and I'm so, so, so glad that he doesn't have his taxi light on.

That's what W called it. I don't know where she came up with this, but around sophomore year she started insisting that there were two basic states when it came to love: being open to a new relationship and being spoken for. Not just technically, in the eyes of the world, but in your heart. If you were really, truly taken, your taxi light was off.

"What about polyamorous people?" I asked.

"You can fit more than one person into a taxi," W said a little thinly, like I was being thick on purpose.

Maybe I was.

"That's not an up-to-date metaphor," I pressed. "People don't use taxis. They just rideshare or take those dumb scooters everywhere."

"*Those scooters*," W said, and then we were off on a sideways rant about the scooters that flock around the city, carrying drunk college students everywhere while the rest of us try not to kill them, or ourselves.

Alec has officially noticed me watching him read. His book comes down one inch at a time, and when it becomes clear that I'm not going anywhere, he finally turns it upside down and rests it across his lap—gracefully covering the Speedo, thank you, Alec.

"Syd?" he asks, waiting for me to explain my sudden presence.

"I have something for you," I say.

I hold out the brown paper bag. Alec's pinched frown interrogates me without words.

"It's not booze or anything weird," I say. Then I remember that I'm offering him magical baked goods I made in an attempt to fix the fact that, with other magical baked goods, I unknowingly pushed his relationship to the brink of destruction.

It is something weird.

"It's a scone," he says with a glimmer of a smile as I pull it out of the bag. "You know, I love that you found time for these."

"What do you mean?" I ask.

"Oh, just . . ." He hefts the sizeable cookbook, showing off all of his marked pages. "I want to bake everything, but, strangely enough, owning a bakery can make it much, much harder. This is my one afternoon off all week, and coming here to cool off was about all I could manage."

I'm standing there in the high beams of the sun, sweating from my neck to the back of the knees, completely stuck in place by Alec's words.

"Enjoy the days of your life that are all about doing what you love. For people like us, this is what it all comes down to, right?" Alec holds up the scone in the world's saddest kind of cheers.

He hides behind his book, makes a few discreet chomping sounds, and about twenty seconds later, he's back. Alec looks a little hazy and gently dazzled, like the sun has gotten to him, but not in a bad way.

And then it's my turn to be dazzled. I look up to find Harley's silhouette, the sun kissing their shoulder.

It's a pretty dramatic bathing suit reveal.

I'm fatally dry-mouthed looking at them in their compact, seamless black wetsuit, cut mid-thigh where their muscles are visibly strong from biking, sliced off at the shoulders, high-necked so that when they turn a bit I can see the curls that stick to their collar.

"Uh, hi."

Alec can probably hear my tongue sticking to the roof of my mouth.

"Are y'all . . . ?" Alec waves his hand, erasing his last words before I can even angst over them. He probably doesn't want to know which of his employees are dating each other. Which is fair.

Harley and I aren't together, not in any kind of official or tangible way. But Harley has become the person I want to talk to when my brain starts to itch, the one I save my best jokes for, the one whose bathing suit gives me a minor aneurysm. And we only met because of the Proud Muffin. In a way, Vin and Alec's magic brought us together, as much as mine took them apart.

I swallow the guilt, but it goes down dry.

"Alec, I think I saw Vin over by the deep end," I blurt. "Just look for the Italian zebra."

Alec looks from me to Harley. From Harley to me. He seems to make a decision, stands up, and tucks his book beneath his arm. "Have a good day, you two."

"Should I follow him?" I ask as soon as Alec is out of earshot. "To make sure the scones work?"

Vin and Alec find each other at the far end of the pool. "You have to let the magic do its thing, right?" Harley asks.

"Right," I say. "Right."

In an attempt not to cramp their style or crowd their private moment, I scan the slope with all the sunbathers on it. And I see someone else I know from the Proud Muffin.

Jessalee is over there, looking entirely too picturesque. She's wearing a cotton two-piece in excellent condition, the kind that you can only find if you shop deep vintage. It's the bright yellow of European butter—yes, it's different from American butter—shot through with blue plaid. Her hair has faded from a vivid blue, pulled up tight enough to show dark blond roots. She's writing in a notebook at top speed. She looks consumed by her own thoughts, otherwise I might wave.

"Did anyone else come by for the scones?" I ask.

"Araceli and Verónica," Harley said. "They showed up separately, but each wandered over to ask about the incredible smell. They were each given a scone and a reminder to wait twenty minutes before swimming."

I whip up a smile. I was secretly hoping some of our other couples would make an appearance. They must need different bakes. Even if we can get Araceli and Verónica back together, that still leaves Kit and Aadi, Martin Thomas and whoever Martin Thomas used to date, and the mysterious all-cash customer.

"So where are the other scones?" I ask.

"I left them outside."

"Where anyone could take them?"

"I mean, they're on top of your car, wrapped up in your T-shirt. It would be pretty weird if somebody ate them."

"Harley." I lower my voice to a confidential pitch, like I'm letting them in on some big secret. "Austin is a weird place."

Keep Austin Weird might have started out as a motto on T-shirts, but now it's emblazoned on my brain. It's a prayer, a plea, a hope. Weird is so much of what I love about this city, and I don't know what's going to happen when it's gone.

"There they are." Harley points out two swimmers at opposite ends of the pool.

Verónica is swimming laps, her arms cutting out of the water, a neon blue swimming cap making her easy to spot as she surfaces for a breath. Araceli floats on her back in the same red fifties-style suit she wore in the photo, serene, unsmiling, big white sunglasses shading her freckled brown cheeks.

They're completely unaware of each other, spinning in their own little orbits around a moment that I hope is becoming more and more inevitable.

Verónica finishes a lap and stops at the side of the pool. She hangs out with her arms folded over the side, shoulders in the sun and the rest of her still bobbing in the water. I can see her more clearly now.

"I made their cake," I say, groaning into my hands. "I made their cake and now I'm the reason they won't have *another* cake."

"We just have to get them a little closer to each other," Harley says, walking us down to the edge of the pool. "The scones will do the rest."

If they're still primed to fall back in love with each other.

"So how do we . . . ?"

Harley's already answered my question by taking to the air, touching their toes, and jackknifing into the water. They come up spitting and glowing with a sort of frozen glee. The water in Barton Springs is naturally, famously cold. "Come on, Syd."

"They really should have waited twenty minutes," I mutter, then leap in.

Water makes its relentless way up my nose. A riot of bubbles releases as I let go of my breath. After the water seals back over me, I tuck my knees and let myself sink for just a second. I pretend that I'm just a normal, bored teenager here with friends, trying to break the heat. I let everything go: all of the relationships I have to save as soon as I surface. It's too cold to stay down for long, though.

When I come back up, Harley is waiting to splash me.

The water explodes into rainbows, refracting as it breaks into pieces and falls cold over both of us. Our laughter breaks just like that. Bright pieces of it fall and then stop as I push a wave of water back at Harley. They dart away from me, fast as an otter. I follow, shouting and spluttering.

"Come on," they say. "You can't catch me."

I really can't. I'm an okay swimmer, but Harley has clearly done this a lot. They bob and weave through the crowded springs, glancing at me over their shoulder, grinning like it's no big deal to do this backward.

But Harley isn't flirting with me—or they aren't *just* flirting with me. They're being strategic, shepherding the rest of the swimmers closer and closer together, until Verónica's laps intersect directly with the path of Araceli's floating.

I wince, waiting for it.

The crash. The cry of "Watch it!"

Followed by the moment when Araceli flips around, trying to see who ran into her. "Is that—?" She takes off her sunglasses and gasps, like she's been holding it in until the moment she's sure that Verónica is the one who collided with her.

I wonder about all of their other collisions. The good ones, the bad ones, the little accidents and sleepy wake-ups when someone's elbow wandered into someone else's face. I want all of that.

Araceli and Verónica are softly treading water now, facing each other.

Harley sticks close as I swim up behind them and casually—very casually—listen to every single thing they're saying.

"It's really you."

"Couldn't stay away, I guess," Verónica says, and it sounds like she might be talking about her inability to stay away from more than Barton Springs. She stares at Araceli for a long beat, then glances away.

Araceli doesn't seem to notice that longing-soaked look, or maybe she's just afraid to really see it. "Why would you be anywhere else, really?" she asks. "Swimming on a hot day is like . . ."

"Being awake while you're dreaming," Verónica finishes for her.

The light seems to go on behind Araceli's smile. "I forgot how good you were at that."

"At what?" Verónica asks.

"Making life sound dreamy."

It sounds like they're working up some sparks, but I want to hear more. The water is deep, though, and my legs get tired faster than I want to admit. I lock my arms around Harley's neck. Just for a second.

They pull me in. My body slides against theirs in that weightless, watery way.

And I swear my legs do this without my brain telling them to. They latch around Harley's hips. They pull me closer than the closest we've been so far. We're face to face, boldly ignoring the fact that our bodies are basically fused. Each daring the other one to mention it. Harley is holding both of us up now, working hard. I can't tell if they're working up to something or holding it back. Either way, a total focus takes over their face. They blink hard, breathe harder.

We bob there, smiling like we've just figured something out. I touch a spot on Harley's face where water has turned a dimple into a tiny well.

"This isn't what we're here to do," I say.

"Then let's go somewhere else," Harley says hoarsely.

When I turn around, Araceli and Verónica are laughing at something one of them said, cackling really, heads back. Verónica touches Araceli's face. They're both glistening with water and glowing with sun as they swim around each other, around and around, a circle that never ends.

If that isn't shiny, I don't know what is.

"Come on," Harley says. "Let's go."

"Where?" I ask.

But I know it doesn't strictly matter. I just want to keep going new places with them.

We swim to the edge of the pool, hoist our bodies into the air. Things have changed while we were in the water. The world has lost a little bit of harshness. Even the air feels kinder, gentler.

We didn't bring towels. I put my arms around Harley, like I'm going to somehow absorb their shivering, make them warm and dry.

"Why don't you meet me back at the car?" Harley asks. "I want to get out of my suit."

My feet pick up wet grass as I walk back to the south

entrance. I stop as soon as I'm out, and catch my breath from all the swimming. Then I get a glimpse of zebra stripes and peer around the side of the little shack.

Vin and Alec are making out back there.

Not like grandpas.

"Oh," I say, so happy and also slightly weirded out.

I run away with my hands over my mouth. When I look back, Harley hasn't come out yet, so I cross the field to the car.

Where W is standing, wearing her shortest shorts with the longest cut-off strings, the ones that dangle halfway to her knees. Where W is leaning over the hood of my car, before she straightens with a jolt.

"Syd," she says, like I've caught her. Like she's guilty of something.

Besides breaking up with me and never really saying why.

"I was going to leave before you came back." I'd forgotten the deep scratch in her voice, like she was always finding some itch I didn't know I had.

"What are you doing here?" I ask. It sounds like an accusation. Like everyone in Austin isn't at Barton Springs, all the time.

"Uh, swimming?" she says with one of her winning smiles. She gives them to everyone, the way I hand out warm cookies. I guess we all have things we hand out to make sure people like us when we're afraid they won't.

But I used to get her *real* smiles. The ones that slid from one corner of her lips to the other. The ones that looked like a string of Christmas lights.

She holds up a pen. "I saw your car and I thought I'd leave you a note." W is the master of the windshield note. I used to love the little scraps of her feelings that she'd leave for me to find tucked between the wiper blade and the glass.

But there's no note there.

"I got distracted," she says, following my line of thought as easily as she tracks my line of sight. "This, uh, smells incredible." She tosses something up in the air. A puck of gingery goodness she has just plucked from a butter-stained paper bag. A scone.

My scone.

"That's not for you," I say, words blazing out.

But none of the other couples showed, and for a lurching second, I want to give the scone to W. I've always wanted to say yes to her, from that first time we kissed in that sweaty middle school bedroom at someone's long-forgotten birthday party.

"How's the Muffin?" she asks. Before I can formulate a response that leaves out the fact I accidentally broke up my bosses, she keeps going. "I saw Gemma and Marisol the other night. They said you were doing okay."

That depends on what you think the ingredients in *okay* are.

But I don't say that.

I say, "You actually *spoke* to Marisol?"

"Sure." W shrugs. Her shoulders are splashed with freckles. Her bluebell-colored tank top is old, faded by sun and every summer of us together. I wish she was wearing something new, even if it was unbearably hot. I wish I didn't look at the bleach spot near the bottom and think about the time we tried to put a Rogue streak in her dark hair because she went through a year-long obsession with the X-Men.

I look at the scone in W's hands. It looks even better than when I first baked it. She was drawn to it for a reason. She could fall for me all over again. If she took a bite, would we fall back together different? Better?

I close my eyes. I see the future.

It's us, together, even if college carries her far away. It's us on the phone until dawn, weekend road trips, every pocket of time that we can find until we're back in the same city, picking our first crappy apartment and filling it with bright furniture. W right there when I open a bakery someday. Me right there when she has a baby someday.

Maybe all that stuff makes no sense to think about when you're still in high school.

But I did. *We* did.

When I open my eyes, though? That future is sun-faded, it's an old photograph, it's already tucked away in a box. Until this moment, I didn't know that an entire future could be part of your past.

"Sorry," I say. "I really need that back." W and I broke up due to natural causes, not magical brownies.

Besides. I wouldn't even *have* that scone if it weren't for Harley.

Harley, who just caught up to me but stopped a safe

distance away. Harley, whose swimsuit is a drenched ball in their fist, whose face I can't read, but for some reason I break out in a fresh round of goosebumps.

The feelings in these scones weren't about W. They had nothing to do with her.

"You couldn't bake another batch later?" she asks, not sounding pushy, just a little forlorn.

There it is again. We're all lorn of something, but whatever I'm missing—it's not W. I still think she's one of the prettiest girls on the planet, and I still want to know if she's applying early decision to NYU next year, and I still wonder what she's doing with all of the time we used to spend together. But I don't actually want to leave Barton Springs with her. She's not part of my day anymore.

I hold out my hand.

And W gives the scone back.

I hold out my other hand.

And Harley takes it.

RECIPE

A Perfect Day

~~~~ INGREDIENTS ~~~~

Harley (sorry, no substitutions)

1 epic trip to a natural spring-fed pool, Barton Springs being the obvious choice

1 to 2 hours at BookPeople

2 milkshakes at 24 Diner (roasted banana brown sugar is my favorite)

2 bikes

4 (at least) street tacos purchased from a truck (not Torchy's, unless what you're really looking forward to are the chips and queso you get on the side, in which case FINE)

2 orders of queso

~~~~ DIRECTIONS ~~~~

Spend as much time as you like at the springs, swimming.

When it gets too hot for anything but AC, wander over to BookPeople. Run wild among the stacks. If you have the funds, definitely buy a book. Maybe one of Ruth Reichl's food memoirs? Just an idea.

Cross North Lamar Boulevard. Sit in a booth at 24 Diner with your elbows on the table, talking about everything. When your roasted banana brown sugar milkshake finally comes, point out the dollop of homemade whipped cream on top, the freckles of nutmeg. Perfection is in the details.

Drink that milkshake.

Drive back to Zilker Park and take a walk along the lakeside. Be careful, though. Those black swans nesting by the shore are just as intense as they look.

As the afternoon turns Creamsicle orange, rent two bikes down by the lake.

Wobble at first. Remind yourself that you've done this before. Bike harder, gaining speed and confidence just in time to fall down. No, don't worry about your bloody knee. Yes, get back on the bike.

Keep riding until your muscles ache, in the good way.

Return the rentals just as the sky turns from orange to blue. Walk to the taco truck. Order all of it.

Wait until the night cools completely and then slice everything into little memories.

7

My next morning shift passes in a sunny haze. It feels like I brought Barton Springs back to the bakery with me. Little bits of yesterday are clinging to me in the best way. I've ridden a bike for the first time in years. I've put W really and truly behind me. I've gotten three couples back together. Now all I have to do is find the rest.

When all of my morning muffins are done, my cakes are in the oven, and my batters for tomorrow are prepped, I drag out the big chalkboard that Gemma calls tacky but lets the counter staff use when they need to move something they have too much of. Alec hates food waste more than Gemma hates bad signage.

I pull out a green piece of chalk and, with my limited art skills, write *Iced Green Tea Sale*.

"Did Vin tell you to do that?" Gemma asks as I drag it out to the sidewalk.

"Oh, Vin would approve," I say.

I have to believe that if he knew, he *would* give me his gruff but genuine blessing.

"Do we have a lot of iced green tea?" D.C. asks, heading to the drink fridge to double-check.

"Tons," I shout. But only because I was here alone at 5 a.m., making about seven gallons.

I go to the kitchen and try to keep myself busy until either Kit or Aadi shows up. I tell myself it's inevitable—even if the tea itself has no magical properties, it's a sizzling-hot Saturday and one of them will have to come in for their favorite refreshment. Then I'll deploy the scone I rescued right out of W's hand.

I've laid the frosty, refreshing trap.

It's time to bake.

And wait.

And wait.

Really, it's harder than you think to keep an eye on anything from the kitchen when you're baking. It involves a lot of sudden, desperate double-checks and random spikes of worry over whether or not you set a timer for the mocha cherry muffins. Marisol keeps looking at me like I've left all of my chill in the walk-in.

Maybe I have.

But I finally get a glimpse of them right before the lunch rush. Kit's short stature and messy blond mushroom of hair.

Aadi's lanky frame and neat black braid. I expected them to show up separately—like Araceli and Verónica did at the springs—but they just walked in with a bunch of friends.

I try not to stare *too* directly as I cut up the scone into tempting bites and arrange them on a plate. When Kit and Aadi make it to the front of the line, D.C. is waiting to help them. They order iced green tea in the largest size that we carry. When they're done, they don't start enthusiastically mapping the depths of each other's mouths. They stand with a firm distance between them and watch a video on a friend's phone. They've never been deterred by the presence of other people before, not when it came to kissing.

So they're here together, but they're not *back* together.

Maybe they just need a little nudge from my scones. After the double success at Barton Springs yesterday, I'm feeling relatively confident. I slide into place next to D.C., behind the counter.

"You came in right when I was going to put samples out!" I say. D.C., who is seamlessly helpful, signs what I'm assuming is the same thing, just in case they missed what I was saying. He wouldn't want anyone to miss out on a sample.

I hold out the plate directly in front of Kit and Aadi. They look deeply uninterested, in the way that only fourteen-year-olds can. But three of their friends, plus a random customer, swoop in with greedy fingers and grab most of the samples.

There's one left. Will it still work if only one of them eats it?

I push the plate forward.

D.C. grabs the last gingery square of scone and pops it in his mouth. "Syd, this is amazing!" he croons.

"Uh. Thanks, I guess." I'm slouching ungratefully past a baking compliment for what might be the first time in my life.

D.C. isn't ready to let go of this moment, though. He's taken with the scone's power, running around acting like this is a sudden holiday, or maybe a full moon, infused with new energy and spark. And he already has a lot of those. "Oh, wow. I can't wait to get home and see Paola." That's his longtime girlfriend. She comes in at least once a week, and everyone loves her. She's usually breezing around in a floral romper and heeled sandals, but I've seen her try out drag when D.C. gets all done up. They make an absurdly good couple, either way. "Do you think I should bring her something? Flowers? A cat? She likes cats. Maybe I should bring her a cake!" he says, like cake is an idea he just invented, despite the fact that he works at a bakery. "Or one of these scones. Do you have any more?"

"No," I say with a tiny sigh. "That was the last of them."

I don't want to begrudge them both the post-scone bliss. But my eyes follow Kit and Aadi as they move down the counter. The scone was right in front of them and they didn't even bother. It can't be the recipe, right?

No. Those are my *best* scones. Even baking nonbelievers like Harley think they're delicious. It must be the magic, then. These two need something besides new-love-interest excitement.

But what?

D.C. keeps signing with them, and I wish I knew more ASL, because maybe I could pick up a little bit about who they are beyond body language and drink preferences. But even if I did know how to sign, I would never be a natural at just whipping up conversation like D.C. does. He's the kind of person who works at a bakery counter mainly because it brings him joy. He could be doing a much more high-profile and well-paid job right now, but he loves meeting people in general, and queer people in particular. He chats with everyone like it's his life's true purpose.

Okay. I have to at least try, right?

I approach the little group, putting my hands up and making the best of my alphabet skills. I feel like I'm back in kindergarten, in more ways than one. "What kind of muffins do you like best?" I'm not sure that anything I've baked today would work, magic-wise, but at least I could get a sense of what they're interested in, like I had with Rae and Jay and Verónica and Araceli.

They both shrug at me, and I can't tell if it's my shoddy signing or they're just not all that interested in muffins.

"I'm going to get their iced teas, okay Syd?" D.C. says, giving me a hearty backslap.

"Yeah. Of course."

As D.C. pours a stream of pale green liquid over two cups filled with crushed ice, I study Kit and Aadi. Their friends are hanging out by the window, but they seem okay to linger here together. They're not mad at each other. They're not even awkward around each other. Which means there's nothing big left unsaid between them.

I sigh. Loud, this time.

Something is getting lost in translation here—and I'm not talking about anyone's ASL skills. I mean the fact that, no matter how hard I stare at them or how many slightly invasive questions I ask, I can't seem to figure out what these two need in order to patch things up. It's like staring at a sheet of pastry that just fell apart in my hands and having no idea how I can turn it back into a viable piecrust.

Kit and Aadi leave, and maybe they're not *together* together, but at least they're enjoying their Saturday, signing rapidly with their friends, and drinking iced green teas the size of their own torsos.

I clock out right after lunch and head toward my car. I'm supposed to go to a study group for a math test on Monday. I have to keep my grades up, I know, and my math quizzes have been swooping down from the usual A- to the mid-B range. I decide to skip the review session, though. I've been working hard all year to prove to both my biological and baking parents that I can handle the double load. But this is more important than a math test. I have to figure out which feeling plus what baked good equals happiness. I'm also learning that everyone's idea of happiness is different. It's like solving for X, except everyone gets to eat.

I backtrack and go in through the front of the Proud Muffin, get myself a glass of iced green tea—mostly out of guilt because I really did make too much—and take it out to the porch. I throw on my sunglasses against the glare of my phone. Setting my drink on a circular wrought iron table, I type in the words *Martin Thomas*.

There are no fewer than fourteen people living in the Austin area with that name. The youngest is a sophomore at Lake Travis High School who plays viola in concert and chamber orchestra. The oldest is a man who lives in East Austin and owns several laundromats. In between, there's a music producer, a software engineer, a law professor, someone who runs canoe adventures in the Hill Country, two bartenders . . .

I can't drop in on all of their last known whereabouts and ask if they've recently gone through a breakup. Or bought a brownie. I can't give fourteen strangers a randomly selected dessert and wait to see what happens.

I finish up my iced tea and head back into the lovely shade of the bakery. The counter is particularly busy this afternoon, with four staff members working at top speed. I edge my way in, and when there's a gap in the orders, I plant myself in front of the computer.

"Just checking my hours," I say to anyone who might be listening.

But really I'm checking our customer database just in case Martin enrolled in our email program to get updates including daily specials and weekly meetups.

He hasn't.

Without knowing which Martin Thomas is mine, I have no way of guessing what his relationship needs are.

I'm failing this emotional math test, and for one fleeting

second, I wish I were at school. Taking the kind of test where the answers can be confirmed by the teacher and the work checked to make sure it's all right and everything is wrapped up in forty-five minutes or less.

Then I look up and I see Jessalee brandishing a day-old dark chocolate and roasted pear muffin. And a handful of cash to buy it with.

Most people who drop in pay with cards. For the most part, cash customers are either over the age of sixty, because nostalgia, or under the age of sixteen, because allowance. But Jessalee is special. She's old-school, without being actually old.

What if *she's* the customer who bought a solitary brownie? She's so into day-old pastries that I never would have thought to consider her. But the muffin in her hand is a reminder that Jessalee's always had a weak spot: deep, dark chocolate.

And she was at Barton Springs the other day. She didn't get a scone, but maybe she showed up after Harley and I both went inside. She would never just swipe one from the top of a strange car.

"Hey, Syd," she says, lifting up on the balls of her feet as part of the greeting. "Want to ring me up while you're here?"

"Oh, I'm clocked out. But . . . I wanted to ask you something."

"Okay!" she says brightly. "Let me just pay for this."

"Oh, that's on the house," I say, a little quickly.

"Are you sure?" she asks, a dash of confusion on her face.

"You're such a good customer, a day-old muffin is the least we can do." But that makes it sound like we give away muffins all the time, and I don't want Jessalee to go around repeating it like it's some new policy, in case the other regulars get the wrong idea. Vin and Alec have generous hearts and would happily give away all the pastries to our regulars, but they *do* need people to buy things. "You're just . . . special."

"Why, thank you, Syd," she says, holding the muffin to her heart.

I run around the counter, whip off my apron, and join Jessalee at one of the cooler tables in the back, away from the window. She puts down her notebooks, her writing pens, her laptop, setting everything up in some mysterious and meticulous order. Jessalee is just as serious about her writing as I am about my baking. I think she works as hard as anyone at the Proud Muffin, and suddenly I'm glad all over again that she has a place to come and do what she loves.

But first: the muffin. I sort of expect Jessalee to eat like a rabbit, but she chomps into it with her entire face.

"Oh, those are good," she says, crumbs flying everywhere.

"I know! I love them. Alec let me help recipe test those." I can feel myself wanting to get wrapped up in an elaborate baking discussion, so I redirect. "They use the same chocolate as the brownies I made last week. Did you see those?"

"Syd! Those were yours, weren't they. Oh, I adored mine. The cherries were . . ." She mimes her heart exploding into a thousand fluttering pieces.

Usually that compliment would fuel me for hours. Right now all I feel is grim satisfaction. "Did you . . . did anything bad happen to you after you ate it?"

Jessalee takes out a folding paper fan that has seen better decades. She bats the air, moving hot particles around. "If you're asking after my digestive health, Syd, you don't have to be so delicate."

Okay, I was definitely *not* implying that my baking gave anyone food poisoning. Swerving around my offended feelings, I switch to a much more direct approach. "Jessalee, are you dating anyone?"

Her face swerves almost as suddenly as my questions. "Oh, bless you, Syd, but I think we'd be better off as friends."

"Wait. What?"

I almost start to protest the idea that I was hitting on her. I *almost* say something about Harley.

But she's already pulling something out of her purple alligator purse. "Here, if you're looking for a place to get started . . ." She takes out a little card with her name on it and *Authoress of love, magic, etc.* written in swirly letters on the other side. She digs up a fountain pen and scratches a few words.

A time, a restaurant, and a day in the not-too-distant future.

Does she want to set me up with someone? Is she going to use her romance novelist skills to train me in the ways of *love, etc.*? What's happening right now?

"Don't worry, I'll be there, too," Jessalee says with a dry little pat to my shoulder. "You won't be going into this alone."

"Oh. Great. Thanks." Even though I have no idea what she's talking about, the scribble on this card is an invitation into Jessalee's personal life, and I need to figure out who she's dating. Or who she *was* dating.

I'm one step closer to settling all of this.

And in the meantime, I have a date of my own tonight.

A real one.

A few hours later, after a quick stop at the grocery store, I drive over to Harley's house. I'm distinctly aware that this is the first time we've hung out without the Proud Muffin involved, *or* the stated purpose of baking to save other peoples' relationships.

I park across the street. When I knock, he answers the door with bare feet, which is new, and a brilliant smile, which is getting to be familiar. Small people cluster behind him. There are only two, I think, but they seem infinite in energy if not in actual number. They pop up around Harley's legs like kernels in sizzling coconut oil. That's the secret to making perfect popcorn at home, if you didn't already know. Coconut oil makes it smell like movie theater popcorn, and lots of real butter and salt on top make it taste incredible.

It's possible that I'm thinking about popcorn to avoid thinking about the small people surprise.

"Hi! Hi!" they say.

"Hi?" I say, looking at Harley. I thought this was the night that he had the house to himself. That was, in large part, why

I showed up here right as the sky melted like a perfect peach sundae.

Harley comes in to hug me with one arm hooked around the back of my neck. "Uh, so the babysitter canceled at the last second and my mom is at work until ten," he whispers on a wave of sage soap and shower-fresh skin.

"Got it," I say.

"Syd! Syd! Syd!" the small ones chant.

"Also, I made the eternal mistake of telling them your name," Harley admits as he opens the door wide. I walk in, but only a single step, because the front doorway is at maximum capacity. And nobody is budging.

"Harley told us more than that Syd is your name!" says the smaller of the small people, who has stubby pigtails and is constantly swaying from side to side.

"Harley told us *allllll* about you," says the taller, skinny one whose eyes are the same brown as Harley's.

"What did he say?" I ask, a little terrified to find out how he talks about me when I'm not there.

"Like you are Syd and you're a baker and sometimes you make magical cupcakes?" the tall one asks, looking for confirmation.

"Brownies," I say promptly. "And scones."

"Scones are English!" they blurt.

"And brownies are chocolate," the small one adds, raising a tiny, pedantic finger.

"So true," I say. "Now I feel like I should know your names

and two things about each of you. To make it fair." From working the bakery counter, I know this much: little kids are big into fair. Also sugar cookies shaped like pets.

"I'm Dean," says the pigtailed one. "And I love cheese and horses and my pronouns are she and her."

"That's three things," says the tall one, squinting with painted-on maturity. "I'm Verity and I'm in third grade and my pronouns are she and her."

"My pronouns are he and him," Harley says, which I know because we've been texting constantly for the last few days and at some point Harley just sent *he/him* with a thumbs-up, and then we kept talking about the time that the Proud Muffin hosted a pole-dancing club and tried to set up some foldable poles in the community space, but one of them fell and hit the emergency fire alarm and everybody kept trying to dance in their neon G-strings and eight-inch platform boots when the fire trucks came.

It's only after getting through that whole story again in my head that I realize Dean and Verity are staring at me: polite, waiting.

"Syd isn't using any pronouns right now," Harley says.

The little siblings "ooooooooh," like that's interesting. Exciting, even.

"Thanks," I whisper to Harley over Dean's and Verity's heads.

"No worries," Harley whispers back. "They might ask every time they see you, though. We do pronouns every morning with juice and a quick rundown of our dreams. In case you were wondering, I had pineapple-orange juice and I dreamed about electric eels filling up the library. It made me anxious at first, but then I taught them how to read and they taught me how to shock people."

"Wow," I whisper.

It hits me like half a dozen eggs cracking at once.

I like this house. I like this family. They *talk* here.

I've gotten so used to not saying things at home. Stepping around certain subjects like piles of laundry that someone left on the floor. And yes, my parents are wonderful people and my sister cares about me fiercely. And no, I'm never going to forget how lucky that makes me.

But it does seem like I'm always the one who has to speak up and tell everyone how I'm different. I have to find a way to help them understand me, even though I don't really understand them either. Having a gender? *Why?* Feeling like your body and who you are inside line up all the time? *How?* Identifying with other folks of your assigned gender as a kid, when I identified with things like extra-fluffy cumulus clouds and nebulas? *What does that even feel like?* I get nervous trying to explain myself sometimes. I get tired. I grow sharp edges where I didn't think I had any. And I definitely get to the point where I just want to bury myself in baking and not deal with any of it.

"I brought something," I say, setting down a reusable shopping bag.

"I made you something!" Harley says.

He runs upstairs and I wait in the little front door nook with Dean and Verity staring at me.

"What should I know about Harley?" I ask, kneeling down. "Quick, while he's upstairs."

"I can hear you!" Harley shouts down.

"Harley's bike is named Shadowfax," Dean tells me in a grave whisper, right before Harley rumbles down the stairs. He shoots Dean a look that says he *knows* she told me something she shouldn't have.

Then he hands me a neatly wrapped little rectangle of a package over the railing of the staircase. He can't even wait until he reaches me. It squishes when I take it from his hands. The paper is candy-colored, tape running in neat lines along the seams. The two small people look up at it with oversized eyes of envy.

I rustle in my bag and find the backup chocolate chips that I bought in case. "You can open these, if you want." They give Harley the hopefully *can-we-really* look of well-trained little siblings.

"Okay. Yeah. But you still have to eat dinner later."

They cheer and tear into the bag.

That gives me and Harley a semi-private moment. He watches me as I pull the tape gently free.

It's a white racerback tank top with black piping and the words *Cupcakes Have No Gender* in green across the front. When I turn it around, I notice a tiny cupcake topped with a heart where the straps meet in the back.

"Shit," I say, then clap my hands over my mouth and mumble, "It's so nice."

"Why did you say *shit* and then say something is nice?" Dean asks. When she hits the swear word, Verity screeches.

"I yell every time my sibling swears because it is like on TV when they go *beeeep*," Verity explains solemnly.

"You really like it?" Harley asks.

"Yes," I say, almost with suspicion. Not of Harley, exactly.

Just, whenever people give me clothes, I look at them and appreciate the style or the color, and sometimes they even fit, but it's hard to wear them. I can already see myself reaching for this on days when I can't decide what else to put on, days when nothing else feels right.

"All right," Harley says, already bouncing on his feet, away from this perfect moment, toward the next thing. "Dinner."

"Where do you want to order from?" I have so many ideas. There are dozens of good restaurants in spitting distance. I made a list on my phone for quick reference. I pull it out and open my notes.

Harley grabs my phone and flips it backward over his shoulder so it lands on the couch. Verity and Dean look up from their feral chocolate feast and cheer again. "We don't need to order anything."

"You want to go out?" I ask. What about the kids? Are they coming with us? I quickly slap together a scheme involving the Guerrilla Drive-In and the P. Terry's Drive Thru.

"No . . ." Harley says.

"Okay, I'm officially confused."

He leads me into the kitchen, where the counter is full of prep work. Bowls of vegetables, chicken, spices. A pot is already simmering on the stove. I noticed the good smell in the air before, but I didn't realize it was coming from in here, that it was meant for us. I take in a deep breath of sticky-starchy air, touched with saffron.

"This bodes really, really well," I say in that deep, visceral voice that only Harley seems to pull out of me.

"That's just the rice." Harley shakes his head at me. "You look like you've never seen someone cook dinner before."

"Not someone my age." I've been assuming that because Harley isn't into sweets that he's anti-food. But I was clearly wrong. Harley is just his own kind of food person. I get a flash of us learning from each other, bumping hips endlessly in a little kitchen as we cook and bake and swap bites and teach each other techniques and trade flavors the other person didn't even know they needed in their life. "You are unprecedented."

Harley's chin quirks to the side.

Then he goes to work, heating a pan, swirling oil, tossing in the vegetables. The instant sizzle of onions is deeply satisfying. "When my mom started working nights," Harley says over the hum of the hood vent, "I decided I was going to cook. I can't handle microwave dinners."

"Harley calls them macaroni and glue!" Dean yells from the other room.

"Harley calls them barf and beans," Verity adds.

"Harley has very strong opinions," I shout back. "Like thinking that baked goods aren't very good."

"Yeah!" Dean screeches.

"What is that about," Verity adds.

"Oh, look, they're on my team," I say loftily.

"Recruiting minors?" Harley asks.

"I don't need children to do my work for me," I say. "Not when I have life-changing cookies." That's what's in the shopping bag. Deconstructed, of course. I lean in from the opposite side of the stove, our heads nearly meeting over the heat. My hands twitch, underused. "Can I help with anything? What else is in the recipe?"

"No recipe."

"You're the most practical human I've ever met. How are you not using a *recipe*?"

Harley sneaks a look at me. "I trust my instincts," he says in a low voice. "And I know what goes together."

Okay, I think I am not the only one applying elaborate food metaphors to life.

Dinner is ready with a shocking quickness, and suddenly all four of us are sitting at a tiny wooden table in the living room, eating rice and chicken and vegetables, except they're better than rice and chicken and vegetables have any right to be.

"What did you do to this food?" My mouth is nearly overflowing and yet I'm unable to stop myself from talking. "This is magic. *Dark* magic."

Harley's face scrunches up against the compliment, but he can't quite get the smile to unstick. He's always fighting them, like if he lets them take over his face fully, he'll never get it back.

By the time I finish eating, my stomach feels a gentle, balanced sort of full. My heart feels the same way.

I've never had this before. Someone cooking for me. A few times people have tried to outbake me and pretended it was a friendly way to bond or repay me for a slice of pumpkin bread, but that's a pretty obvious passive-aggressive tactic.

This is something else.

I wish I knew how to tell him that. I wish I was as good at talking as everyone in this little house. Dean and Verity are chattering over their food, which means it takes them an extra year to finish.

Finally, unable to wait any longer, I push my chair back. "Ready to bake," I say, because that's what I know how to do.

Harley follows me into the kitchen, dogging my steps. It feels like we've reversed our dance. Before, Harley was leading, and I was following. Now it's my turn to lead. I start unstacking ingredients from my bag. Flour, brown sugar, white sugar. Eggs, vanilla, another bag of semisweet chocolate chips.

"This feels so indulgent," I say. "It's been weeks since I baked just to bake." I've been too busy trying to counteract those brownies—and keep my whole world from toppling if Vin and Alec actually broke up.

I think about them making out behind the Barton Springs ticket shack again. Seeing that might have been awkward, but it was a good awkward.

"What do you think happens when it's over?" Harley asks, arranging the items I've unloaded on the counter. "Does the magical baking just . . . ?" His fingers sparkle through the air, in what I'm assuming is the act of magic dissolving into nothing.

I don't know. I've been so focused on fixing my brownie catastrophe that I've hardly been able to think about what comes after it. Can I still be a professional baker if I've got this unpredictable power inside of me? I've been so careful at work the last week, making sure that anything I feel while I mix and pour out muffins is mild enough not to affect the customers in a big way. I tested a few crumbs, just to be careful. Nobody has left the bakery screaming or crying.

But could I really keep that up forever?

For the second time in recent history, my future wobbles.

"As soon as everyone has the bakes they need to get back together, that should put things right," I say. I hope.

Harley fiddles with an egg, turning it over and over in his fingers. "That depends on why it started, I guess."

"It started when W broke up with me." That much is pretty clear-cut, even if the inner workings of the magic are, well, magic, and not strictly logical.

"Sure." The egg slides and Harley barely catches it. "But correlation is not causation."

"Some of us haven't been to college yet," I remind him. "You're saying that just because it happened at the same time doesn't mean that the breakup *caused* the brownies? I guess that's possible, but there's no reason to think another explanation would be better. That's Occam's razor, right? Everything else being equal, why multiply our theories?"

"See, you're totally in college," Harley says.

I laugh, but something else is pressing on my brain. "What else could have done it?"

"I don't know," Harley says, fighting another one of those unruly smiles. "Maybe if you work at the Proud Muffin long enough, you become a magical queer baker."

"I do like that," I admit.

"Oh," Harley says, eyes flicking to the clock on the oven display. It's 8:45. "I have to put them to bed." He heads to the living room, and I'm left staring at the ingredients from my bag. Ingredients that somehow don't add up.

"Sorry, you have to be this tall to ride the Stay Up Late Train," Harley says.

Dean jumps and jumps, hitting the bottom of her head against his hand. Verity just sighs and trundles upstairs.

Harley disappears for a few minutes and I hear him saying brisk, non-negotiable things about brushing teeth. Then there's a quick song—yes, he is actually singing to his little siblings, it's fine, I'm fine—and he comes back.

I think back to the grocery store. The quick, scattered way that I traveled through the aisles. The unseeing rush of checking out, bagging without thinking because I was too busy picturing my night with Harley.

"Noooooooo," I wail like a horrible baking ghost. "No, no, no, no."

"What's wrong?" Harley asks, running back into the kitchen.

"I don't have *coconut.*"

"That's okay, right?" Harley tries, putting a hand on my shoulder. "You can just leave out the—"

"No!" I nearly shout. "Do you have any?"

Harley pokes through the cupboards, but somehow, I already know it isn't there.

"You really can just make it without the coconut," Harley tries again.

"I need the coconut, it's what makes these cookies . . . these cookies." I'm trying to swirl calm into my voice, but I can feel panic coming for me, and I don't know how to stop it. Harley's about to see me at my worst. When I can't make something I've been planning on—when a recipe goes wrong or simply doesn't get a chance to be baked in the first place—I can't keep it together. I turn into the soggy bottom of a poorly baked pie.

"Then make something else," Harley says firmly. Like he's sure of it. Like he's sure of *me.*

"There's nothing else to make." He flings the cupboards and the refrigerator open wide. It's sweet. It really is. "It's not that *simple,*" I say, thinking of how long it took me to pick this recipe.

Then I see something on the side of the fridge. A near-full container of heavy cream.

"Do you have powdered sugar?" I ask, voice still scratchy with my last defeat.

Harley turns to the cupboard and then turns back, holding

a bag over his head with both hands, triumphant as a boxer in a big-budget movie.

And then I'm throwing frozen peas out of the freezer to make room for my best metal mixing bowl, and I only wait five minutes for the bowl to chill, because it's after dark and it's not over ninety degrees. And at the same time that the temperature is finally dropping, my impatience is rising. I pour all the cream in the chilled bowl, grab the mixer Harley unearthed for me, and skim the beaters through the cream. Harley hovers just behind me.

"What are you . . . ?"

"Shhh," I say, like even the smallest word might disturb the molecules of cream as they start to gather.

Soon, we're staring at an enormous bowl of fresh whipped cream. I've added a tablespoon of sugar, so it's barely sweet, which I know Harley will like, and there's no shortage of things we can slather it on. I spotted an Entenmann's raspberry cheese Danish twist in the bread box. A carton of wild blueberries in the fridge.

Harley can't wait for any of those, it seems.

He dips a finger straight into the bowl. The whipped cream goes right between his lips.

He smiles, his fingertip still hooked there, his tongue pressed up behind it, his teeth looking very close and very white. And then he dips his finger into the whipped cream again and holds it out for me.

My lips close around his finger, and my first taste of Harley is skin and salt and cream, silky soft, a hard surprise at the center. His finger moves in my mouth, pushing a little deeper and then drawing back out.

"Um," I say, when I have my mouth back.

Then we switch, and I feed him a bite of whipped cream, and then we're giving it to each other by the handful, smearing it into each other's faces. Getting creative about what parts of the body we're aiming for.

We laugh and shriek and run after each other around the kitchen.

I dearly, dearly hope his siblings don't wake up.

But even that fear can't stop me tonight.

I fling a five-fingered star of whipped cream at him and run toward the living room. He catches me right by the door, pulls me back, spins me up against the counter. Harley pins me there, hips to hips. His face is close, eyes sparking like the candles on top of a cake, and they're mine to blow out whenever I feel ready. Then there will be nothing but darkness and cake and plenty of time to eat it, and it's all so overwhelmingly good that at first I don't notice the feeling of something hard against the front of my shorts. I remember Harley's joke about packing with a scone, and way after the fact I realize that Harley is packing something *else*.

We both pull away at the same moment—and then look at each other with thrilled, nervous, we're-really-getting-close-to-the-edge-of-something glances. I've been hoping to get closer to Harley pretty much nonstop the last few times we've been together. Even while I was baking. *Especially* while I was baking.

Wait. I step back and test another bite of the whipped cream. "I think it happened again."

Harley is sitting up on the counter now, spooning it into his mouth.

"I think the whipped cream . . . wait, stop eating it." I grab the spoon. He smiles, mouth rimmed with white.

"I think the whipped cream has my feelings in it," I say.

"What kind of feelings?" Harley asks.

"The kind that end with someone pinning someone else against a kitchen counter."

"Ohhhhhh." He pushes off the counter. I don't know if he's going to ask me to leave. I don't know if he's going to throw the rest of the whipped cream in the sink, add water to the bowl until it's a thin, unappetizing white, and let the rest of my horny feelings drain right down the sink.

"I didn't mean to put the way I feel on you, not like that . . ." I say, ready to launch a full apology.

"How is it different?" Harley asks, cocking his head.

"What?" I ask cut short.

"If you came onto me, and I was into it and felt something back, you wouldn't apologize, right?" I shake my head so fast a gobbet of whipped cream flies off. "How is this different from you telling me, or kissing me?" Harley comes at me slower this time, eyes just as bright as before.

"I guess it's not," I admit.

"If anything, this is an extra brave way to do it, because if I was into someone else, I would have run out the front door to go find them and then you'd be stuck here alone, babysitting."

"Right," I say. "I'm very brave."

One of his hands goes to the back of my neck, and the moment feels warm and ready and ripe.

Harley plunks a little whipped cream on my nose. "I like this."

He could be talking about the whipped cream, or the way we're using it, or just me being here.

Me being this close.

"I'm glad," I say, stepping back, digging both hands into the whipped cream bowl. "Because it's on."

When I wake up the next morning, I smell like milk.

After a quick and necessary shower, I go downstairs to find my parents and Tess perched around the little kitchen island like birds of prey, eating out of the mixing bowl with spoons.

I got in late and shoved what was left of the whipped cream to the back of the fridge, wanting to eat the rest in private and think Harley-sweetened thoughts. In my happy daze, it didn't occur to me to label it *Syd's Only* or write *Do Not Eat on Pain of Death*.

Big mistake.

My parents are serving each other little love-bites and cooing while my sister makes short work of a bite that's piled nearly as high as her eyebrows. I run into the kitchen and snatch the bowl away.

The bottom of the bowl gleams back up at me. There are only a few snowy tracks of cream left.

"Please tell me you didn't eat all of that," I groan.

"We did!" my dad says, looking far too joyful. He swats Mom's butt. My mom giggles and swats him back. Tess and I look at each other, deeply horrified. "All right, have to go pack."

"Where are you two going?" I ask.

"We decided to get away for a few days," Mom says. "Just the two of us. A spa in the Hill Country, very relaxing." Her words are reasonable enough, but I know what this whipped cream does.

Oh. God.

I just sent my parents on a Sex Vacation.

My dad runs down the stairs with a flapping-open bag in his hands.

"We're going to book the room while we're on the road, which is ridiculously spontaneous of us, but we'll let you know when we check in," Mom says. "After that—"

"Our phones might be off," Dad adds.

"Our phones might not work there!" she says, sounding more giddy than guilt-ridden.

Dad steps into his shoes. "But you can get us by . . ."

"You know, that other thing." She snaps a few times. "Email!"

"You'll be fine," Dad decides. "You're basically adults."

They fly out of the house faster than I've seen them do anything in years. Tess is left staring at the backside of the door.

"I can't believe I only have a week at home before I go back to Northwestern and they just *left*."

I think about the power of the whipped cream, and what it might have led to if Harley and I had kept eating it instead of having the world's most epic dairy battle. The truth is, I'm not in a hurry. I'm hungry to do more with Harley, but I also want to savor every bit of this.

Tess clears the bowl off the kitchen island. I see now that they were nominally eating the whipped cream on top of French toast, but there are only a few bites out of each piece. "At least we can hang out, right?"

"Yeah." I switched out of a few shifts at work, so I'd have free time while she's home. "What sort of thing are you feeling up for?" I ask tentatively, aware that thanks to my whipped cream I might be about to walk headfirst into my sister's very private private life.

"Nothing?" She shrugs. "Nothing sounds good."

Watching Tess rinsing out the last clingy bits of whipped cream, a question rises like the water steadily filling the sink. What if her not dating isn't a sign that she's picky, or busy, or into something she wants to keep secret?

Tess could be asexual.

Aromantic, too.

First thought: *My sister is a rainbow!*

Second thought: *Wait, I'm the resident rainbow. How did I not notice this sooner?*

I've always been sad when she didn't hear or see or understand something about me, but what if I've done the same thing to her? I groan as I slide a few bites of cold French toast into the trash. Honestly, assuming that she wants a partner *at all* is just as bad as when we were younger and Tess assumed I would fall for a boy just because everyone was so invested in calling me a girl. In some ways it's worse. I'm older now than she was then. Plus, I should know better.

Tess sets the bowl upside down on the drying rack, then looks back at me, like she's waiting for something.

What do I do?

What should I *say*?

Because this is me, I want to throw my arms around her, throw a party. I want to mix up some don't-be-afraid-to-talk-to-your-dumb-but-loving-sibling cookie dough and let her eat the whole bowl.

Because this is Tess, I want to give her plenty of space and not suffocate her with enthusiasm.

There are so many resources about how to come out to your family, what to do if they're not understanding or accepting. But what about when you're the queer one knocking on other family members' closet doors? Can I come right out and *ask* my sister if she's considered that she might be aroace? Do I let her figure this out in her own way? Do I just keep leaving space—like Harley does in our conversations—and wait for her to tell me?

There are a few things I know I can do. I can make it really, really easy for her to say it. And I can make sure that Tess knows she doesn't have just me—she has an entire community in her corner.

I slip my feet into flip-flops and head for the door, which banged open a little in the wake of our parents' exit.

"Yeah," I say. "Let's do nothing, but with muffins."

This Whipped Cream Can Get It

(BUT ONLY IF YOU WANT IT)

~~~~~ INGREDIENTS ~~~~~

1 carton heavy whipping cream (Yes, heavy cream and whipping cream and heavy whipping cream are all basically the same thing. Don't freak out, just grab whatever your grocery store carries.)

½ tsp vanilla extract

1 to 4 tbsp fine sugar (Either superfine granulated or powdered sugar work here. If you use powdered sugar, you can sift it first to make sure there are no clumps. I use organic powdered sugar and it never seems to be a problem.)

That's it.

No, really.

There are no other ingredients.

~~~~~ DIRECTIONS ~~~~~

Most people don't understand why it's worth making their own whipped cream. They can't see past the tubs of vile Cool Whip in their freezers and the spray cans of fluffy topping that actually tastes okay but leaves a layer of slime all over your mouth.

Congratulations! Very soon you will no longer be one of those people.

You can—and should—put this on top of pies, cakes, bread pudding, even your morning waffle. You can slap it on ice cream, add generous glaciers of it to your hot cocoa.

If you live in a hot place, or it's summer in your temperate place, stick the bowl and the whipping attachment of your mixer in the freezer for about ten minutes. I like using a hand mixer, but you can absolutely use a stand mixer; just know the whipping process will go *much* faster.

Dump the cream into the frosty bowl. Make sure it has high sides, otherwise your kitchen is going to look like a dairy-related crime scene. Start beating on low, working up to a higher setting, until it's spinning so fast it's like a carnival ride in your kitchen! If you're using a hand mixer, this will probably be the highest setting you have. If you're using a stand mixer, it probably won't be.

When the cream starts to visibly thicken, mix in the vanilla and sprinkle in a tablespoon of sugar. Keep mixing, add another tablespoon of sugar, then taste again. Do this until you've reached the desirable level of sweetness and . . . whipped-ness.

If you're into the spray-can style, you can throw in more sugar and keep mixing until it froths and peaks. But if you want my advice? Whip until you can stick a finger in and have the mixture just hold. And a whisper of sugar is all you really need.

8

Walking over to the Proud Muffin with my sister feels like a parade of two. I'd forgotten how much I like spending time with her. Between her applying to college and leaving for college and all the time I used to dedicate to W, Tess and I haven't properly hung out in what feels like years. She tells me about her professors. I tell her about Marisol teaching me how to make her favorite piecrust: the secret is lard. She tells me about her roommate, Raina, who's quickly becoming her best friend.

I tell her about my new friend. Harley.

She gives me a perfectly calibrated sister stare, and I add that I want to make out with Harley. I *don't* tell her about the part where I'm not with Harley yet because I'm still cleaning up the catastrophes that rippled out from my last relationship.

Tess is too naturally dubious to believe in baking magic.

We could keep walking for hours, filling in the blanks of the past few months, but it's not far to the bakery. It's a quiet morning at the Proud Muffin. The little garden tables are empty, the porch dotted with a few people making the most of their morning coffee and freshly baked muffins.

"What are those smells?" Tess asks. "I want to eat those smells."

"Lemon lavender muffin, marzipan dream muffin, chocolate oatmeal stout muffin," I say in one long string. I could name every muffin here in my sleep.

It's a little surreal to walk in as a customer. It's like I'm floating through the halls at school and everyone else is in class, but for some reason I don't have to go. Or I'm driving through rush-hour traffic in Austin, but I don't need to keep my hands on the wheel. I should probably enjoy this sort of freedom, but it just makes my fingers twitchy and my throat tight. I can't shake the sense that there's something else I should be doing.

I peek into the kitchen. Marisol is back there, along with another baker, Carlos. Everything looks perfectly fine. Gemma and D.C. are working the counter this morning, along with Lex.

"Can I get a gingerbread latte and, um, whatever my sister wants?"

"On the latte," Lex says, going to the espresso machine.

"It's hard to choose . . ." Tess says, facing down rows of muffins. "Now that I live in Chicago, I want to eat everything in

Austin. Do you know what they think is delicious in Chicago? Smoked meat. As if they could ever do better than Texas barbeque. How have I only eaten dry rub ribs twice since I got home? That seems like an oversight."

This is the first time I've heard Tess split her allegiances between Austin and the Midwest. Maybe she really does think of this place as home. Or maybe home isn't just one thing for her.

"Well, we don't have a smoked meat muffin, per se, though now that I'm thinking about it, that would go over well," D.C. says. "We do have a few with bacon in them. What kind of flavors do you like?"

"Oh, you know . . ." she says, and proceeds to list every flavor in the universe. We're alike in that way.

Tess has been in here once or twice before, but I've never really brought her in on purpose. Now that I know she might be aroace—and need this community as much as I do—I can't help picturing a future where she comes in all the time. She's already hitting it off with Gemma and D.C. Soon they're cutting a host of muffins into sample squares so she can try them all.

"Wow, okay, this roasted pear and balsamic one is . . ."

"Good, right?" D.C. asks. His usual perkiness is in place, but I swear there's something buzzing under his voice.

"Hey. Syd." Gemma pulls me to the side. "I just want to make sure you know what's going on."

My head immediately racks up all the things that could go

wrong. All the cakes I could have forgotten to bake, the special orders I might have written down wrong. Did something happen with Harley? Did I throw everything off between us, did Harley wake up this morning and feel different about me? Or worse—feel *nothing* about me? Maybe Harley asked to be switched off my shifts.

Gemma runs a rag over the counter, picking up espresso grit and muffin crumbs. "Vin and Alec called a meeting of kitchen staff and counter managers yesterday. I guess you had to switch out. I just wanted to make sure that you heard . . . that it's not a surprise the next time you come in . . ."

Gemma tosses the rag in a bucket of cleaner.

A queasy feeling sloshes through me.

"Vin and Alec are breaking up," Gemma whispers, and I feel like the little kid who missed the family meeting, the one who's hearing about the divorce secondhand from a neighbor.

"No," I say. "They're not."

"Wait, did you hear that they're getting back together?" she asks.

I forget my sister and the nice day we were having. I abandon all thoughts of Harley. I march around the counter, straight into the kitchen, and fling open the door to Vin and Alec's office. It was closed. It's never closed.

Vin is in there, his fingers sliding through papers. He keeps writing numbers even as he looks up at me, shifting pages like he doesn't have a second to spare for my splitting, splintering life.

"This isn't right," I say.

Vin looks apologetic, wincing behind his reading glasses. He pushes them up onto his forehead. "Close the door, please."

I click it shut behind me, and as soon as we're alone in the tiny room, words fly out. "Did you cheat?"

The worry drains out of his face. He goes dangerously quiet. "Did you just ask me that question?"

His fingers are paused, pen still in the air. He's giving me one chance to take it back. I should take it back.

I stare at him, stubborn as anything.

"Syd, it is none of your business what happened or did not happen in our private life." I think he's going to leave it at that. I get ready to keep pushing for a sentence that resembles the truth, even if it hurts. Then Vin sets down his pen, presses his lips together, scrubs a hand over his chin. He looks awful. A restless, gray sort of awful. "There was no cheating. Of any kind."

Is he lying to me about being wooed? Is he lying to himself? Or did I get it wrong somehow?

"But I heard—"

"No."

"Then you can't break up," I say instantly.

A look rumbles across his face. "Syd. You don't get to set what happens with our lives like you set the daily special."

I think about the scones, the clandestine kissing at Barton Springs. "But you love each other."

"Yes. We do."

Well, that's not what I expected.

"Sometimes that's not what breaks it. You understand?"

"No!" My voice could smash an egg all on its own. "If you both still love each other, you should fight to keep it!"

He laughs gruffly, not a mean laugh but an old and very tired one. For the first time, he genuinely looks like the queer grandpa Marisol and I joked about. "You have so much energy to fight with, Syd. And your fights . . . they're different. They're not fake and they're not unimportant, but they're not the same as ours. When you grow up, it gets easier in some ways and harder in others."

The moment slips like a knife that I was holding wrong.

Vin still sees me as a kid. Of course he does.

"What about the Proud Muffin?" I ask.

I hold my breath. This is the question that's been layered into every one of my fears since the moment I realized what my brownies had done.

"We don't know yet," he says blankly. "Alec and I both love this place, but there are a lot of factors."

Tears storm my face, so I storm out of the office.

I can't stand here and listen to *factors*.

In the kitchen, Marisol doesn't look up from her baking even though I'm being loud as all get out. She's doing exactly what I would be if I was on shift today—dumping her mind into her work.

I get my face under control, pulling the tears back into it by force. Then I walk out to the front counter and find my sister in a state of complete, muffin-fueled joy.

"This is the best thing I've ever put in my mouth," she says, holding up the remains of the marzipan dream muffin. "Why didn't I spend more time here when I actually lived in Austin?"

"I don't know," I say raggedly. "I told you exactly how great it is."

For years, I've been dedicated to two things: W and the Proud Muffin. I've lost one of them.

I'm going to fight for the other.

I put my head down on the table, swamped by cookbooks and defeat.

It's a good thing I don't care about looking pathetic in public. Every person in this café can probably hear me whimper while they wait for iced chai and perfectly plated salads and panini neatly charred with thin black lines.

"There's nothing here," I mumble. Which is sort of a lie, since there are literally thousands of recipes all around me, and millions more scattered throughout the café.

But I need the *perfect* recipe. The one that's going to get Vin and Alec back together—and keep them that way. I still owe Jessalee and Martin and Kit and Aadi their own perfect bakes, but Vin and Alec come first.

I really thought I'd fixed them with the scones, but sometimes a make out—even a full-body, dizzy-making make out—isn't enough to fix things. I should have known that. I mean, W and I had sex in the middle of our breakup.

Vin and Alec are still attracted to each other. They're still *in love* with each other. But they're stuck in some kind of awful limbo where they believe that nothing they can do will save their relationship.

How am I supposed to bake my way out of this one?

I started with my home cookbook collection and a few dozen internet searches. A restless Sunday turned into three furiously upset days, while Tess alternated between hovering anxiously and getting bored and disappearing for long stretches of time. As soon as I was done with work and school on Thursday I drove downtown to the Cookbook Cafe.

Now it's half an hour before closing time and I'm surrounded by more than five hundred tomes on the alchemy of food, from an ancient and revered copy of *The Joy of Baking* to Ottolenghi's *Sweet*. The collection spread over wooden tables and shelves was originally owned by Virginia B. Wood, who started out as a pastry chef and went on to become a famous Texas food writer. After she died, her friends decided the café at the new downtown Austin library was the perfect spot to house her books, where everyone could flip through them.

This is usually one of my happy places.

But today, I'm a miserable creature hunched over books in a dark hoodie and stringy cut-offs. My fingers are more papercut than skin. My porcupine of frizz is longer and sharper than ever because I don't have W to give me a fresh buzz like she's been doing on a regular basis for the last two years.

I feel an open palm on my back, gentle but with a

little pressure to it, and I look up expecting to see some nice employee about to tell me that I'm abusing the very generous cookbook policy and I need to leave, forever.

But it's Harley.

Hair getting curlier the closer we get to true summer. Smile starting to collapse under the weight of worry.

"Um. Hi." I push away the cookbooks stacked in front of me, as if that will keep Harley from noticing the damning evidence.

"Hey, Syd."

I check the pronoun pin—he.

"How did you find me?" I ask.

"Harley!" shouts the barista back at the counter. He runs over to gather a tiny cup of espresso, then drinks it in one swift motion, his body creating a nice long line with his head thrown back.

Okay, maybe coffee isn't the *worst* thing.

"Your sister said I should try here," Harley says on his way back to me. He straddles one of the chairs with a sort of lumbering slowness that I've never seen from his usually quick, agile body. It's possible I'm not the only one who's had a long night. "Well, either here or passed out in one of the booths at Austin Karaoke."

"That only happened because she dared me to sing every Queen song in the catalogue and . . . you saw my sister? As in, Tess?"

Harley stares at the brown sludge in his tiny espresso cup, like he might be able to frown until it magically refills. "She was hanging out at the bakery. She seemed pretty convinced you'd be here."

"Oh," I say, and guilt cuts me up, a perfect dice, because it's Tess's last full day in town and I'm spending it like *this*.

"Find anything good?" Harley asks.

"There are so many things I want to bake." Sour cherry slab pies and mango cream tart and, courtesy of Ottolenghi—who started his career as a pastry chef—chocolate, tahini, and halva brownies. They all sound amazing. They all make my mouth water and my stomach get opinionated. "I just don't know what I *need* to bake. For Vin and Alec."

Harley's face instantly slumps. So he's heard the news.

"I still don't know how this works," I say. "I've been baking for so many years, but I've only been *magical* baking for two weeks." I whisper the word *magical* like my great-aunt Margo whispers the word *gay*. Like it's obviously real in the world but still improbable in her head. "How can I tell which recipe will yield the right results? What feelings do I even want Vin and Alec to feel?"

Harley drums long, overcaffeinated fingertips on the table. "What if they just need time? For things to work themselves out?"

My fears about the Proud Muffin come on as strong and fast as food poisoning. If Vin and Alec don't get back together quickly enough, the best bakery in the world could be on the line. "I can't bake them *time*," I say, trying to keep the sharpest knives in the drawer out of my voice. "So it's going to have to be pie."

"I like pie," Harley says brightly.

I perk up a little, peeking an inch out of my hood.

"Well, I like piecrust. Actually, I just like rolling out piecrust. Who wants to eat a lump of butter that's been stretched and touched and, like, turned into a lid? You're eating butter Tupperware."

"I don't have the energy for anti-baking sentiments," I say, pulling the strings of my hood so tight that my face is basically pinched into a sweatshirt dumpling. "This is all I have going for me, okay?"

Harley grabs my arm and pulls me up, leaving my fallen cookbooks everywhere. I try to run back and take a picture of a stovetop summer berry buckle, but Harley just drags me back toward the library entrance. It doesn't matter. I've already screenshot enough recipes to keep me baking until February.

We walk into the library and start up the ramp, which runs through a big open atrium that connects all the floors. There are a hundred different types of chairs throughout the library—a sort of collection of its own, celebrating different eras and types of design—and Harley seems determined to sit in all of them. I follow his ramblings through the different sections: the YA room that's just for teenagers, the little tech library where Harley jokingly asks if I want a 3D mold of his hand.

That sounds pretty nice, actually. I like Harley's hands.

By the time we get to the roof, with its wooden slat tables and potted greenery and incredible views, I'm ready to throw my hood back and let the breeze ruffle my grown-out shave.

"Tell me one thing about you that has nothing to do with baking," Harley says.

"I don't have time for this."

"Okay, now it's four things."

"That math doesn't even make sense!"

"You skulking around the library when it's a gorgeous afternoon and there's a bakery to save makes no sense."

"Fine." It takes a superpowered effort to come up with four facts that have nothing to do with baking and also nothing to do with W. "I've always liked to sing, just in the car and stuff, really loud, mostly to bad pop music. Someday I want to get in my car and drive across the entire country and eat at a really good roadside diner in every state. *Without* planning stops. Finding the diners is part of it." It's been so long since I've tapped into these parts of myself, and once I start, there's momentum—like when I was a little kid, tossing myself down a hill, getting dizzy and liking it. Or when I was riding a bike and really picking up speed, in the days before I canceled bikes. "I used to wish on rocks because I thought wishing on stars was just wishing on rocks that are really far away. I think my parents think I watch queer porn on my computer late at night, but it's mostly *Schitt's Creek* and the *She-Ra* reboot."

"Mostly?" Harley asks with a meaningful eyebrow raise. He leans back against the railing, elbows on the wood. "Do you feel better yet? This place always makes me feel better."

"Really?" All I can see is how much Austin is changing, all the time. There's so much construction equipment that it looks like they're trying to graft a whole new city onto one that's already here. For every building that I recognize, there are four I feel like I've never seen before.

"I like maps," Harley says, breeze lifting up the bottom of his shirt just a hint and messing up his curls in a way that somehow makes them look even better. "When I was little, out in the country, I'd go to a high hill nearby and spend hours drawing everything I could see, and then the next day I'd make it all move a little, so it felt like the map was alive. This is like being inside of a living map of Austin."

"Living maps sound pretty magical," I admit. "That's probably why you're so good at biking around the city." Pride flickers around his face. "Hey, maybe you can be the navigator on my road trip."

Harley ducks his head, grabs the back of his neck, and looks up at me. It's hopeful and sad at the same time. Like he's pretty sure we're never going to do that. And I get mad at him for deciding it. We haven't even kissed yet, and he's putting limits on what we could do together, what we could be to each other. There's nothing stopping us from dreaming and then making those dreams real. Vin and Alec did it. They made the Proud Muffin together. They're the proof in the legendary pudding.

The bakery is over there, nestled in with the homes and shops and taquerias of South Austin. Even though I can't see it from here, I know exactly where it is. But I don't know how to keep it there.

"So what pie are you going to make?" Harley asks, like he can feel my mind circling the problem.

I look out at the city, and for the first time all day, I feel inspired. Not because I've figured out what to bake for Vin and Alec, but because I'm not going to let that stop me.

"All of them."

The next morning, Harley shows up at my house.

When we left the library, I made Harley pack his bike into my trunk and drove us both to HEB for a tornado of a shopping spree, during which I debated the merits of going to the Proud Muffin or invading Harley's kitchen again before realizing I'd need every one of the dozen pie plates I've collected over the years. Mom and Dad made me stop at twelve, arguing that we'd never conceivably need more pies than that, even in the apocalypse. I'd argued that the end of the world called for *at least* a baker's dozen pies. But Harley insisted it was too late to start baking, so now it's morning and he's at my front door.

"So . . . this is your place," Harley says.

Maybe this moment was always coming, but that doesn't mean I'm ready for it.

"It's boring? Kinda normal. It's just a house."

"Okay," Harley says with a sweet, crumbly short-crust laugh. "Is that a problem?"

"It's just . . . your house is so much like *you*." This house is like my parents. It's like my sister.

Speaking of sisters, Tess stomps over to us and I can tell that she's pissed. I know I've been spending way too much of her break distracted by this situation. I must feel guilty, because my neck lights up like a red-hot pan. She doesn't say anything to me. Not a single word. Instead, she focuses on Harley. That's how I know she's going to give me hell later.

"Hey," she says brightly, in a tone that could easily be mistaken for nice. "From the bakery!"

"From the bakery," he agrees gamely.

"Tess, this is Harley. Harley, this is my older sister, Tess, though I guess you two already met."

"We are acquainted," Harley says, offering a handshake like the politely reared southern kid he is.

"I've been hanging out at the bakery because I don't have anything else to do. Even though it's *spring breaaaak*." She says those last two words in a faux-party mode, waving her arms half-heartedly in the air.

I rush into the kitchen and poke my head out of my hoodie.

"Um . . . Syd . . ." Harley says, pointing at my hair.

"You have to take care of that," Tess finishes for him.

"I don't have time to shave my head!" I cry. "There are pies to bake!" I touch my hair and it fluffs up in a disturbing way. It must look like the previously mentioned porcupine got electrocuted. "Besides, W used to do it for me," I mumble. "The one time she was out of town and I tried to do it myself, I had a patch on the back of my head that looked like Australia and nobody told me for two days."

This is the first time in two years that I haven't had W

here to notice when I went from softly fuzzy to seriously over-grown. She would always take care of it before it could get out of control.

I feel out of control.

I can't seem to stop my hands from grabbing the balls of pie dough I made last night out of the fridge.

"We're going to help," Tess says. "Where are your clippers?"

"In the bathroom," I say, tossing flour into my bowls.

Tess comes back a minute later, drags me outside, and plugs the clippers in near the front door. From our spot on the front steps, I whirl around to watch Harley through the window, banging a ball of dough with a rolling pin.

"Stay. Very. Still." Tess pushes the clippers over my head. The rumbling sensation on my scalp is comforting, but I wonder if Tess has any idea what she's up to.

"Do you even know how to do a fade?" I ask.

In response, she turns the clippers off and snaps on a different plastic guard. "I'm a quick learner."

Instead of worrying too much about what's happening on top of my head, I focus on the scene in the kitchen, where Harley is pushing a round of pie dough flatter and flatter, sprinkling it with flour as he works.

"So that's your bike messenger," Tess says flatly, daring me to read into it.

"That's Harley."

Little bits of fuzzy hair cling to my shoulders, and I bristle until Tess brushes them away.

"It's nice to see you doing something you care about with someone you like," she states.

My immediate reflex is to argue that W and I did things I like all the time—but the truth is that we did *couples* things together. Date-like things. And yes, she was willing to help with events like shaving my head on a regular basis, but mostly because I start to act prickly when I feel like a tumbleweed.

"All right," Tess says, waving me away. "You're shorn."

I run inside to change out of my T-shirt, which is covered in tiny flecks of hair, and when I get back to the kitchen and check how things are going with Harley, he smiles up at me with an earned glow.

"You did a great job with those balls. Dough balls. Pie dough balls. Wow, I'm sorry for saying any of that."

"What comes next?" Tess asks, hanging around the kitchen island and swiping little bits of pie dough—she really will eat anything in dough form.

Normally, I would let the dough chill a little longer, because Austin, and heat, and I don't want any of these crusts getting messy and leaking butter while they blind bake. But I've wasted too much time already.

Vin and Alec could be splitting up their possessions right now. Figuring out who gets to keep their stoneware bowls, their rainbow whisk. They could be talking about the future of the Proud Muffin, figuring out who gets custody.

Or if no one does—if it's better to cut their losses.

I glove my hands in flour and then smack them together a few times. "Let's make some crusts."

Harley grabs the rolling pin, sprinkles more flour over it, and gets to work on the rest of the dough balls while I settle the finished bottom crusts into pie tins with a level-handed care. Harley eyes the overhanging bits and slices them neatly. He pinches the outside edges of each, a perfect crimp. Then he carefully squares a foursome of bottom crusts in the oven to blind bake. While he waits, Harley works on the top crusts. He even finds cookie cutters in a cupboard and creates little cut-outs of apples to put on the lid of the apple pie.

He *lattices*.

"Okay," I say. "That's impressive. Tess, isn't that—?"

I look around. My sister's gone.

I could pretend it's because there's no more excess dough to steal, but I know that she vanished for other reasons, too. Quietly, I promise that once the pies are baked, I'll spend the rest of her last day at home hanging out with her. As a thank-you for giving me a fresh buzz, and alone time with Harley. And for making me feel like I can survive without W.

"You're good at that," I say, pointing at Harley's intricately woven piecrust. He made it on a piece of wax paper for easy transfer once the fillings are done. Speaking of which, I unstack bowls and start throwing together fillings.

Harley shrugs. "I spend so much time braiding Verity's and Dean's hair, it's kind of the same thing."

By the time we're done, we have twelve pies: apple, salted caramel apple, blueberry with lime zest, strawberry rhubarb, mocha pecan, sweet potato and buttermilk, lemon chess, blackberry with Italian meringue, old-fashioned chocolate, coconut cream, peach, and peach strawberry basil.

Tess comes back in right around the time that I pull the last pie from the oven. It's already midafternoon. I can't tell you how many times I've been so distracted by Harley's presence that I nearly dropped a hot pie.

I grab three forks from the drawer. I don't even know where to start.

"Wow," Tess says. When I pry my attention away from the pies and look over, I see that she's packed to head back to school.

"Wait, you're leaving?" I ask, already missing her. I've been running around all week, but I feel closer to my sister than I have in years.

"I should get back," she says. "Exams to study for."

I point to the pies cooling on their perches around the kitchen. "At least have a piece before you go." I'm making a peace offering. I'm also testing out my pies on my sister to see which one will work on Vin and Alec.

Magical multitasking?

There's a scuffle in the living room, the door flapping open and shut a few times, bags being dumped.

"Hello, hello!" my mom calls.

Harley looks at me, a little wild-eyed.

"Don't worry," I say. "They're nice." A little too privileged to understand queer culture and a little too busy flirting with each other to notice anybody else, I want to add. But nice.

My parents arrive in the kitchen. Mom looks from Harley

to me, then sharply back to him. "Did you two bake together?"

Harley seems unprepared to skip straight to the interrogation. He holds out a hand to shake, walking it back to the simple introduction part. "So nice to meet y'all. I'm Harley. He/they pronouns. He is good right now."

"Excellent," Dad says, shaking Harley's hand.

It's an awkward thing to say—but parents are awkward people.

And I've missed them, so I give Dad a big hug, then Mom.

"Syd, you haven't let anyone bake with you since you were nine years old," Mom says, unwilling to let this drop.

I put my hands over my face.

"Is that true?" Harley asks.

"I bake with Marisol every day," I point out.

"Yeah, for work," Tess says, piling on.

It's true—I've had company in the kitchen, but I can't remember the last time I baked *with* someone. Even as a kid, I would listen to my mom's list of the kitchen rules: Don't light your hair on fire! Don't light the house on fire! Always set an oven timer! And then I would do all the work myself.

When I wanted to make something for W, she would hover in the next room, reading or watching TV, insisting that she'd ruin whatever I was making if she even breathed too close to it. But Harley isn't afraid of the kitchen. More than that . . .

"Harley isn't afraid of me," I say, crossing my arms.

"Should I be?" he asks.

"I've been told that I'm formidable when I'm baking."

"Scary," Dad says as he moves the bags from their trip to the stairs. "She's scary when she's baking."

Harley looks at me, and I can feel him silently asking if I've talked to my family about my gender. Or lack thereof.

I shake my head, certain that nobody else will notice.

Sometimes, I wish they would. But then I'd have to sit down and explain myself on their terms.

I'm worried that Harley will judge me for not being brave enough. But his brown eyes stay soft. It feels like he's here for me, in a moment that I usually have to get through on my own. And somehow that softens the edges. It makes this one more thing that we share.

I sit down abruptly on a stool as another truth hits me.

Love is about sharing the hard bits. Not just the happiness.

W and I were good at the good. But we mostly ignored the bad, the awkward, the uncomfortable. We just kept moving like nothing would be able to catch up with us. Like if we didn't look at it directly, it might slink away.

Tess is adding plates and forks to the stack that I brought out for pie testing. My parents are exclaiming over each one in turn. My mom won't stop talking about Harley's lattice. My family seems determined to eat, so Tess, Harley, and I load the kitchen island with pies. I figure the more of us are eating, the better chance I have of figuring out what to feed Vin and Alec.

Of course, I'm a little terrified that whatever one my parents are drawn to will just cause them to run away in another sudden fit of getting-it-on. But even though Harley was with me and I was definitely aware of his presence in the kitchen, today felt different. Harley kept me grounded enough to deal with difficult things. Including the fear that Vin and Alec—the couple I've always looked up to as the gay dictionary definition of love—might have been drawn to my brownies because they really do need to let go of each other.

Maybe I shouldn't base whether or not I believe in love on two people whose lives are just as messy as mine. I'm not giving up on them, though. If they're too tired to keep fighting, I'll have to do it for them.

"This is quite the thing to come home to," Dad says, and sticks his fork straight into the chocolate pie, completely forgetting about slices and plates and all of that traditional but technically unnecessary etiquette.

Harley looks briefly scandalized. And then, just as quickly, delighted.

Mom and Tess dig into the *same pie*. "Wait," I say. "Don't you want to try different ones?"

"Oh, we'd hate to take up all of these," Mom says, waving around, her eyes still glued to the chocolate pie.

It really does look good. All right, I guess we'll all start there.

Harley clinks his fork with mine.

"I hope I didn't mess up the magic," he whispers.

"Oh." It didn't really occur to me that Harley *could*.

In about four minutes, half the pie has been excavated

from the pan. Mom is patting her stomach and blinking heavily. Dad is producing elaborate yawn-like noises. Tess is frowning deeply, kicking her duffel bag with a thudding foot. "I don't think I should drive back tonight," she says suddenly.

"Ohhh, that's very smart, and I am very sleepy," Mom says.

I pull Harley aside and whisper, "I think this one is Tired Pie."

No matter how much I want to fix things at the Proud Muffin, a part of me is exhausted by this whole mess.

And the part of me that thinks about gender every day— mine and everyone else's and just in general—could use a break. It took me until middle school to realize that most people *don't* think about it every day. Because they don't have to. Because the world is set up in a way where they just take it for granted.

"This is the best piecrust you've ever . . . crusted," Mom says as she falls into one of the armchairs in the living room.

"That was Harley," I say, my words slowing to a crawl.

"I like piecrust," Dad burbles as he heads up the stairs. "I like Harley."

I look at Harley with a held-in smile. He's curled up on one end of the couch. He's made himself smaller than I thought possible, but then suddenly his eyes go wide and he tosses a wild punch into the air, the kind of stretch that randomly bursts out of someone before a long, deep sleep.

"I like Harley, too," I whisper, because everyone is too much of a tired mess to notice.

As my muscles fill with heavy sand and I rush to throw clean dish towels on top of my pies before I can't move ever again, a single thought wafts through my mind. How much my family doesn't notice is a good thing *and* a bad thing.

My sister is passed out on the kitchen floor. Completely unable to lift her, I grab a knitted blanket from the couch and fling it over her body and dab the chocolate off her nose with a napkin. I had grand plans about getting up and joining Harley on the couch, but I can't seem to get my muscles back in the game. I close my eyes right there on the floor next to Tess.

When I wake up, it's morning, and a nightmare of uneaten pies.

Pie, everywhere.

There are eleven of them all over the kitchen counters, which I see as soon as I stand up, because I've been on the hard, cold kitchen floor since yesterday afternoon. The lines of the tile are etched into my cheek.

Harley arrives behind me, looking like he just came out of a coma.

I grab a pie server, wielding it like a battle axe. "We have so many things to test before I go to work in—"

"Now," Harley blurts. "I have work right now."

He runs for the front door, shoving his feet into his sneakers without socks. The shift I picked up for switching with

Carlos doesn't start until after lunch, but Harley's delivery shift started half an hour ago. Not to mention that he fell asleep at my house, most likely without telling his mom first.

My parents like Harley, but his parent is definitely not going to be predisposed in my favor.

"Go," I say.

"Wait, how are you going to test the other pies?" Harley asks, and the fact that he still cares even when he's got one shoe on and he's late for a shift and his mom hates me—he really believes I have the ability to fix this.

"I'll figure it out," I say.

Harley leaves. My family doesn't look like they're waking up any time soon.

My brain does a little spin and lands in a new direction.

I dig up the card Jessalee gave me. Today's date is written on it. The start time for her meeting—whatever it is—is an hour from now. The restaurant is up near Round Rock, which means I have about four minutes to leave if I want to get there in time.

I dress in a flurry and load pie after pie after pie into my car. They blanket the back seat, they fill a cooler in the trunk. The apple pies ride shotgun. I talk to them as I drive—very slowly, no sudden turns.

"Don't worry," I say. "You're getting eaten. All of you."

* * *

The card Jessalee gave me leads me to a Mexican restaurant with well-priced brunch specials and margaritas that people who are old enough to drink margaritas in public refuse to stop talking about. I'm sure they're great, but let's be honest that anything based on a fruit-and-alcohol combo is going to be at least moderately delicious if you add a strategic circle of salt around it.

I go in and don't see anyone. My hope withers like a week-old party balloon.

I check the card. Did I get the time wrong? Is there another branch of this restaurant somewhere else in Austin— somewhere I couldn't possibly drive in time?

Then I hear Jessalee's voice carrying on a sudden curl of wind that moves through the open side door.

I leave the indoor dining room with its marigold booths. The tables and chairs outside are covered in bright chips of tile. Around a long table are about fifteen people, with Jessalee holding court at the far end. Everyone looks older than me, but still young-ish. They're Latinx and Black and Asian and white and people who are more than one of those things, and they all give off a distinctly queer vibe. They're digging into conversations and bowls of chips and salsa. I'm still not entirely sure what these people are all doing here, but I know this: they look hungry.

"Syd!" Jessalee says, popping up from her chair the second she sees me. She runs over and gives me a dainty side-hug.

"Hey, Jessalee," I say, knowing better than to attempt a

nickname. The only time I've seen someone do that—D.C. tried "JLee" once when he called her drink—I honestly thought she would drop the delicacy and stab him. Or maybe stab him delicately.

"I'm so, so glad you made it," she says. "There's an empty chair right by me!"

She points at this chair like it's the best thing ever. I squish in between her and a stranger, trying to look grateful.

As everyone else attacks the appetizers, I watch Jessalee like a beady-eyed grackle, tracking whether she pays more attention to one particular person or ignores someone ostentatiously. I stay on the lookout for emotionally saturated glances. She just keeps walking around, chatting, giving out more side-hugs like they're her signature move. Everyone is warmly smiling and sharply dressed. I'm suddenly, absurdly glad that I let Tess and Harley shave my head yesterday.

Jessalee circles all the way back around and sits next to me, propped on top of a folded leg. I look around for her notebooks, pens, laptop, any sign that I've crashed a writing group. All I see is a tiny clutch by Jessalee's place setting with the words *ethical slut* hand-beaded onto it. "All right," she says, clinking the side of her mimosa with her fork. "I think we're all here. Welcome to polyam brunch!"

Baby's First Polyam Brunch

~~~~~~ **INGREDIENTS** ~~~~~~

1 open mind

1 breakfast special

2 mimosas (virgin, if you're under 21)

~~~~~~ **DIRECTIONS** ~~~~~~

Get into conversations with people, most of which aren't even about polyamory.

Learn a few things that you didn't know before, like the difference between a V and a triad.

Start with your own breakfast special but be open to sharing plates. Realize that this is not a metaphor for anything in particular but a way for everyone to try the restaurant's seven equally delicious breakfast enchiladas.

Drink a mimosa.

If someone asks, and you feel like doing it, share your own dating history. Admit that you've been in a single relationship, and you went into it headfirst when you were in middle school and only recently surfaced.

Drink another mimosa. Realize it's basically just fizzy orange juice.

Don't let that stop you from having a good time.

9

I'm having so much fun that it takes me until the food is starting to go cold to get back to my investigation.

At the bakery Jessalee is always engrossed in her work and eating day-old pastries at a tiny table by herself. Here she's playing hopscotch all over the table to make sure she gets a chance to talk to everyone. No amount of watching her is helping me figure out her love life, though. I'm going to have to start asking questions.

The person on my right side is so deep in a rant about cat insurance that it feels rude to interrupt. On the other side of Jessalee's empty seat is a twenty-ish person wearing a striped blue T-shirt and a look of total abandonment. Maybe they're relatively new to this, too. Maybe they're still figuring it out. Maybe they're looking around at everyone and trying to see where they fit—and in the process, noticing how everyone else fits together.

I slide over into Jessalee's seat.

"How long have you been coming to polyam brunch?" I ask. "Did Jessalee invite you here, too?"

"Oh!" They look up at me. They have the kind of dark, shiny hair that flops over their eyes and makes it seem like they're always peeking out from behind a hedge. "No, I have been here many times. And yes. She did invite me."

"Does Jessalee have any partners right now?" I scramble to add, "I'm not asking for me."

"She is not seeing anyone," they say in a weary way that makes it obvious there's more to *that* story. "How do you know Jessa?"

They're allowed to use a nickname for her? Hmmm.

"I work at the Proud Muffin," I say, beaming. I can't hold back the shine that comes with those words—but then I remember that the bakery might be in trouble, and it's my fault. Guilt spreads like the stain from the guacamole I dropped on my shorts.

"Ah. I thought maybe you were a writing friend of Jessa's?" Their words have a soft accent, an upward lilt.

"I write recipes," I say impulsively. I like the idea that someone here assumes I'm creative.

"Even better, because you can't eat a book," they say, and their laugh seems spring-loaded, ready to burst out at any moment. "Javi. They/them. Your name and pronouns?"

"Syd. She . . . they?"

I've been thinking about it a lot. The truth is that "they" doesn't feel perfect to me either, but maybe it's not any one pronoun that's the problem. Maybe it's the assumption that one of them is going to fit *all the time*.

This feels like a good place to try out something new.

We angle toward each other a little, and it feels like an island of privacy tucked among everyone else talking in pairs and small groups. This might be the best chance I get to ask questions. "So. Jessalee. Do you think she's got her taxi light on?" Javi wrinkles their nose. I explain the concept in a quick, condensed way. "I think one of my friends at the bakery might be interested."

"They should join us next time," Javi says in a generous tone. Then their voice gets a little darker, a scattering of clouds over their sunny demeanor. "I'm not sure Jessalee wants to date anyone at the bakery again."

"Again?" I mumble over a cold, soggy bite of enchilada.

Jessalee was dating someone at the Proud Muffin? Marisol? She's in the right age range and she was alone at the last community night, which would scan with a recent breakup. But we work together in the kitchen every single day. Marisol might not be the chatty and forthcoming type, but I would have to miss a lot to miss *that*.

"Wait, who was Jessalee dating?" I ask in a needy whisper.

"We were together," they say wistfully.

That's why they looked abandoned. They aren't nervous

and lonely in a general sense, but missing Jessalee specifically. I glance over and find her still bouncing around and talking to everyone.

Everyone but Javi.

"You don't work at the bakery . . ." I say faintly.

They've started up again, though. "Jessa and I met through a friend who knows I love her books. She does not get involved with fans, usually, but we began to talk, and we had so many things to say to each other. It felt like Bergamot and Ambrosia discovering they were connected by the magic of the great palate gods of old."

I have no idea who Bergamot and Ambrosia are. Or who the great palate gods of old are, for that matter. But Javi talks about Jessalee in a sweet, sad way that makes it clear: they still care about her.

"You read her books?" I ask, my curiosity edging forward.

"You don't?" they ask, their hair flopping around in shock. "And yet you're friends with the author of the best queer foodie fantasy series in all the lands."

"I . . . am?"

They hold up their glass. I think they must be twenty-one, at least, judging from the way they wave it, and the slight hint of alcohol mixed with sweet mango. "You've never heard of *The Sweet Sorcery of Ambrosia P. Jones*? The *P* stands for *Patisserie.*"

I spit a laugh. A bit of virgin mimosa comes out with it.

Spilling out the content of my pockets, I find her business card with the meeting time on the back. *Authoress of love, magic, etc.* I've got a much better sense of what *etc.* means now. It's sugar.

"You think the books sound silly," Javi says. "They're not. Well, sometimes they are, but Jessa's humor, it's one of the best parts—"

"I'm laughing at myself," I explain. "Really, I should have known." When I guessed that Jessalee was camped out at the bakery writing romance novels, my imagination hadn't put all the pieces together.

Right as I'm thinking about the Proud Muffin, Gemma bursts onto the porch. People flock to her, giving hugs and pouring out praises for her bright yellow jumpsuit and her makeup—she's reigning queen of the bright blue lip.

Jessalee is the only one stuck to her seat, watching Gemma's entrance with the dismal look of someone who used to share her spotlight.

Javi gently makes their way through the crowd and gives Gemma the warmest welcome of all, complete with a lingering kiss. This is Gemma's space, and she's my coworker. I find myself looking away out of a potent combination of embarrassment and politeness.

I expect Javi to rearrange the seating so they can squeeze in next to Gemma, but they come right back to me. They seem committed to their conversation with the awkward newcomer, which makes me like them.

I can see why Jessalee and Gemma would like them.

"So all three of you were together?" I ask.

"We started as a V," Javi explains. "Gemma and I knew

Jessalee. Through this group, Gemma and I met each other."

"You became a triad?"

Javi nods. "I thought everything was perfect between the three of us. It takes a while when relationships change, and there's a lot of talking. But as you can see, I like to talk. Jessalee is so good with words. And Gemma, you must know her well."

I nod—but the truth is that I wish I knew Gemma better. I've been so focused on W and baking. When I'm done fixing all of this, I'm going to spend more time with everyone. Of course if I don't get Vin and Alec back together soon, I might not get the chance to know people like Gemma and Jessalee better. By the time I arrive at this thought, I feel as downhearted as Javi looks.

"I thought we were all in the same place. Together. Happy. But Jessa wasn't sure. She broke things off with both of us."

With a little help from my brownies.

After what happened, I might have been stupidly looking for pairs of people, but now that I see the shape of this relationship, I'm catching up quickly. Jessalee, Gemma, Javi: this is what I need to mend.

There are so many questions I want to ask, but they would be way too personal and prying for a first talk over tortilla chips. When did Jessalee start to pull away? Did Javi or Gemma have any guesses about why? The one thing I know is that Jessalee showed up the day we had the scones at Barton Springs. She wanted to find some kind of fresh spark.

So, when did she lose the sparks she had?

I watch Jessalee's love interests as yet another round of

chips and tomatillo salsa are passed around. Even across the full length of the table, Gemma and Javi are tossing each other little looks of adoration. Jessalee is ostentatiously chatting with someone else.

She's making a pretty big point of not caring.

I see it happen though—the moment when Jessalee runs out of salsa and Gemma reaches over several people with a nearly full dish. She waits until Jessalee grabs it, then grabs her eyes and doesn't let go.

Now that I think about it, Gemma always made herself busy at the exact moment Jessalee came to the counter. I've always assumed that was just a factor of how busy we get during the morning rush, or maybe that Jessalee wasn't one of Gemma's favorite regulars.

I have been reading this romance novel *all wrong*. And apparently it's about baking wizards anyway.

In unrelated news, Gemma keeps eyeing *me* across the table. She probably wonders if I'm trying polyam in the wake of my breakup with W, and if W knows, and if that's maybe part of why we broke up, and oh, wow, this is getting complicated really fast.

"Is it complicated?" I ask. "Being in love with two people?"

"It takes work, but so do all good love stories," Javi says. They can't seem to help adding, "That's one of the things Ambrosia learns on her quest to find the world's last secret flavor." They sigh at Gemma's sadness when Jessalee turns her back.

My heart pinches tight on their behalf.

"I brought pie!" I shout.

All of a sudden, I'm up and grabbing Gemma. "Can you help me?" I ask as we pass through the restaurant, back into the parking lot. "I brought a little more than I can carry and . . ." I open the car door, its window cracked, revealing a half dozen pies on the back seat. Gemma clears her braids off one shoulder and gives me a worried stare. She hasn't even seen the ones in the cooler yet.

"Are you okay, Syd?" Gemma asks.

"What?" I ask.

She picks up the lemon chess pie. "When Marisol gets upset, like really upset, she can't stop baking. I know we don't know each other as well, but . . . you seem a lot like her." She pauses. "In that way."

I line my arms with pies, as many as I can carry without gravity getting involved.

"I'm great," I say, a lie the size of Texas—the only state that constantly tells you how big it is. I'm not going to be great again until everyone who ate my brownies is back in love, Harley and I can finally make out, and the Proud Muffin is safe. "I just didn't know how many people would be here and . . . I overbaked!"

"Yeah," Gemma says, with a tight-pressed smile. "You really, really did."

I look down at all the pies we're carrying, and for some reason my eyes are drawn to the peach strawberry basil. It's got a fluffy crumb on top, like the perfect muffin-pie hybrid, but it's more than that. Something about it is calling out to me, letting me know that the magic inside is what Jessalee needs.

As we head back onto the patio, I ask Gemma to swap pies with me. Peach strawberry basil for plain old peach. She looks at me like I've lost the last bit of sense that I have. "Can you offer a piece of this one to Jessalee? Please?"

"Why?" Gemma asks as I slide the peach strawberry basil pie on her overburdened arms.

"It's the best pie here. And she's always so nice to me at the bakery," I say. "It would mean a lot."

"Why not give it to her yourself?"

"Well, you two are the only people I know here and the whole point is to meet new people, right?" Gemma shakes her head and shimmies the peach pie onto my arm. "I'm not trying to date . . . yet. Just thinking about new possibilities."

No lies there.

"Okay, Syd," Gemma says. "But this is a group for people in their twenties. I think Jessalee assumed you were a little older because you work in the kitchen."

"But you know I'm a baby child?" I mutter.

"I know you really shouldn't date adults until you're an adult," she says in a mild, reasonable tone. "When you're old enough, you bring pie around any time you want."

I set my pies down on the long table and make several new friends instantly. Javi is eyeing the blackberry piled high with fluffy Italian meringue that I lovingly blowtorched, and I can't really blame them. I make sure a big piece makes its way over to them as the pies are divvied up.

The restaurant probably has a policy about outside food,

but the waiters quickly start joking with Jessalee about which pies they want to try. I'll leave behind whatever I don't need for Vin and Alec.

In my head I'm calculating an enormous apology tip.

Gemma heads around to the far end of the table, and Jessalee grabs the peach strawberry basil pie right out of her hands. She looks at it like it's the answer to a question that's been haunting her. Then she digs a fork in and takes three bites so fast they blur.

When she talks, it looks like she's talking to the pie. "I miss you and Javi so much."

"Why won't you talk to us, then?" Gemma asks, shooing someone down the table so she can sit next to Jessalee. That person is so busy scarfing apple pie that they don't seem to mind.

Jessalee takes another huge bite. Chews it over. "I don't want you to think that it's okay that you left me out when you took that trip to Marfa."

Gemma takes a step back. Javi leans forward. Everyone else is eating, eating, but I'm watching.

"Is that what you think?" Gemma asks. "That we left you out? You were too busy for us. You told us you had to write."

"I did!" Jessalee hangs her head, blue hair in the pie. "I still wish you'd invited me. I could have brought my book along. I could have worked on it at that little motel you stayed at, with the typewriters in every room. You both knew how much I wanted to go there. You and Javi could have gone out and taken photos all day and then we could have stayed up all night together, looking for the Marfa Lights."

"We already had plans to take you back there for your birthday, Lee." Wow. I guess Gemma is allowed to shorten her name, too.

She reaches for the pie. Cuts her own sliver, but sets it aside and fills her fork from the uncut pie instead. It takes her a full minute to chew and swallow or maybe she's just working up her courage. I can feel the swell of magic, the simmering sense in the air that something is about to change.

"You pulled back so hard and so fast that I worry it'll happen the next time you get upset about something," Gemma says.

Javi leans across the table. Digs into the pie with their own fork, halfway out of their seat. Around a bite they add, "I was afraid that you were looking for an out. Because . . . you didn't like us that much?"

"What?" Jessalee holds a hand to her mouth. "It's the opposite. I felt so much about both of you. All three of us together. And then you left me behind. I thought . . . I thought the magic was gone."

That explains the spark Jessalee was chasing that day at Barton Springs.

"No, no, no," Javi says.

"Absolutely not," Gemma adds.

Jessalee and Gemma and Javi are all digging into the pie now, but whatever they need to say must be spent, because the only thing they're doing with their mouths between bites now is kissing.

It's so sweet, and I'm so happy for my coworker and my best regular and this very nice-seeming person I've just met that I don't notice how much of the pie is vanishing until they're down to the last slice.

I run around the long table and get there right as their forks tangle over the last piece. Jessalee splits it in two and feeds a bite to Gemma and one to Javi. I've never seen three people demolish a pie so fast.

Jessalee looks up at me. "Thank you, Syd. This is the best thing I've ever eaten. Please make it for every special, ever."

I take a breath. I inhale the compliment.

But the pie is gone. I needed a slice of that for Alec and Vin. They're the ones I did all of this for.

Jessalee and Gemma and Javi deserve their happiness, though.

We all do.

But even with magic in the mix, we have to work for it. And it looks like I'm not done working. "All right, I'm only seventeen so I guess I should cut out, but have fun with the rest of the pies!"

Now I know what I need, the pie that will fix everything. There's a secret at the center of Vin and Alec's relationship, and until they let everything out and let each other back in, we're all in trouble.

I look back at Gemma, happily scarfing a slice of the salted caramel apple pie with the apple cutouts on top. I hope it's the one I made when I was thinking about how cute Harley looks with a rolling pin.

And I start to run.

Something is wrong at the Proud Muffin.

I feel it the moment I walk in the door and see Marisol's shoulders. She's usually relaxed when she's baking—it's like her natural state—but right now the muscles around her neck are bunched in angry clusters. I've seen Marisol bake through bad tropical storms, bad breakups with people who keep coming to the bakery to bother her, and a birthday when everyone in her family decided to ignore her.

Whatever has gone sour, it's bigger than all of that put together.

"Hey," I try as I toss on an apron.

"Did you really accuse Vin of cheating on Alec?" she asks, whirling around on me, whisk in one hand. "Seriously, Syd?"

I go into a defensive mode that involves not making direct eye contact, and instead I pretend that I'm taking inventory of the coarse sugar cupboard, where we keep little metal drawers filled with every color of the rainbow. "In the walk-in . . . you were right there with me . . . we heard—"

"We don't know what we heard," Marisol snaps. "And you shouldn't assume you know anything about anyone else's heart when you know so very little about your own."

Whoa.

I'm not going to dignify *that* with a response.

No. Wait. I whip around, getting undignified. I'm tired of being held to a different standard than everyone else in this bakery just because I'm a teenager. Why do I always have to take the high road? Why is that road paved with more patience and maturity than people expect from *actual adults*?

"What about you?" I ask. "What's the longest you've been with anyone? Seven dates? Eight?"

Marisol shakes her whisk at me. "Locking someone into a relationship when you're both in middle school is not an accomplishment," she says, crisp and tart as a Granny Smith. "And quantity and quality are two different things." I think she's done, because she turns her back and keeps on baking, which usually signals the end of a conversation. But after her hands push out a few rolled lengths of bread dough, she adds, "You know those cakes they sell at Costco?"

"The ones with the slimy white frosting and sugar flowers that could rot a tooth out of your head?"

"Yes."

"The ones that are the size of a football field but eating even a tiny slice feels like a crime against real baking?"

"Yes."

"Are you comparing my love life to a *Costco cake*?"

It's a good thing I don't have a pie with me right now, because if Marisol turned around it might be headed straight toward her face. I've always thought pieing people would be a waste, but I'm quickly reconsidering my stance.

Marisol bangs down a finished pan of miniature bread

loaves, the ones we serve at lunch. "W tells me enough to know it's a good comparison."

I throw her loaves in the oven and snap it shut. Even when we're pissed, we're still a precise team. Otherwise no one gets baked goods. Otherwise the Proud Muffin falls apart, and that's exactly what I'm trying to avoid. "What, are you and W friends now?" I push it, even though I know I shouldn't. "Or are you just flirting with my ex because you're bored, and you know she's going to get a little crush on you?"

Marisol shakes her head, too disgusted at me to do anything but hold up a stop-with-that-mess hand. "I would *never* flirt with W. Are we friends? That girl is like my little cousin."

"And what am I?" I ask.

My voice might sound coarse, like I don't care.

But I know that my face is open and scared and giving the whole thing away.

Marisol finally turns around, snatching up a wet rag that I forgot about. She tosses it into the barrel in the corner without even looking. "You're some infant who keeps messing up my kitchen."

At that moment, three people in full hipster regalia and one in a dark, perfectly cut business suit enter the kitchen. A lot of people confuse hipsters and queer folks. Maybe there *are* some queer hipsters, but for the most part they just steal queer fashion and make it look boring.

Marisol goes stock-still.

"Right, you've already met Marisol," Alec says, trailing behind the invasive newcomers. "And this is Syd."

225

I try to catch his eye, and I only succeed for half of a second, but it's enough to see the truth.

I've seen that look on my parents' faces, when they were barely keeping it together, when there wasn't enough money to keep the bills at bay, when they were sad all the time and trying so hard not to show me and Tess how bad things were.

Alec is in pain.

"We know that you have a very loyal staff," one of the hipsters says. He's got a dark crescent of facial hair and is wearing a leather apron over jeans that probably cost as much as my entire wardrobe.

"We'll be bringing in some of our own people, of course," the person in the suit adds, like he's the walking embodiment of reading the fine print.

"Of course," Alec echoes emptily.

"And no staff under eighteen," the one in the suit says, eyeing me. "We need everyone to be able to serve alcohol."

"And appreciate black pearl quinoa," the hipster adds.

All three hipsters—I'm starting to think of the other two as backup singers—laugh and add little jokes. They say the word *aesthetic* a lot. When they start talking about how they obviously have to repaint the tacky rainbow porch, I'm just about done.

"What's your business?" I ask, crossing my arms, proudly underlining the name of the bakery on my apron.

The lead hipster doesn't notice how much loathing is loaded in my voice, or he doesn't care, because he answers with enthusiasm. "We run the Grain Bar up in North Austin, and we're hoping to expand."

"The Grain Bar?" I've heard of it. They serve overpriced bowls of "ancient grains" and pair them with hard liquor.

I hate it.

I hate everything about this.

The hipsters trail toward the offices. Alec follows at a marked distance. Marisol thinks these people are here because of me. No wonder she's mad. My survival instincts go into overdrive.

I need another peach strawberry basil pie. *Now.*

I can't just start baking whatever the hell I please while I'm working, though. I need to make it look like this is for the bakery, at least until Vin and Alec realize the glory of this pie. I saw the cascade of honesty it inspired for Javi and Gemma and Jessalee.

My bosses need that.

I run for the phone tucked on the other side of the wall that separates the kitchen and the counter. And I dial the only phone number I know by heart.

"Hello!" W's voice hits me like someone ran an electric current through the phone. It takes me a second to figure out why. She's happy. I'd forgotten what she sounds like happy. "Gemma? What's up?"

I can't figure out how to answer. To ask what I need to ask. None of it makes sense, out of context, and W and I aren't in each other's contexts anymore.

I didn't just lose the person I cared about most. I lost the person whose life fully overlapped with mine.

"Is this Marisol?" she asks, then rolls off a few words in Spanish.

God, they really *are* friends.

"Syd? Syd, is that you?"

"Call the bakery back in two minutes, please," I say.

"What? Why?" There's anger in her voice now. It shocks me right back into our breakup. "This is some weird ploy to get me to talk to you. Sorry, no thanks. Not after you blew me off the other day."

I hadn't thought about how our encounter at Barton Springs must have felt to her. But she's the one who ended us, right? Does she get to feel bad for herself? Does she get to act like *I'm* the one keeping us apart?

"You don't have to talk to me," I say. Honestly, I don't have the time or emotional capacity to deal with W and whatever we're both feeling or not feeling. This is about Vin and Alec.

No—it's more than that.

"Just make the call," I say, fear trickling into my tone. "This is for everyone at the bakery, okay? This is about all of us."

I know that I can trust W to understand that *us*.

Even now, even if she and I are never close again, there are some things she'll always understand.

"Okay," she says, and the phone goes dead.

I go back to the kitchen, back to sprinkling rainbows of coarse sugar on muffin tops.

Two minutes later, the phone rings and I rush to answer it, grabbing an order slip.

"Whatever this is, it had better be important. And you'd better explain it to me later. You can't just act like I'm nothing and then need me out of nowhere."

It takes everything I have not to hiss back, *Neither can you. You never really explained why you broke up with me. And then you showed up at Barton Springs like I was supposed to be thrilled about it and give you scones.*

But I just nod my head and write things down on the order slip, pretending that a customer is urgently requesting a strawberry peach basil pie. "Pastry crust or crumb topping? Yes, we can do that right away."

The phone goes dead again.

"What was that?" Marisol asks as I stride back into the kitchen.

"Pie," I say. "I got it."

I go to the walk-in and grab a ball of pie dough. I weigh it in my hand. It'll cut my baking time down by half, but will it mess with the magic? I made this dough myself, even if I didn't do it today. I recognize my scribbled date on the plastic wrap.

Besides, Harley rolled the dough last time and it didn't seem to ruin anything.

I'll put extra magic into the pie to make up for it, I swear.

Honest Pie

~~~ INGREDIENTS ~~~

FOR THE BOTTOM CRUST

1½ cups all-purpose flour

1½ tsp granulated sugar

½ tsp salt

½ cup (1 stick) cold unsalted butter, cut into ¼-inch pieces

3 tbsp cold water

1 tbsp apple cider vinegar

FOR THE FILLING

4 cups sliced peeled peaches (about 4 to 6 peaches, depending on size)

1½ cups sliced fresh strawberries (just buy a pint and put them all in)

2 tbsp lemon juice (zest the lemon first)

½ cup sugar

2 tbsp minced fresh basil

7 tbsp tapioca flour, or 5 tbsp cornstarch

FOR THE CRUMB TOPPING

6 tbsp granulated sugar

1 tsp baking powder

1 ⅓ cups all-purpose flour

A pinch of salt

Zest from 1 lemon

½ cup (1 stick) butter, melted

DIRECTIONS

Real talk: pies are a lot of work.

But this one is very much worth it.

First, make and chill your dough. This can be done up to a day before you bake. Mix the flour, sugar, and salt in a bowl, then add the butter and cut together with a pastry blender or your fingers. Sprinkle in the cold water and then the apple cider vinegar, tossing to mix. Bring everything together, kneading the dough a few times to make sure the butter is fully distributed. You might need to add a bonus tablespoon of water to get it to come together. I'll be honest: this is the ONLY recipe for pie dough that I've never had fall apart on me. In a world that feels like it's constantly crumbling, this dough is one reliable thing.

Cover the dough in plastic wrap and shove it in the fridge for at least an hour. (Fifteen minutes in the freezer works in a pinch.) When you're ready to start actively baking, preheat the oven to 375 degrees.

Roll your dough out on a clean and floured surface, until you have a ½-inch-thick disk slightly larger than your pie pan. Carefully transfer it, settling the dough into the pan and cutting any overhang. Crimp the edges, otherwise they might shrink up.

It's time to blind bake! This is another one of those baking things that sounds intimidating but is actually pretty simple and deeply satisfying, because it'll keep your crust from getting soggy. More real talk: nobody likes a soggy pie. Line the dough with baking parchment and pick your weapon: the shell can be filled with pie weights, dried beans, or rice to keep it from puffing up. I use rice, because it covers the bottom so evenly. If you are my grandma, you can skip the parchment and dock—aka prick holes in—the bottom crust with a fork, but if you are anyone other than my grandma, the docked crust will still puff up. (How does she do it?)

Blind bake the shell for 25 to 30 minutes, until it's nicely golden. In the meantime, make your filling and get the crumb topping ready.

Combine the sliced peaches and strawberries in a bowl, tossing in the lemon juice and sugar and tasting as you go until you reach your preferred tart/sweet balance. Add in the basil and test again. I promise, the juicy sweetness of the fruit and the bite of the basil will change your life, or at least your idea of what a pie should taste like. Thoroughly mix in the thickener—I like tapioca flour if you can get it, but I've used cornstarch and the pie was still amazing.

To make the crumb topping, stir the sugar, baking powder, flour, salt, and zest into your melted butter with a fork until crumbs form.

When your shell is out of the oven and slightly cooled, spoon the filling in, then scatter the crumb topping evenly over the fruit.

Bake for 45 minutes to 1 hour. You should see fruit starting to seethe around the crumb topping, but the real secret to knowing when a fruit pie is done is in the sound. When you hear fruit bubbling beneath the surface, your pie is really and truly done.

Let the pie cool fully. Realest talk: this is nearly impossible to do. The scent of the simmered strawberries is at its peak, the basil-laced peach is welling up in pools between boulders of golden topping, and all you want to do is attack the pie with abandon, possibly smothering it in vanilla ice cream or some of that perfect homemade whipped cream. But it really is best if you can wait until it's no longer blazing hot, when the fruit has settled and the filling won't run.

Now cut a slice and dig into the truth.

10

The truth is that I'm pissed.

As I make this pie, those Grain Bar people are touring the offices, asking pointed questions about Vin's business practices, bragging about how much money they have to invest because they just *have* things. Maybe they had to work hard for them and maybe they didn't, but did they have to fight? For every inch of space, every truly safe moment, every person who sees them and likes them for who they are?

My arms fly twice as fast, slicing peaches and mincing basil with a fury.

Honestly, I hate the world that we live in for making it so hard for places like the Proud Muffin to exist. And then keep existing. I hate that this is normal—that places I love disappear overnight, and the place that I love most is on the chopping block and the worst kind of assholes are wielding the overpriced Santoku knife. It's true that Austin is an oasis of queer life, but there are still no guarantees. We can lose whatever we have, at any moment.

I stir in the thickener with tiny, ferocious flicks of my wrist and I sincerely hate, hate, *hate* that I can already picture this place as the Grain Bar, the kitchen retrofitted with every expensive useless tool, the community space turned into an overpriced apartment for people who just moved here from Brooklyn because they *fell in love* when they went to SXSW that one time, the counter turned into a hookup spot for over-paid startup employees who have a thousand other places to meet people just like them.

My hands are slippery with righteous rage as I tip the filling into the crust, a little of it spilling on the floor. Ferocious tears show up as I top the pie with butter crumbs, and I barely hold in salty drops that nobody wants on their dessert.

I throw the whole thing in the oven.

After another forty-five minutes of wobbly, nerve-ridden work, I take the pie out and carry it to the front. Vin and Alec are both on the porch, saying a prolonged goodbye to the Grain Bar people. It looks painful and stilted, even from a distance. I should put the pie down and walk away—wait for them to be drawn to it, naturally.

I march out onto the porch.

"I need you to taste this," I say, holding out the pie.

The Grain Bar people are looking at me like I'm a little *too much*, and I know that if they buy this place, I'm the first employee to go.

"Syd . . ." Vin warns, but either Alec didn't get the memo about how much trouble I'm in for storming into the office and acting like a complete baby or he *really* needs to say something true, because he reaches for the pie like it's a life preserver.

"Fine," Vin grumbles. "Can we offer you some?"

The hipsters wave off the pie like it's personally offending them.

Mr. Fine Print, on the other hand, looks like he's trying to keep a lid on his enthusiasm. "Yes, please."

Well, that wasn't really part of the plan, but I don't care at this point. As long as Vin and Alec eat the pie. As long as they break down the secrets and lies that have solidified into a brick wall between them. I grab three plates and cut three pieces and watch as all three of them chew, breathe harder, chew more.

Vin and Alec look at each other.

There's a fire in their eyes, and it's about to happen. That stare is going to spark into passion, and settle into love, and they're going to send these rich entitlemuffins back to North Austin with nothing.

"I can't believe you," Alec says.

"*You* can't believe *me*?" Vin growls.

And then they're shouting, shouting, about how they each blame the other one. For the breakup. For letting things get this bad. For letting the Proud Muffin slip away. For not fighting harder.

"Wait . . ." I say.

"Well, this is intense," one of the hipsters says with a nervous laugh.

"And I hate *this*," Alec says, pointing at the hipsters, who are stuck in place by the sudden downpour of strong emotions. I can't tell if they're staying out of shock and respect, or if they want to take out their phones and put this whole thing on the internet. "I hate that I even let them in the front door."

"I hate that I'm their accountant!" Mr. Fine Print pipes up, wiping away a bit of crumb from his mouth with a napkin. "Absolutely fucking hate it. I don't think they even *know* that I'm gay and this is my favorite bakery."

Huh. I didn't see that twist coming. Though, now that I'm looking beyond his suit, he *does* seem familiar.

The lead hipster backs up, down the steps, away from the earnest display of emotion. "Oh, dude, you should have said something . . ."

"It's not my job to tell you basic things when we've been working together for eight years, *Kevin*!" The guy in the suit grabs the rest of the pie, squares it up with Kevin's beardy face, and lets it fly.

It lands with a squelch of cooked fruit, bits of broken crust sticking all over Kevin's face as the pie slips down and finally falls.

Now the cameras really are out, the customers on the porch and in the little garden and sitting in the windows holding their phones up to catch this. I turn to find D.C. and Lex and the rest of the counter staff looking stuck halfway between laughter and horror.

"I hate that we can't do that every day," Vin says, looking at Alec with green-brown eyes that go from gruff to puppy in about two seconds. "Hey, at least we agree on something, right?"

Alec looks disgusted, and not just by the collateral damage of fruit and buttery crumbs on his best shoes. "No," he says. "We're a mess." Vin shakes his head and follows Alec toward their car—fighting all the way.

I back away, retreating to the safety of the kitchen. As much as I loved watching Kevin take a pie to the pretty face, I'm pretty sure I just made everything worse. I didn't give Vin and Alec Honest Pie. I baked something else into the peaches, the strawberries, the pastry. A truthful feeling, yes, but a very specific one.

I was rage baking.

That was Anger Pie.

I run back to the walk-in and collapse on one of the crates. The tears that I was holding back before start falling, hitting the concrete floor, turning it from pale gray to a darker, stormy color.

A minute later, I hear another crate scraping over toward me. Marisol sits down and drapes an arm around my back.

"They weren't fighting because Alec thought Vin was cheating," I say in a finely shredded voice, finally getting it. "Alec thought Vin was secretly planning to sell the bakery.

He thought Vin was being wooed by buyers who wanted the Proud Muffin, not guys who wanted to date him."

"That's why they were fighting," Marisol confirms.

"Are *we* still fighting?" I ask, looking up suddenly, my face red and my cheeks hot with the aftermath of tears.

"We need to stick together, you and me. Just . . . no more messing with Vin and Alec. They have it hard enough right now."

"I'm trying to make things better," I say.

Marisol nods like she knows this feeling, like she's already tried in her own way and run into her own walls. She ropes me in close with her arm, spreads her fingers over my shaved head. "You just have to keep baking, right?"

"Yeah," I say, thinking of all the ways I might be able to salvage this with sugar. "I can do that."

After everything that just happened, it feels wrong to go out with Harley, but it also feels like the only right thing left.

The night is fresh-baked, warm, scented with April leaves and the vanilla of Harley's body wash. They're standing on the top step, hands in their pockets, rocking on their heels. Harley is wearing a shirt the color of bluebells, black jeans, and cowboy boots. Real, cracked in the grooves, ground down at the heel, dusty, dirty, these-have-chased-after-cows cowboy boots.

I flash on W just long enough to realize that despite

everything she and Harley *don't* have in common, they both have these boots.

Apparently, this is my type.

"I thought we'd go dancing," Harley says, rocking forward in a way that brings them right into my space. "Since we never got to at the gay bar."

"That sounds great." My words are so confident. My feet feel a little less certain. They're worried that we're not very good at dancing. My hips are also pretty nervous about this plan.

We get in my car anyway, and I follow Harley's directions to a place over on South Lamar, with wooden porches slung all the way around it, big Christmas bulbs wrapped around every post, and rocking chairs all lined up and waiting for butts.

We shuffle into the dance hall. The air in here feels smoky, even though people obviously aren't allowed to smoke inside. The dance floor is packed tight with couples spinning and swapping and reeling. The age range is impressive: from late teens to what looks to be early nineties. The crowd is pretty one-note in other ways, though. It's a lot of white people, with a few Latinx and Black folks. And while I can see one old, delightfully dykey-looking couple with fringe vests and clipped gray hair dipping each other with vigor, the overall vibe seems pretty straight.

But Harley looks comfortable here. I try to absorb a little bit of that feeling.

They hold out their hand and lead me onto the dance

floor, and soon I'm a half-beat behind them, whirling and stamping and clapping and generally confused. The music is a fiddle-heavy sort of country, not the kind of country they play on the radio, laced with pop or cut with classic rock.

I try to find a way into the music—a sort of flow where you stop overthinking and just keep moving—but I can't quite manage it, and Harley's smile, when I look up from my awkward feet, sets me back a full beat.

Every time.

There's also the fact that, in the few cases where I've done any kind of couple dancing with W, I've always taken the lead—the part that's traditionally reserved for guys—so even when I start to find the patterns in the dance, I'm always pushing forward when I should be going backward, mashing into Harley's face.

At least it makes them laugh.

After five or six or seven botched dances, I tug at Harley's hand. There's a stitch in my side, and I wore the wrong shoes based on the vicious blister rising on the back of my heel, but I'm still smiling. My face is wide open, without any kind of defense. We go outside, collapse into side-by-side rocking chairs, and sip at the cooling air.

"This isn't exactly what I expected when you said dancing," I admit.

"This is only our first stop," Harley says, jumping right back up. They stroll across the parking lot and I follow, enough distance to appreciate the way they swagger in those boots. They make Harley's hips jut out and their torso settle farther back, a balance that's totally different from their usual forward bounce.

I like them both.

We park in a lot and head into the downtown crowds, quickly becoming anonymous like we did that first night together. This crowd is mostly students, young and—otherwise—diverse. I should feel more at home here than I did on the country-western dance floor, but this just feels like high school, the sequel. Like a big party that I'm crashing, where I'll always be stuck in some corner, not because everyone hates me, exactly, but because I never bothered to learn the rules or play the game.

After a few blocks of being pushed and pulled and pitched around by everybody moving at different speeds on the sidewalk, I grab Harley to the side. I know that they have ideas for our night, but I want to show them that I can contribute, too.

There's a pocket of an outdoor club, nestled into the nightly pandemonium, where the band is dressed in full eighties regalia—pegged jeans and neon—and they play stunningly accurate renditions of radio smashes that were big when my parents were my age. I know all of these pop confections and power ballads; this is what I grew up listening to on car trips, or jump-dancing with Tess on our twin beds. When I made my first-ever batch of cookies, I was listening to "I Would Do Anything for Love (But I Won't Do That)" while Tess did a highly dramatic lip sync in the background and stole bites of dough.

Even now, the sound of this music finds a matching groove

in my brain. I shout-sing Paula Abdul—"Straight Up"—while Harley looks at me with this incredible crinkly face, amused but also concerned.

"Don't you know this?" I ask as the band hits the opening lick of "Jessie's Girl", which is the gayest '80s song, and a personal favorite.

"Um, the music I know is the stuff we were just dancing to!" Harley shouts.

We bop along to a few songs, but I can tell that Harley is having more fun watching me do the Molly Ringwald than actually listening to the synthesizers, so we head back into a night as warm and clingy as a heated swimming pool.

"Okay, now that we've had our warm-ups . . ." Harley says, grabbing my sweaty hand. "Time for the best dancing in Austin."

We push our way up Sixth Street, people giving way around us.

I check my phone. It's already eleven, but my curfew isn't until midnight and I've tested that fence with W so many times that I know exactly where the holes are, and how to duck through them. Being proactive is key.

I thumb a quick text with one hand, not willing to let go of Harley. *Home by one. Extra salted caramel in the fridge. Put some on the vanilla ice cream! See you soon!*

We end up at a club on Red River, where we cut straight to the back door. A large, burly person who accepts deliveries seems to know Harley. Apparently, that's the magic of being a bike messenger. They let us in and snap NO DRINK bracelets on our arms, and then we're set free in the fake-fog-and-laser-strewn darkness. There's a long bar, a few banquettes, a back room with a pool table. Most of the club is taken up by a sunken black dance floor. And most of the dance floor is taken up by total weirdos.

Every kid who didn't fit in at every high school in the greater Austin area must be collected here. There are about a hundred people on the dance floor, and another dozen on a small stage in front of a screen that plays music videos. Usually that bothers me, the feeling that you're supposed to be watching TV instead of dancing, but in this club it's like moving wallpaper, a page for our bodies to scribble our own ideas on top of. People are swirling their arms, slashing steps in all kinds of interesting directions. Some are dancing in loose, barely knotted groups. Others are completely alone in the crowd, but they don't look lonely. They look deep into what they're doing. People are wearing everything from goth velvet to candy-plastic stilettos to frayed denim overalls with very little beneath them. One person is rocking frayed pointe shoes. They're all dancing in little worlds that rub up against each other. Worlds that only need to be big enough for two things: a body and a beat.

Harley and I find an empty patch of the dance floor, pushed so close by the presence of so many other people that we're nearly touching. And then we are.

I sigh against Harley's skin and loosen into the music.

Their hands slide over my shoulders, then down, but they don't linger in the same places W's did. They travel and discover things about me, and I feel like I'm discovering those things, too, finding my own shape.

And I smack into something in the dark. Not another dancer. I'm too aware of everyone else's bodies for that. I slam into the way W used to touch me—the way she gave so much special attention to my chest and hips and everything people consider girly. She thought it was cute for me to play-act the boy part sometimes, to dance the lead at other peoples' weddings, but at the end of the day she touched me like *she* wanted to be touched. She touched me like I was a girl.

Even when I told her I was agender, W was so used to me being a girl—in her mind, in her arms, in her bed—that she never treated me like anything else.

It was bothering me, and I didn't even know it. And because I didn't know it, I never told her, I never asked if she could change. Knowing that is like a tiny stone in my shoe, throwing me off. It scares me that I could be feeling something so important and also holding it down so completely.

But there's a new feeling rising through my feet and my legs, my hips and my chest and my arms, spreading all the way to my fingertips. A floating rightness that has everything to do with how Harley touches me.

They bring their face close to mine, and there's something about how close our cheeks are hovering, how our lips are *nearly* kissing, how long we're able to hold off while our hips are already pushing into each other, a slow pour of feelings that we're not even pretending to hide. "I'm glad that we let that guy in the purple baseball cap at the gay bar have his fun,"

Harley whispers. "Because you're really, really good at this."

I won't ruin the moment, but in my head I rush to disagree. W is the good dancer.

But maybe W is just the one who's always known steps that work for her.

When nobody needs me to be a girl, or a boy, I *can* be really, really good at this.

I put my arms around them, slide my entire body up and down theirs, shake out a year's worth of stale worries. I want to tell Harley that their body has whispered something true, and now it's shouting through my blood, warm and unstoppable. Their dancing is a blur of wild, joyful motion—but they look a little nervous about keeping up with me now that I'm really letting go.

"You're amazing," I shout, but it's so loud in here that I might as well be whispering straight into Harley's ear.

They grip my waist, palm my hips. They keep up with me.

But this isn't just about me. It's about everyone in this room, it's about all of us, and what shape we get to be when nobody asks us to fit in.

I know where I want to end the night.

"I thought you didn't want to think about the Proud Muffin," Harley says as we pull into the mostly emptied-out parking lot.

I turn to Harley in the dark, their curls faintly backlit by a streetlamp filtered through the trees. "I changed my mind. After all that dancing, I need dessert. And I don't know a better place, do you?"

"No," Harley says. "Perfect ending, for sure."

"Don't talk about things ending, please," I say quickly. "Not right now."

Harley nods—then reaches out and touches my hand, not really holding it, just stroking a finger along the back of my knuckles. "Is that . . . is that okay?"

After the way our bodies pushed together on the dance floor, it's strange how this tiny touch makes my heart flare up.

"Better than okay."

Harley's smile widens. There's a silky silence in the car— that perfect pre-kiss silence. I could lean in right now, I could ask Harley *right now*, but our first kiss deserves a bigger, better moment. Something unforgettable. And the truth is that I want to kiss them in my favorite place in the world.

Especially if I'm about to lose that place.

We head in through the front door right as the last shift of the night is winding down. Harley doesn't hold my hand, but I'm aware of exactly how far their fingers are from mine, the way they stir the same space. Gemma and Lex are wiping down the counter and wrapping the cakes and cleaning the espresso machine, steam from the wand making that unmistakable hiss. It hits me with the kind of familiarity that you can't fake—the kind that only comes from knowing a place by sound and smell and touch as well as you know it by sight.

I was planning on picking out a Harley-friendly dessert

and taking it upstairs to the community room for some privacy. We always close it a little early so the counter staff can clean it before they start on the downstairs. I start perusing the sweets behind the glass, but Gemma pulls a little plate up from below the counter.

It's a dreamy slice of golden pie.

"I saved this for you," Gemma says. At first, I think it's a slice of Anger Pie that somehow didn't wind up in Kevin's face—not exactly the perfect ending to a perfect date—but then I realize that the crust is definitely Harley's handiwork. Those perfect crimps are unmistakable. "I found this while cleaning up, and I hated to think that you'd made the whole thing and didn't even get to taste it."

"I'm glad that you and Jessalee and Javi enjoyed it so much," I say as I grab the little plate, plus a napkin and forks from the silverware stand.

"Oh, we did." She shakes her head emphatically. "We really, really did."

"It feels like I missed a story there," Harley says.

I want to tell Harley what happened at brunch—they've been my partner in magical bakes since the beginning. But nothing can really stop me from getting up to that community room right now.

"You want to play a game of Truth or Pie?" I ask, heading for the stairs.

"Always," Harley says. "Wait, what's Truth or Pie?"

Gemma gives the counter a long wipe. "I'm going to head out soon," she says. "Lock up when you're done?"

"You have a key," Harley says as we climb the narrow stairs. "How have we not been sneaking in here all along?"

"Most people don't sneak *into* work."

Harley puts one hand to their chest, mock-offended. "We aren't most people."

And this isn't just some after-school job. I feel the magic of the Proud Muffin all over again as we top the stairs and arrive in the community room. The floors shine like a mirror glaze. The scent of cinnamon in the air never really fades. The room feels enormous with only the two of us in it. I've never seen it empty before—I've never had it all to myself.

"Okay," I say, holding out the little plate in front of Harley. "Truth or pie?"

"I need to know how this works," Harley says, looking far too serious, which is far too cute.

"This pie inspires quick and complete honesty. It's highly magical and not to be meddled with. It's also the most delicious peach-based pie I've ever made, and I've seen you attack a Texas Breakfast muffin when you think nobody's looking."

Harley's eyes go wide. "You saw that?"

I cross my arms and squint in a decent imitation of Vin. "I see everything that happens in this place." I push the pie a little closer to Harley's nose, waiting for the toasted scent to work its wonders. "So, if you pick truth, you have to answer a question. If you pick pie, you have to answer *three* questions."

"Those rules make no sense," Harley points out.

"Oh, they absolutely do. To get a bite of this superlative pie, you have to spill more truth."

"There's that baker's logic," Harley says, following up the sass with a shyness that I never see coming. It gets me every time. They tug at a back-of-the-neck curl. "You really want to know more about me?"

"Everything," I correct. "I want to know everything about you." I feel a shock of nerves at my own boldness—and the fact that I'm ready to reveal anything Harley wants to know about me, too.

"Truth," Harley says, diving right in.

"What's the first time you remember flirting with me?"

"The day we met?" Harley says, sitting on the arm of a couch, leaning back with a flicker of a smile.

"Really?" I ask.

"You were working at the counter and I showed up for my first delivery day. We bantered a lot. You told me you liked my shorts."

"Ugh, I did?"

"To be fair, they are my best bike shorts."

"Ahhhhhh," I groan as I locate the memory. Yeah, I did that.

"I flirt a lot, I guess," Harley says with a shrug. "It's easy and it doesn't usually mean anything. People assume that being demisexual means you don't like flirting, and for some folks I'm sure that's the case, but for me it's like . . . a fun game with really low stakes."

"Ah," I say. "So you didn't mind me awkwardly admiring your shorts?" My face must be the color of a strawberry rhubarb tart right now.

Harley shakes their head. "Your turn."

"Truth," I say, matching Harley's opening move.

"Okay. Okay. What's the thing you're awkwardly admiring about me *right now*?"

"Your cowboy boots," I say a little too quickly. Harley laughs. "I just . . . really like them." I breathe harder, and it's only partly because I'm wearing a binder that I picked up at the Proud Muffin clothing swap.

"*These* boots?" Harley asks, kicking them off with a sigh. "I'm glad you enjoy them, but they're murder to dance in."

"Hey!" I say. "You can't take those off. It's a health code violation."

"Truth," Harley says, kicking off the other boot in complete defiance of my baking boss attitude, then sliding around the wooden boards in sock feet.

"What's your favorite flavor?" I ask.

They tilt their head, let their thoughts collect. "Turkey?"

"Ughhhhhhh."

"You asked for truth, Syd. You get what you ask for."

"Truth," I say, heel-toeing off both of my sneakers to catch up with Harley. I want to slide around the room, too. I take off in my socks and find a heart-wobbling moment of slippery bliss.

"What's *your* favorite flavor?"

"All of them," I say, spinning around with my arms out, embracing everything delicious.

"That's not a real answer," Harley challenges.

"Fine, if you need me to pick a favorite above all other

favorites . . ." I discard half a dozen choices before landing on "Butter."

"Is butter a flavor?" Harley asks.

I skid to a stop. "Think about croissants. Shortbread. A perfect slice of toast. *Of course* butter is a flavor."

"Huh. I guess I like it too, then."

"But not as much as *turkey*."

Harley boldly skates over to the spot where I left the little plate. "All right. I'm ready. Pie."

I follow and load up the fork with a fruit-heavy bite, cupping a hand under it as I fly it over to Harley. They chew with their eyes closed, a look of utter confusion spreading over their face.

"Do you like it?" I ask, shy for maybe the first time ever.

Harley licks a bit of filling from their bottom lip, and then I die. "Yeah. I do." And I know it's the truth, which is pretty amazing. I never wanted to push Harley into liking something they didn't. I just have this need to know every single flavor they love. "Wait, is that one of your questions?"

"No!" I scramble. "That's just a warm-up."

"Hmmm," Harley says dubiously. "Okay, let's go."

I have three questions to ask. I have to make them good ones. Harley's letting this magic of mine take hold, and I can't waste it.

"Do you want to dance?" I ask while their eyes are still closed.

That flicker of a smile, again. "Yes."

I go over to the shelves and get to work. Even with all of our stops tonight, there was never really a slow song. I plug my phone into the sound system and cue up the first good thing I see: "Carefully" by the Little Brutes.

Harley's mouth quirks as the beat bounces from speaker to speaker. When I get back to them, they're already lifting their arms to hold me. It's late, and we're tired, and our bodies have already done the hard work of getting to know each other. We've been funny and sweet and fearless, and even though we've barely spoken all night, it feels like we've been talking for hours and hours.

We can just sway now.

In our socks.

It's dark outside, dark enough that when I catch a glimpse of the windows, it's just us, an echo of us. I play with one of Harley's curls, teasing it apart into red-brown strands.

"This feels like a ninth-grade dance in the best possible way," Harley says with a laugh.

This is it, the moment we've been working up to all night. Or apparently since the first time I saw Harley in bike shorts.

"Do you want to kiss me?" I ask softly while we sway.

"Yes, yes I do."

Harley looks at me, and without the boots they're barely an inch taller, which makes it absurdly easy for them to stare straight into my eyes. They get closer, closer, until I can see the individual dark chocolate lashes as Harley blinks, looking eager and nervous and ready. And I'm so happy that when the third question arrives too early, right before Harley's lips meet mine, I blurt it out.

"Do you want to date me?"

"No," Harley says.

I back away, fast, my body responding before my brain can even manage.

Harley spins away from me, like they can't believe they said that. They walk in tight circles, distressing their curls. "I mean, part of me really does, but . . ."

The pie is in Harley's system, working its magic, which means that what they just told me is true. Part of them wants to date me, but . . . "But you said no."

There's this horrible, hovering silence, the opposite of the pre-kiss silence.

"Wait," I say. "Are we going too fast? Is this . . . is this too much all at once? We can take it slower! I know that W and I were having sex and everything, but we were together for a long time, and I want you to know that I'm not in any kind of hurry."

Harley nods, still not looking my way. Suddenly the community room is too big, with all of this untouchable distance between us. "I'm not really worried about that, exactly," Harley says, with painstaking slowness. For the first time, that drawl is *not* my favorite thing.

"Then what are you worried about?" I ask.

"I like you so much," Harley says. "An absurd amount."

"Then why wouldn't you want to go out with me?" I press.

"Hey, I thought you reached your question limit . . ." Harley tries, but there's no way I'm sticking to that rule now. This game feels very much like it's over. And the song ends, making the silence between us even sharper.

"You were with W for a long time . . ." Harley starts.

"You think I'm not over her?" I rush to fill the next blank, to fix this problem. "I'm completely over her."

Harley waves their hands, finally frustrated. "I'm not afraid you're still hung up on W. I've *seen* you getting over her and talking about what you had with her and . . . honestly it scares me. Yeah, I sometimes take things slowly because I'm demi, but it's not . . . it's not just about timing. That's making it all about sex, when really it's about feelings. Whether you want this in the same way that I do. And I'm really, really afraid that you don't."

Wow, this pie is not messing around.

I take a few steps closer to Harley, but I don't want to crowd them, so I stop short. "I like you, Harley. An absurd amount."

"Okay, but . . . I need to be in love."

"That sounds good to me," I say, trying for a smile.

Harley stares down at their socks. "I'm afraid that I'll fall in love with you and you . . . won't feel it back."

"*Why?*" I know I'm pressing, but I can't let this go. Where is this coming from? What have I done to make Harley think I won't fall in love with them?

Harley is staring at me with this heavy sort of

disappointment—like the answer is obvious. They head over to the forgotten plate of pie. Slide a bite onto the fork. "It's your turn, Syd."

"Absolutely," I say. "I'll tell you anything you want to know."

My lips close around the bite, but I can't feel the loveliness of Harley feeding it to me, or even the taste of the pie. All I can feel is the tremble from their fingers taking over my whole body.

I swallow. Hard.

"Were you ever really, truly, wildly in love with W?" Harley asks.

The answer rushes up, and even though my hand moves to cover my mouth, I have to let it out.

"No."

Harley takes a step backward, hands in their pockets, a wilted smile on their face. I can feel their sadness filling the huge room. No surprise, though. I didn't see this truth coming, but they did.

And now we both have to put on our shoes and walk away.

RECIPE

The Worst Night

~~~~~~~~~~ **INGREDIENTS** ~~~~~~~~~~

1 or more parents who fell asleep on the couch waiting for you to get home

1 bedroom waiting for you, where you will probably never bring your crush

1 or more siblings who usually helps you get through your hurt, who aren't around for whatever stupid but also perfectly valid reason, for example, college

3 half-hearted attempts to clean the room you now hate

2 fitful hours of not-really-sleeping

1 dawn that comes gray and sickly, reminding you that the rest of your life is still a disaster

1 thing that can't even be called a breakup

1 heart that feels broken anyway

~~~~~~~~~~ **DIRECTIONS** ~~~~~~~~~~

Mix all ingredients in one big, horrible bowl.

Add tears to taste.

11

The next twenty-four hours are a blur of baking.

My flavors won't balance. There's too much salt in my short crust, not enough lemon in my lemon poppy muffins. Nobody wants a plain poppy muffin. My hands slip when I hold spoons and—more ominously—knives. I burn an entire pan of cardamom sugar cookies right at the end of my shift and don't have time to replace them. I go home and stage a complete kitchen takeover, but my textures won't behave. My crumbs are stodgy, my frostings are grainy, my batter splits.

From the living room, I can feel Mom watching. She's sitting on the one couch cushion that gives a decent view of the kitchen, pretending to read a book. But I know that she's tuned in to me.

I line a baking sheet with parchment. I cut my finger on the little metal ripping part, bleeding copiously onto the kitchen island. I grab a Band-Aid from the first aid cupboard, rip the Band-Aid, then try again.

Mom just watches.

Does she think this is all about W, another wave of loss ripping through me? Does she think this is all part of the process? *Is* falling fast and hard for someone new and then having it split—like this batter—part of it?

I think about Harley's face, and the way that pie brought all their worries right to the surface. The weight of their sadness after they said they were falling in love with me. The texture of their disappointment when I confirmed that I was never really in love with W.

How did they see that? How did I *not* see it?

I drop an entire tray of cookies, and it hits the floor with a heart-shaking clatter. I kneel to see what can be salvaged, but I've flipped the whole thing upside down. The dough is sticking to the floor, and the floor hasn't been cleaned in a month because that's my chore and I've been a total mess and Mom and Dad have been giving me a pass.

Mom comes over and quietly helps me pick everything up. Only when the last of the cookie dough is in the bin do we look at each other. She is squinting at me exactly like Tess would. Her rose-colored plastic reading glasses are up on her forehead, but other than that she looks more like Tess's older sister than our mom. Her hair is the sand-brown color of coriander, and she pretty much always keeps it in a loose bun. Her skin only wrinkles around the eye creases when she's worried about one of us. Which she is.

"Sorry," I say.

"For what, Syd?" she asks. "Flipping some cookies no one asked for? Or keeping secrets from your mother?"

"I don't have secrets," I mumble automatically.

But that's such a huge lie it hits me like the wall of heat from a blazing oven. I sink into the nearest stool, knocked out.

I have *tons* of secrets. They're just mostly things I don't tell myself.

I didn't even know that I wasn't wildly in love with my own girlfriend. Who doesn't notice that? It's like forgetting to put the flour into a cake. It's like forgetting to put eggs in an egg wash.

"How did you know you were in love with Dad?" I ask. "I mean . . . *really* in love." I am not in love with asking my own mother these questions, but I need answers. And nobody else I know has a functional love life right now, so here I am. Leaning over the kitchen island and waiting for her to dole out romantic memories.

"Your dad was a lifeguard the summer I was home from college between sophomore and junior year," she says, like that explains everything.

"Please don't tell me he saved a toddler from drowning and that's how you knew he was the best man you'd ever seen or some extremely straight thing like that, I can't handle it right now."

She laughs and picks a few bits of floor-crud out of an unbaked cookie before she gives up and throws it away. "He was a horrible lifeguard. I mean, nobody *died*. But it wasn't something he picked out because he was noble or a great swimmer, it was just his summer job. I took my little brothers and sister to the pool to swim almost every day, because it was more fun than babysitting them at home, and while a bunch of girls swam around in their new suits trying to get your dad's attention . . ." At this point I yelp about how upsetting and unnecessary a detail this is, and my mom insists that it really happened. "Anyway, I found myself at the snack bar at the same time every day, right when he was there, and we talked and it just . . ."

"Added up?"

That's how it felt with W. That if we just kept going, putting together all those meaningful moments, they would add up to a love story.

"Oh, no," Mom says, smiling at some unseen thing. A slice of another life, when my mom was sneaking away from adult responsibility to get curly fries and Sour Patch Kids and my dad was apparently hot enough to be the hot lifeguard. "No, it was more like by the tenth time we talked I realized what had been there since the beginning."

I think about Harley, instantly.

About me flirting on that first day, complimenting Harley's bike shorts.

But that wasn't enough for us—that instant ease, that

hopeful sense that I'd met someone I could banter with forever.

"Are you going to ask me what's wrong?"

She sighs, like she's working up some kind of parenting wisdom that takes a lot of energy to dispense. "Syd, you're seventeen years old. Old enough to hold down a real job and finish high school at the same time. I hope that you can tell me things when you need to, without me having to pry."

"Oof," I say.

"Big oof," she says.

"How can I tell you what's going on with me when I'm not even sure half the time?"

She cocks her head, and her messy bun slides. "That's a really good question. Very mature."

"You don't have to make fun of me."

"I'm not." She turns her back and starts cleaning up some dishes I left in the sink. She hasn't cleaned up my baking messes since I was ten. My parents made it very clear—if I was going to trash the kitchen, I was going to untrash it, too.

"I have things I want to tell you," I admit, "but I don't know how." Things like disaster brownies and cute bike messengers. Things like wanting to be with someone only to find out that you might not be what they need.

Things like not having any sort of gender when I woke up today and spending twenty minutes trying to decide which T-shirt and torn-up jean shorts make the most sense when nothing really makes sense at all.

"The last time I saw you bake like this . . ." Mom says,

twisting around to look at me, the sink filling with suds. "You were such a sensitive kid, and you didn't know how to talk about a lot of it, so you would just bake it out. I let you take over the kitchen and I tried not to worry too much, but now I know that *you* were worried."

"What do you mean?" I ask.

"When you were around twelve? Right before we moved down here?" I try to pinpoint that time in my head, but it's mostly a swirl of school goodbyes, moving boxes. "You wanted to come out to us, but you . . . you didn't know how."

"It was never hard for me to tell you," I say automatically. I've been saying that for years.

Mom sits down at the kitchen island, letting her hands rest in a loose knot in front of her. "We wanted you kids to be happy with whoever made you happy, but . . . your dad and I didn't realize that it wasn't enough. To believe that and not *say* it. You were still just a kid growing up with these signs around you that maybe it wouldn't be okay. If you told anyone. Your dad and I were so busy trying to keep the family together and barely managing, and the summer we separated it was like . . . you couldn't hold it in anymore. I thought you were upset about the split. But you were trying to tell us who you are, and . . ." Her eyes get salty, but she pushes the tears away, like she's mad at them for showing up. Like she's mad at her own tear ducts for making this about *her*.

"You and Dad almost broke up."

I remember it now. The past leaks into me like a spill of melted butter, oily and warm and way too much.

She grabs my hands. She holds them inside of hers. "We did break up, muffin. And then we got back together, because we never really wanted to be apart." I think about Vin and Alec. How much they still love each other.

How sometimes it's enough, and sometimes it's not.

There are so many other measurements to take into account.

"I baked a lot before I came out to you?" I ask. There's something there, waiting in these memories, a truth I can almost taste.

"You made such beautiful things, even when you were just starting to learn. One time you made a batch of cookies without even going to the store first, oatmeal and cherry and dark chocolate. I think you snuck a little bit of cinnamon in there. We ate them together—you, me, Tess. I thought I was going to cry every day after your dad left, but those cookies made me roll down the stairs, I was laughing so hard. And then there was this tart, I think it had chocolate almond brittle in it? Do you remember that one?"

"Mom," I say mock-seriously. "I remember everything I've ever baked."

"Anyway, Tess was at a sleepover, and you and I ate that tart and talked for hours. I couldn't stop talking about my childhood crushes, for some reason. Oh, it was wild! I made a list of every single one leading up to your father."

"But how many lifeguards were on it?" I ask.

She smiles faintly at the thought of that list. "Fourteen people! And you told me you'd been having crushes all year.

You kept eating and eating like it was making it easier for you to finally tell me—"

"Wait," I say. "Repeat that part."

And when she does, I see what's hidden inside those memories. She's talking about my magical baking.

She's saying it started when I was *twelve*.

I've been so sure that it all came back to W. My first heartbreak ripping out of me and reordering the world. But this was never really about her. Magical baking was part of my life way before I met W. I'd just forgotten that it was *real*.

When I was young and full of feelings I didn't know how to share, when I was afraid nobody would understand me, I found a language everybody knows. Sugar, flour, butter. The comfort of a perfect cookie, the joy of a celebration cake, the bittersweet importance of chocolate. I put everything in my heart into my baking. Years later, I lost the one person who I thought would see me and love me for exactly who I am—and the magic started up again. This has always been my way of sharing what I feel. Especially when things get hard.

Speaking of which, I get up and start throwing everything I've been making into the trash. Every scoop of subpar frosting. Every bite of stiff, cardboard cake. Every scrap of parchment paper. Nobody needs the taste of what I've been feeling since Harley walked away from me.

"Done for the day?" Mom asks.

"Not exactly," I say.

* * *

I arrive at Vin and Alec's house with empty hands.

It feels wrong, the absolute lack of a baked good.

But sometimes things feel right because they're routines. And breaking them is the best choice we can make. At least, that's what I tell myself as I have a mild panic attack and ring the doorbell.

Vin and Alec's house is a sweet little white one-story with cinnamon red trim, a pocket-size front porch, and a garden that seems as edible as it is pretty. I can smell the herbs in the little squares of dark earth. Lemon basil, thyme, mint.

Alec answers the door wearing double oven mitts. I honestly don't know how he turned the doorknob like that, but if anyone could do it, Alec could. He pinches his face, looking appropriately surprised.

In the years that I've known them, I've never visited their house. In my head, Vin and Alec lived at the Proud Muffin, the way teachers live at school. Even if I knew it wasn't strictly true, it was the only way I could picture them.

I peek inside. There are no boxes. Has Vin already moved out?

I haven't seen them since yesterday, when they left the bakery mid-fight. Nobody has. They didn't show up at the Proud Muffin this morning, and they didn't call in. They were completely missing. I've been imagining all the horrible ways they might have spent the last twenty-four hours.

"Come in." Alec waves me in with a mittened hand. "Unless you just came to gawk at your boss in his house clothes." Alec looks just as stylish as usual, in dark jeans and a slouchy T-shirt.

"Thanks," I say, taking a single step into the entryway. It's decorated with food photography, a few of Gemma's prints. Ruby pomegranate seeds strewn on a perfect slice of yellow cake. A filled and frosted chocolate cupcake cut in half and photographed like architecture. There's a spot over by the couch, though, with a bare nail.

A close-up of a detail on Vin and Alec's wedding cake has been taken down. It's sitting on the coffee table.

Are they going to get rid of it?

Did that fight they had because of my pie finally seal their doom—the way my fight with W sealed ours?

"I need to tell you something," I say.

I've been thinking about this on the walk over. Twelve blocks, no sidewalks—thanks, Austin. It's time for me to be honest, to say exactly what I did, even if it means Vin and Alec never look at me the same way again. They love each other, and maybe that's enough, and maybe it's not, but they deserve a real chance to work it out. Not just an endless string of my guilty baked goods.

"Sure, Syd. But if this is about work—"

"It's not." Deep breath. Okay. "I baked a batch of brownies that broke you up." Alec drops his smile like a hot pan picked up with a bare hand. "Actually, it broke up a lot of people, and I've been working really hard to fix that, but that's why the Proud Muffin is in trouble."

Alec blinks a few times. I wait for him to ask me questions about the brownies. Demand the recipe. He just sighs and crosses his arms, mittens resting on either bicep. "Syd. The Proud Muffin has been in trouble for a long time."

That stops me from delivering the rest of the little speech I'd prepared. "It has? How long?"

"Oh, honey. *Years.* South Austin has been prized real estate for a long time, but ever since downtown rents skyrocketed and pushed up the prices over the bridge, we've been fending off developers left and right. Keep Austin Weird might be the rallying cry, but most people fold when you wave enough cash in front of their noses. Vin and I made it clear that this wasn't about money for us. We've tried to keep y'all safe from the property wars, but . . ."

I try to adjust my apology, my plea, my prayer. "If you and Vin stayed together, you could fight it . . ."

"That's what we've been doing for years," Alec says. "That's the *only* thing we've been doing, in fact. Syd, I'm a baker. When's the last time you saw me in the kitchen?"

"Never?"

"That's right." He sets his oven mitts down. "We opened a bakery so I'd have a place to bake. But it takes everything we have and then some just to keep those doors open. Can you imagine *not baking* nearly every day for five years?"

No.

No, I really can't.

But this can't be the end, either. "Please don't sell our bakery to the terrible grain people."

"Oh, we're not going in that direction," Alec says, waving off one of my biggest fears. "They ran away from that deal after the little pie incident went viral." He slides his jaw. Squints. "That was your pie, wasn't it?"

"Yeah. Sorry about that." But not really sorry at all. "I just can't handle the thought of losing the Proud Muffin."

"Syd . . ." He steals a glance toward the kitchen. The air is filling up with that almost-done toasted butter smell.

"Will you talk to Vin?" I ask. "Please?"

"Talk to Vin about what?" Vin asks, gruffly strolling into the room in his pajamas.

"About the brownies Syd baked that broke us up," Alec says dryly.

"Oh," Vin says, sliding Alec's glasses back up his nose, the sweetest kind of reflex. "*Those* brownies."

"Wait, you're not fighting?" I ask. "When I saw you leave the bakery the other day . . ."

Alec laughs. "That tiff was exactly what we needed to clear the air. When I first found out that Vin had been talking to people who wanted the property, we got stuck halfway through an argument. Couldn't see the other side of it."

I nod, pretending I didn't hear part of that fight from the walk-in.

Everyone says couples fight, but I still don't get it, if I'm being honest. W and I had a fight and it definitely didn't fix anything. It just went on and on until we were broken up. "How could a fight make things better?"

"Syd," Vin says in his best I'm-the-boss-of-everything

voice. "Fights are like cleaning up after yourself in the kitchen. It's not the fun part, but you gotta do it sometimes. Any relationship that doesn't have fights just has mess building up until you have to move out and find a whole new house."

"Oh," I say quietly, suddenly seeing all the fights W and I *didn't* have. All the times we glossed over a problem. I pretended that "just fine" was enough to keep us going, when W knew it wasn't. "Just fine" was our mess.

And the truth is, I didn't want to clean it up.

I wanted a new house.

I don't feel that way about Harley, though. I desperately want to clean up what happened between us the other night. I just don't know if I can.

As I work through all of this in Vin and Alec's living room, Vin cozies up to Alec, and I wait for them to top this moment with a kiss. To prove they're really and truly back together. Instead, Alec grabs his mitts and runs to the kitchen a split second before his timer goes off. I can't see him open the oven, but the smell finds me quickly. I deconstruct it. Hazelnut. Brown butter. A few moments later, another smell mingles with the first two. "Chocolate ganache," I whisper under my breath, to keep myself from shouting questions at Vin about the status of their relationship. Any human who's ever constructed a nine-layer cake knows when things are delicate.

"Hey there," Vin says, studying me as I hover near his couch.

"Are you going to kick me out?" I ask.

"No," he says. "It's good to know that you still exist when

you're not baking. And it's good to see *this* one baking again."

Alec comes in with a plate that holds a simple but perfect cake, with chocolate sliding down over the sides.

"Stay for a piece, Syd," Alec says firmly.

"That's okay . . ." I say, backing toward the door. There's an unspoken code of baker's etiquette that says I should take what's being offered, but all of a sudden it feels like I'm intruding. What if they're still in some half-broken-up twilight zone and this moment is what they need to agree that going their separate ways was definitely a bad plan? Alec can talk all he wants about how much trouble the bakery was in, but right now it feels like we're so close to everything getting better.

"You know you can't leave without getting fed when there's cake sitting right here," Alec says, setting down the plate on the coffee table as he makes the unspoken code spoken. "And a piece of this will do you good."

Vin points at the armchair where, apparently, I'm allowed to sit.

So I sit. And we eat. And it's not what I came here for, but it's something I needed more than I knew. The hazelnut and brown butter are perfectly balanced. The chocolate is warm and melty. As I reach the bottom of my piece, I find secrets that have been waiting for me to wake up and notice them.

"I think the Proud Muffin was my first love," I say.

It's not the same thing as falling in love with another person, but it feels just as big in its own way. And just as hard to let it go. "So, if you're not selling to the Grain Bar . . . ?"

"I only started talking to those people because I knew

things couldn't go on as they have been," Vin says. "I was sure that Alec here, who is incredibly stubborn when it comes to my happiness, wouldn't agree to let go of the bakery because of me, so I tried to make the first move without him to prove I was ready. Which, as we all know, just proves that I'm a complete stunad."

"Vincenzo," Alec rumbles, shaking his head with so much affection that I can barely stand it.

Also: *Vincenzo?*

"We know what we want now." Vin looks at Alec like he invented the recipe for the entire universe.

Alec looks at Vin, and his eyes are full of warm, melty love.

I want to ask them what that means for the Proud Muffin, but I promised that I wouldn't push too much about work while I'm in their house, and besides, this cake is beckoning me. I take my last bite, the fruity undertones of chocolate filling my senses, and as I swallow, I get a hint of one more secret.

I've been trying to follow the same recipe for my relationship with Harley that I did with W. Meeting, flirting, kissing, dating, without ever facing the question of how much I truly feel. Watching Vin and Alec together like this, seeing how much they love each other even in the hardest moments, makes it clear that I want more than what I had with W. Back in eighth grade, I was just so thrilled to find someone I liked, who liked me back, another queer person who understood this part of me that no one else did. I wasn't even thinking about falling in love.

But I am now.

And—here's the secret bit—it terrifies me. I just lived through a little heartbreak, and the worst damage wasn't actually the sadness it dragged me through. It was the fear of what a full heartbreak would feel like.

I've been telling myself that I'm holding back with Harley because I need to finish cleaning up my mess from the breakup with W, that it's my duty to get all of these other relationships back together before I could focus on one of my own.

But mostly I'm just scared.

Harley thinks that I'm not falling as hard as they are—they've got it backward, though. What I feel for them is already so big and deep and we've barely gotten started. So I've been flirting, and dancing, and whipping cream, but I've also been tamping down how much I want this, how much I worry about this, how much of a mess I am at the idea of falling in love with Harley just to potentially lose that someday.

It's time to stop holding back—which means I *have* to stop hiding feelings from myself.

And I have an idea.

Get Comfy with Your Great Big Feelings Cookies

~~~ INGREDIENTS ~~~

1 cup (2 sticks) butter, softened

²/₃ cup granulated sugar

²/₃ cup packed brown sugar

2 large eggs

1 tsp vanilla extract

2¼ cups all-purpose flour

1 tsp baking soda

1 tsp sea salt

2 cups (one 12-oz bag) semisweet chocolate chips

1 to 1½ cups sweetened, shredded coconut
(depending on how coconutty you like things)

~~~ DIRECTIONS ~~~

Preheat the oven to 375 degrees. Line two cookie sheets with parchment paper. Yes, it will feel fussy and unnecessary the first time you use it. Yes, it's worth it to never scrape up a stuck cookie ever again.

Cream together the butter and sugars with a hand or stand mixer until light and fluffy. Beat the eggs into the mixture one at a time, then add the vanilla.

Okay, this next bit might be the most controversial, but I'm a one-bowl chocolate chip cookie baker. Meaning: I measure my flour, baking soda, and teaspoon of salt directly into the same bowl I just used for everything else. I don't sift. I don't get another bowl dirty.

I trust that everything will turn out right.

Mix on the lowest setting until the dough is just combined. I can't legally tell you to lick the beaters, but if you believe in living life to the fullest, you know what to do.

I'll turn around. Tell me when you're done.

Stir in the chocolate chips and coconut by hand.

Roll out balls onto the parchment, making sure you give them a good 2 inches between cookies (they spread!).

Bake for 12 to 15 minutes, or until golden brown. Trust your instincts here. If you like pale, soft, ultra-chewy cookies, take them out sooner. If you want them to be dark and caramelized at the edges, keep going.

Whatever your preferences, there is nothing more comforting in this world than a perfect chocolate chip cookie, and these ones are full of big, bold flavors that will help you settle into every one of your big, bold feelings.

Don't be afraid.

Or you know, be afraid, and feel it anyway.

12

After I get home from Vin and Alec's, I bake what might be the most important batch of cookies in my entire life. I don't drop or overmix anything. My hands are steady and confident as I throw balls of dough onto my best cookie sheets. I don't sneak any bites. While they transform in the oven, I sit at the kitchen island with my hands wrapped around an oversized mug covered in rainbow narwhals—for extra emotional support—until about twelve seconds before my timer goes off, when my inner sense that my timer is *about* to go off has me leaping to my feet.

I open the oven door, releasing a wave of heat and the most brazen vanilla scent.

With my oven mitt, I pull them onto the counter. The chocolate glistens, because it's melted and hasn't reset, but

I can't wait for that moment; I grab the biggest one studded with a completely unreasonable number of chips and I take a bite and burn my mouth and I don't even care because I'm already crying, and they're the best, saltiest, most important tears. They mingle with my bites and bring out every flavor: mourning for what I thought my future was going to be before this breakup; wonder at meeting someone like Harley; anger at making it this far without knowing myself a little better; and love, *so much* love, whether or not it lasts.

I lick my fingers, then move the rest of the cookies onto my cooling rack, where they sit in imperfect rows, waiting to be devoured.

Then I sit at the kitchen counter, and I eat them one by one.

And I feel *everything*.

At some point, Dad comes in and tries to steal one, but I swat him away with an oven mitt.

"These are mine," I say through an unexpected burst of laughter. "Find your own."

He backs away with his hands up, and I laugh harder, because I realize my dad just found me, post-breakup, demolishing an entire sheet of cookies, *literally* eating my feelings.

I collapse over the kitchen island, laughing so hard that I'm crying again. There's *joy* in these cookies, and it overpowers the uncertainty of Vin and Alec and the Proud Muffin, and two more couples out there, still heartbroken, and me and Harley hitting what felt like a dead end.

I didn't know there would be so much joy.

Harley is a big part of that feeling, too, and soon I'm sifting through all the tiny moments that felt so big. Harley lingering in the alley to talk to me for five extra minutes. Harley bouncing into action with cake boxes. Harley's curls in my hands, finally. I was waiting for those moments to add up to a love story instead of letting myself feel the simple fact that we were already in one.

At some point my stomach reaches its limit and I have to set aside the rest of the cookies—and then I bake a few more batches for good measure. I box them up, knowing that these will help other people get in touch with their deepest feelings.

I'm still scared that I messed everything up the other night, and I don't know how to fix that. But I'm going to see Harley again, soon, and one of the biggest feelings that just hit me in waves, cookie after cookie, was hope.

When I get to my first break the next morning, I haven't actually seen Harley yet. I check on the rest of my Big Feelings Cookies, which I double-wrapped to make sure nobody catches a whiff of them and decides to help himself. When I get off break, I check the back door. Harley's bike is nowhere to be seen. Harley is officially late.

Marisol calls to me without even turning away from her three-tiered tiramisu cake. "Harley's not coming. They called in sick."

"What?" Harley hasn't been sick once the entire time we've worked together.

Did they call in because they're upset with me? Or is this about the bakery? Maybe they can't deal with being here if this place really is slipping away. Is Harley ghosting me, or the Proud Muffin? Or both? How am I supposed to tell Harley all the feelings I just sorted out?

What if that's exactly what they're trying to avoid?

I put my hand to my upper stomach and press down.

Marisol shoots me a harsh look.

"Don't tell me you're sick, too."

"No," I say. "I'm good." It's the biggest lie I've told in a while, but at least I know I'm lying, right?

It might be progress, but it doesn't exactly feel like a win.

Vin and Alec come around the kitchen a few minutes later, with their arms wrapped around each other. They look happy—blissful, even. And for a moment, all of my worries about Harley dissolve.

"All staff meeting," Vin says. "Four p.m. Bring your appetites."

Marisol sighs like she's the captain of a ship that was about to go down and we've finally stopped taking on water. We go to the walk-in and toast with those little fizzy Italian lemon drinks she loves. Then we sit down on crates and enjoy the frosty cold air and the silence in the kitchen.

When I open the door a tiny sliver, I see Vin and Alec kissing.

That feels like a win.

* * *

I'm not going to stop there. I still have two more couples to get back to *official.*

Right before I clock out at 2 p.m., I single-handedly drag the chalkboard out to the sidewalk and scribble: *Iced Green Tea, half price all afternoon!* It doesn't look remotely as nice as when Gemma does it, but desperate times call for really bad handwriting.

I sit down at one of the little tables in the garden, with a plate covered in a tempting tumble of cookies and a paper right next to it with another scribbled invitation. *Syd's Home Bake, Help Yourself!*

I'm setting the iced green tea trap again—but this time is different. I couldn't figure out what Kit and Aadi needed to get back together. Now, my cookies are going to help them figure it out on their own.

But first, a dozen people coming in or out of the bakery take full advantage of the many, many cookies that I made last night. And then they stand around telling me how they feel. Their eyes get a faraway glaze as they tell me everything they've been holding back. One person says they're working up the bravery to break up with someone who clearly doesn't love them anymore, as evidenced by the fact that all they do is watch Netflix in separate rooms. Another waxes poetic about how much they love their new apartment, the first space that's ever really felt like was *theirs.* Another pours out the fear that they'll follow the life plans everyone else is laying out for them instead of pursuing their real passion—needle-felting anime characters. One person gives a soliloquy about how awkward online dating makes them feel and how lonely they've been lately. But then they start happy-crying about how great their friends are, and I wonder how often our big feelings contradict each other.

After forty-five minutes, I'm getting worried I'll end up with a lot of emotional new friends, but no Kit and Aadi.

Then, as a fifty-ish woman tells me about her deep nostalgia for the lesbian karaoke bar where she used to live and how all she thinks about is opening her own—and I encourage her, of course—Kit and Aadi drop their bikes in the rack and pass by, their sneakers pounding up the porch stairs. They head straight into the bakery, undeterred by my sweet distraction. I push a few more cookies on the future lesbian karaoke bar owner and say goodbye. When Kit and Aadi come out with enormous cups clutched to their chests, straws fused to their lips, I hold out the cookie platter and point to the sign.

They both light up. Then they scarf three to four cookies in quick succession. I wait with an impatient ticking in my heart. Will they make up right in front of me? Will they sign heartfelt love poetry to each other? Will they kiss with the teeth-bumping urgency of high school freshmen? Will they get on their bikes and ride off together into the sunset—okay, the blazing hot afternoon?

Kit smudges melted chocolate from their fingers onto their lemon-yellow denim shorts. Aadi shrugs happily.

Nothing seems to change.

Then Kit's brow wrinkles. They pull a cell phone out of their pocket and type into the texts, then turn the phone around to show me what they've written. I'm thinking it will be some kind of secret, urgent missive about how Kit wants to win Aadi back.

What it says is *These make me happy! Can I get the recipe? I want to make them for my mom.*

Aadi also pulls out their phone, types rapidly, and then shows us both what's in their heart: *So good but now I'm feeling mega-thirsty! Need more igt to wash this down.*

Aadi heads back into the bakery for seconds on the tea. Kit waits, and then they join back up, strapping on those helmets with the cat ears before they pick up their respective bikes from the rack.

"Huh," I say, nibbling at the edge of a cookie.

I have this intense longing to see semi-sweet chocolate eyes so close to mine that I know no one is pulling back, an urge to stop waiting for the so-called right moment and let this one soften into a kiss and then set itself on fire.

Harley. My feelings are Harley.

So the cookies still work.

I guess I really don't need to get Kit and Aadi back together—they're not hiding some great big feeling from each other, or even from themselves. They already know they're better off as friends. I stop myself before I blurt out, *It's ridiculously mature of you to be so in touch with your emotions!* They wouldn't hear me.

And besides, they're not babies anyway.

I pack up the last few cookies, feeling unsure about how to find Martin Thomas and fix the last relationship on my list. I won't give up until I'm sure everyone is okay. But maybe my brownies didn't only wreak havoc. Maybe in some cases they put people exactly where they were supposed to be.

At exactly 4 p.m. that day, the community room is filled with a dozen proud muffins in their matching aprons, T-shirts, tank tops, and hats. We've shown up in force, with our pride on the outside.

Vin and Alec don't stand on the stage today. They sit down with us, in a big circle composed of chairs and couch cushions and patches of floor. You can't tell queer people where, or how, to sit. We'll always break those rules.

Vin and Alec are facing down the entire staff—minus Harley.

I can feel my hands flying around nervously, like Mom's do. I strangle them into stillness on my lap.

"We want to make a few things extremely clear," Alec says.

"With no room for interpretation," Vin adds, looking right at me.

I feel more than a little called out, but it's fair. I did storm into his office. And then his house.

Alec looks from employee to employee. "This place means so much to us. *You all* mean so much. But Vin and I realized that if we don't start fighting for each other instead of for the bakery, we're going to lose what made the Proud Muffin exist in the first place."

"We need time we can actually spend together. We've been running in opposite directions for too long. I've been so busy keeping those doors open that I haven't done any real community organizing in years. And Alec . . ."

Alec needs to bake.

I think about what it would be like to hardly bake for years, and it causes me instant physical pain.

"I've been offered the chance to work in some wonderful kitchens," Alec says, adjusting the stem of his glasses with undeniable excitement. "Places where they know exactly who I am and what I stand for, and they're excited about that. I'm talking about taking this message of love and muffins all over the world."

Okay, that sounds amazing. But does it really mean leaving the bakery behind? Why can't Alec just go to those places and then come back home? To us?

Even though the day is just as hot as any in Austin, I'm shaking. I got Vin and Alec back together. That was supposed to fix things. Instead, I feel like I'm the one who signed away the deed for the place I love most.

"We've accepted an offer on the property," Vin said, grumbling and final. "The papers have been signed."

I expect an uproar, but there's the exact opposite—a dull, expanding silence.

It reminds me a little too much of the horrible moment

when Harley spun away from me. It doesn't help that I'm back in the community room.

"The bakery will remain open for the next two weeks," Alec says. "After that . . . we'll write your references. We'll help you find places to work. And when we're back in Austin, we'll invite you all over for backyard BBQ and bake for a crowd."

"We're not done with what we started here at the Proud Muffin," Vin says. "And you haven't seen the last of us. Not by a long shot."

"Syd, I need to lock up," Marisol says. "Let's go."

I've been sitting at the kitchen counter for hours now. Ever since the staff meeting got out.

I don't know how many self-pity muffins I've eaten.

I texted Harley: *Did you hear what happened at the Muffin?*

And heard back, ten minutes later.

Yeah.

Harley's been shy with me before, but never short on words. Is this just about the Proud Muffin, or is it about us too? Can those things even be separated? With most of the brownie relationships mended in their own ways and the magical bakes dispersed and the bakery closing, does Harley assume we're just . . . done?

I grab a bag of the bakery's most bracing black tea and pour water from the hot tap even though it's a blazing day. I have a chill that I can't seem to shake. When I turn around,

Gemma is calmly taking down her photographs from the walls, Marisol is sitting cross-legged on top of the bakery counter with her head down near her knees. "Stop it," I nearly shout.

"Stop what?" Marisol asks listlessly.

"Accepting that it's over."

It was one thing to walk away from W, to respect her decision to end things. But the Proud Muffin doesn't *want* to close. Vin and Alec love this place. They love it so much that they've been fighting for it harder than they even fought for their own marriage. But they aren't the only ones who care about the bakery.

What if it's our turn to take up the fight?

"We shouldn't be sitting here," I say. "We should be doing an enormous fundraiser to save this place."

"Syd, they already sold it," Gemma says.

I slam my tea down, sloshing a little bit of liquid over the side. Marisol doesn't even act disappointed or glare at me while she wipes it up. She just draws little shapes in the spill. Things really are bad.

"They can back out," I say, taking out a fresh cloth and wiping the counter. "Or buy it back. I don't care. We can't lose this place." And honestly, I still feel like it's my fault that it's on the brink of closing. I'm not going to apologize for getting Vin and Alec back together, though—even if it means they're leaving the Proud Muffin behind.

I would never go that far.

"Come on, we have to figure this out," I say.

If I can make broken-up relationships whole again, I can get a bakery back into one piece, right?

But only if I have other proud muffins to do it with me.

I can't bake my way out of this one alone.

Gemma and Marisol look at each other, wordlessly trying to decide if they should accept a baby-child as their new leader. But I'm the only one serving up hope right now.

I'm not giving up on the bakery, and I'm not giving up on Harley. These love stories aren't over yet.

"I don't think Vin and Alec are wrong about the property," Gemma says slowly. "Even if we could raise money to keep this place, we'd never be able to keep up with skyrocketing utilities and taxes. We'd get forced out just like they did. But if we could find another place . . . farther south, into the Hill Country? It could be a sort of art space, too. It would be so much cheaper, and we could be there for queer and trans folks who've never had anything like the Proud Muffin in their daily lives."

Yes. Yes.

"So we do a bake sale?" I ask.

"Not enough money in that," Marisol says automatically. My heart perks. She's shooting down ideas, but she's talking about this like it could be real. "Besides, a bake sale is basically what we do here every day."

"What about a party boat?" Gemma tries, setting her prints in a pile, the great unhanging forgotten. She leans into the counter, and I lean in from the other side, Marisol sitting in the middle. "Queers love a good party boat."

"On Ladybird Lake?" I ask. "It would cost a lot up front, but we could make a lot back..."

Marisol tuts. "Don't either of you remember Splash Days?"

"Oh," Gemma says. "The Hippie Hollow incident."

"I don't know what that means," I say.

Marisol and Gemma exchange a *look*. Marisol says, "Well, this community organization teams up with bars downtown every year for a fundraiser, and a while back they rented a party boat on the lake, but when it passed by Hippie Hollow... you know what Hippie Hollow is, right?" She looks me over, trying to gauge just how naive I actually am.

"Nude beach," I say. "The only one in Texas. W and I snuck in there once and went night swimming." The memory comes without the harshness that others have. They're getting hazier, softer, farther in the past.

Marisol even looks mildly impressed with me.

Gemma takes up the story where she left off. "Well, when the party boat passed Hippie Hollow, everyone piled on one side to see, you know, *everything*—"

"And it sank," Marisol finishes flatly.

The three of us laugh so hard that it feels like the seams of the bakery could split with the sound. We keep laughing and pounding the counter and Gemma even starts to hiccup because she's laughing so hard she can't breathe. Marisol throws a muffin right at her face to scare her.

The hiccups stop.

We all start laughing again.

Ten minutes ago, I didn't think laughing was possible.

"What else could we do?" Gemma asks. "A blowout party would be fun, but Austin has hundreds of parties every night. We need something special to pull people in . . . something that everyone will want to be a part of."

I have an idea, but I'm afraid to say it out loud.

"We should do the Big Gay Texas Bakeout." I take a sip of my tea at the end of that sentence, trying to look old and wise.

"That's a joke," Marisol scoffs.

"No, Syd's right," Gemma says slowly. "Bake sales are basic, but people love baking competitions. The first annual Big Gay Texas Bakeout. We could make it a yearly thing to support the bakery." Gemma's digging into this idea like it's a three-course meal. There's a reason she runs both the counter and the QTPOC nights—she's organized and she takes initiative. "We can have folks from all over the area come and bake, charge an entry fee for bakers, and people who want to come see it can vote by giving money to their favorites—"

"Syd and I are judging," Marisol interrupts.

"We can't have any gross, over-sugared cakes winning," I say. "The Proud Muffin stands for quality."

"And love," Marisol says, out of nowhere, planting her booted feet down on the counter. She stands up, her head almost brushing the ceiling. "This is all about finding the person who bakes with the most love."

Marisol might have surprised me with that, but it's true. Baking is where we put our hearts when there's so much in them and we have to let it out. We put a piece of ourselves on a plate and hand it over to someone else.

"Forget love is love," Gemma says, tossing aside the well-known phrase. "Our motto is *love comes in every flavor.*"

"Jessalee would like that," I say. Gemma ducks her head and bats off my compliment with a cleaning rag, but she can't hide her lovestruck smile.

"But where are we going to do it?" Marisol asks. "The bakery can hold a community event, but—"

"We need something bigger," I finish.

Big enough to hold the biggest, gayest bakeout we can imagine.

I picture the great sweep of Austin. The metal and glass, the new high-rises and the low shady spots. There are so many beautiful parks, so many green spaces and rooftops and clubs where you could host an unforgettable event. But we need an outdoor lawn with room for hundreds of folks to roam. And ovens. Catering ovens? Are those a thing? A big tent would be nice.

My heart speeds across the city.

"I know someone who might do us a favor."

I take out my phone and text Harley, my heart in my thumbs. I know things are weird between us, but I have to believe that Harley wants to save the Proud Muffin as much as I do.

Can I have Rae and Jay's number?

It comes back to me almost immediately.

* * *

I spend two days in constant contact with Gemma and Marisol, planning for the bakeout and recruiting help. We decide that to keep everyone's spirits—and donations—high, we have to bring it together before the original Proud Muffin closes.

Every minute of the next week that I'm not working or sitting in class, I'll be making fliers and slapping them all over the city, writing posts about the event and putting them up all over the internet.

Between planning and publicizing, we go to Vin and Alec to ask for their blessing. Five employees have banded together to found a new Proud Muffin if we can raise enough startup money: Marisol, Gemma, D.C., Carlos, and Lex, which surprised everyone considering how new she is. Since I'm not eighteen, everyone thinks I'm too young to be part of it. Which makes sense, but that doesn't mean it goes down smooth.

"What do you think?" Gemma asks our bosses. "Is this . . . okay?"

Alec gives all of us hugs that lift us off our feet. Vin cries a little bit, growls at us for making him cry, and then cries a little more.

"I'm already scouting new locations," Gemma says, "and almost everyone who works here says they'll stick with us if we move."

Almost everyone.

Harley hasn't committed yet, and that's making me nervous. Nearly as nervous as every time I text about the bakeout and get another helpful but completely impersonal response.

Yes, Harley is going to bike around the UT campus and hang up fliers. Yes, Harley can help set up a bike stand for everyone who rides to the bakeout. No, Harley won't say anything about what happened between us, or what nearly happened and then dramatically didn't happen—probably because they think there's nothing left to say. And every time I start composing a massive I-need-to-tell-you-everything text, I stop myself halfway through and erase it.

I might have to stop waiting for things to line up like I'm following a recipe instead of falling in love, but that doesn't mean I'm going to text-bomb Harley with everything I've figured out, everything I feel.

They deserve more than that.

As I watch the final details of the bakeout settle into place, I start thinking about what's going to happen when Harley and I see each other at the event on Saturday. I try not to play it through my head a thousand different ways.

I keep myself too busy to worry. Most of the time.

When the morning of the bakeout comes, I'm sitting on the couch with the last of the Big Feelings Cookies and a cup of coffee. In the middle of the planning whirlwind, I packaged up the extras and overnighted them to Tess at college. She called me to tell me that she feels really great about being single, actually, and also feels like she's probably always going to stay that way, at which point I might have snuck the word aroace into the conversation. You know, just in case she wants to look it up.

She also feels, very deeply, that these cookies are perfect with her new favorite drink, and I'll admit: coffee becomes exponentially better when it's soaked into a chocolate chip cookie. That doesn't mean I'm a convert, but I pull out my phone to tell her she's right.

When I open my texts, I see Harley's right at the top. I scroll backward, past the awkward messages we sent this week, back to the time when we were taking magical bakes all over Austin. When we were flirting so hard that every single sentence we sent back and forth was rich with hope and sweetness and anticipation. I miss that.

I miss it more than I ever missed W.

I can't imagine spending today with anyone but Harley. No matter what is or isn't going to happen between us. So I text:

See you at the bakeout later?

A reply comes right away. *See you there, Syd*

Another few moments pass. Harley's typing.

It's going to be great

What's going to be great? Is Harley just talking about the bakeout, like we have been all week? Is this something more? Or am I so hungry for that sort of message that I'm seeing it baked into a simple text?

I'm so nervous about what's going to happen on absolutely every level today that I bolt most of the coffee and jitter my way upstairs to get dressed, leaving the rest of the cookies uneaten.

I pad softly past Mom and Dad's room. They'll be up soon, and they're determined to come to the entire bakeout, even though it's set to run all day and into the evening. They might not understand every dimension of my life, but they know what it's like to need money to keep your dreams alive. Now that they have some money of their own, they're a little too eager to donate. Plus my mom keeps offering to sew aprons for everybody, and my dad says that he'll design our new website for free.

I told them I would meet them at the main tent around nine, because their extra hour of sleep on Saturday morning is vital. I pull on an outfit—my best jean cutoffs and a tank top—trying not to second-guess it.

There's a knock at the door.

My heart wobbles like an underbaked custard as I run for the door.

What if Harley decided to come see me before the bakeout?

But when I open the door, it's not Harley. It's not even Gemma or Marisol. It's an older Black man, about seventy, with dark brown skin and a starched white shirt. His gray hair puffs out near his ears, under a Panama hat. He's wearing linen pants, polished oxfords. To be honest, a lot of the queers I know would die for his style. I don't recognize him, but there's a weird floating sense that I should.

There's someone in the car on the street, just behind him.

Someone sitting in the passenger seat with their head leaned back in a way that spells frustration.

"Is everything all right with your car?" I ask.

I stare at it in a vague way. I've always admired muscle queers who know about cars and lift weights and look like they should be in *The Outsiders*. But the closest I've gotten is changing my flat tire one time on the left side of MoPac while cars nearly tore my clothes off passing by at eighty miles per hour on the expressway. Once I got the spare donut on, I drove straight to Gourdough's and celebrated still being alive with one of their cherry-bomb doughnut holes. It seemed appropriate.

"We're just fine," the old man says. "But we've been driving around this neighborhood for a while, looking for a coffee place I used to like so much, and we got lost. I was wondering if y'all have a map."

"The maps are in their phones!" the person in the car shouts, waving a hand out the window. "Every damn thing is in their phones."

"This neighborhood switches around every time I turn my back," the old man says. "Not changing as fast as where I live, though. You know East Austin?"

"Oh, definitely." I've been to a breakfast place in East Austin where the Benedicts kill you with butter and then resurrect you with the tang of fried green tomatoes. I've visited a tent where they carry out boiled crawfish in metal buckets, by the pound. I've bum-rushed a food truck where you can order an entire roasted chicken for lunch, spritzed with lime, swimming in a hot spring of savory juices. I've also, year by year, seen those places vanishing. Houses ripped up and replaced by condos with blank faces and New York City prices. All of Austin's starting to look like the mash of sameness you get when you chew things up and spit them back out. But East Austin's the historically Black neighborhood, and it's been hit extra hard by gentrification in the last few years.

"Hey, I know you," the old man says. His smile is the white of a perfect buttercream. "From that bakery with the rainbows."

"I'm Syd," I say. "And the bakery is closing." *That's* why I thought I should know him. He used to come by when I worked the front. When you give people coffee and treats, they tend to think of you in a glowing way forever.

"Oh, that's a shame," he says.

"We're trying to save it, though." I grab my phone from my pocket and pull up the flier that Gemma designed.

"This is today?" he asks, his face very, very close to my phone. "Sounds like good fun. I am busy on the weekends though. I'll have to check in at work. You know, people think laundromats run themselves, but they don't."

"Laundromats?"

I look at the car behind him, and I realize that it isn't just carrying a single, sulking passenger. It's loaded up with boxes. Cardboard boxes, moving crates. This is one of the couples I broke up. The *last* couple.

This is Martin Thomas.

"Sorry," I say, focusing back on him. "I just . . . thought I recognized the person in the car, too. You know. From the bakery."

"That's Josiah," he says, back to that smile. "And I'm Martin."

I almost slip and say *I know*.

Something inside of me snaps as I shake his hand. I'm not letting that car go anywhere. I run into the house again. I grab the last two of the Big Feelings Cookies. It's all I have, and I hope it's what Martin needs.

I run back out with the cookies on a napkin, along with a mug of black coffee.

"I just brewed this," I say. "And I made the cookies myself. Since you didn't make it to the bakery, is it weird if I offer you some?"

"Maybe I'm older than I thought when I last checked," Martin says, "but I would call it polite."

He accepts the mug and the napkin. He takes a single bite of the cookie and chews in a slow, considering way. Martin Thomas is the kind of eater who is not going to open his mouth to speak until every last crumb is swallowed or brushed away.

"I want to tell you a story," he says.

"All right," I say. I was sort of hoping that he would run back to the car and tell Josiah that he still has feelings, that he wants to stay together. A quick reunion would really help me out right now—I don't have time for anything longer.

I have to leave for the bakeout.

But I also have to let this magic do its work. I promised that I would help the people who ate my brownies.

I sit down on my front steps to let Martin know I'm ready to listen.

"I used to come south of the bridges all the time. I was with my wife back then; I had a wife when I was young, and I loved her very much, which some people find hard to believe now."

"I get that." I do. Even when people know you're bi or pan or otherwise not-all-one-gender-oriented, they can still get stuck on a single way of seeing you. Especially if you've been with one person for a long time. As excited as I was to start dating W, I could sometimes *feel* people deciding I was a lesbian. Lesbians are amazing; it's just not the right word for me. I can only imagine how much harder that would be for a man who was probably born during World War II.

"My wife passed on when we were still young, after three children," he says with a sigh that's slipped back in time, past sadness, all the way back to pure adoration.

Then it passes, and he looks back at the car, where the person inside is ignoring him in a passionate, pointed way. "When my children were grown, I found Josiah. He waltzed into my life right when I thought I was done with being in love. This was literal waltzing. Josiah is a dancer, you know."

I don't, but I like how he keeps saying that, as if we've been meeting like this in the street for years.

Josiah has apparently been waiting in the car for long

enough. He snaps the car door shut behind him. The way he moves is like air threading through tree branches. He's probably in his sixties, but he's wearing clothes that look comfortably ageless: stretchy pants, a big, flowing T-shirt, a delicate silver chain down his chest. His hair is shaved close, cut into ninety-degree angles that frame his long, oval face. His shoes, in high contrast with Martin's, are flawless white sneakers.

"*What* are you doing?" he asks, and at first, I think he's talking to me, that he's figured out the deep, uncomfortable truth of my offering. But he taps Martin's arm. "You're keeping this young person from enjoying breakfast in peace."

The love I feel for Josiah and that breezy way of not gendering me is immediate and intense. Why can't more people do that? Just waltz right around words like *boy* and *girl* until they know more?

"I was just telling Syd here about a foolish old man who fell in love," Martin says. "And wants to stay that way."

"Oh, him," Josiah says, rolling his eyes. Then his gaze hooks on me. "Are those cookies homemade?"

"My own coconut chocolate chip recipe," I confirm. "I brought them out, since I was already bringing coffee and . . ."

"We can't possibly," Josiah says in a way that makes me think the only thing holding him back are the rubber bands of social nicety.

"Oh, I already did," Martin admits, taking another bite.

"Well, if we're not putting you out . . ."

"I made enough to share," I say. Which is true.

There's a delicate footwork to offering people food. You can't actually *make* anyone eat. Basically from birth we have opinions and feelings and fears and cravings when it comes to what goes into our bodies. What passes through our lips and becomes part of us. It's instinct and it's what we've learned and it's what we like, it's culture and personal history and how hungry we are at any given moment. It took me a long time to figure out that I can't push too hard. I just have to lead and hope Josiah follows.

I edge the cookie forward.

He looks away, like it's a too-hot sun.

"You're going to love this," Martin says, right before he finishes his own cookie. "I just have to feeling about it." Josiah throws a hard look at him, but something in Martin's face makes him soften.

Josiah grabs the cookie. He takes a bite.

Then he goes still. Very, very still.

There's something about a dancer's stillness that's different. It feels studied and simple and complete, like the moment before everything bursts into new motion. Josiah closes his eyes and I can hear my breath as I wait to see what happens next. All down the street, the wind kisses the trees, and the leaves shiver.

Martin gets down on one knee.

"Um. A little help?" he asks me, handing the coffee mug back.

I help him make it the full way down. Martin pulls a

simple, beautiful silver ring out of his chest pocket. "This is how I feel. This is how I've felt for a long time." Josiah is watching him in something between shock and wonderment.

I take a few steps back, because I don't want to completely intrude on their moment, but I'm also completely caught up in it. I watch as Martin shakes his head and smiles up at the person he loves. "You've taught me that it's not enough to be in love, you have to show it every day. Sometimes that's hard for me, but I know we have so much more to show each other. So, this is how I'm doing it, right now."

Josiah shakes his head, and at first I think he's saying no—but then I realize he's laughing. "This is why you went silent on me two weeks ago? I thought you were pulling away, when you were just working yourself up to propose?"

"That's the one," Martin says. "I was . . . well, I was scared."

Josiah puts a hand over his mouth, and a few tears run around it. "Why?"

Martin presses his lips together. He's feeling something big, and I know that battle—he's trying to let it out. "I thought that if it wasn't perfect, if it I didn't do this right . . . I thought you might say no."

"Yes," Josiah says, overlapping the last word. "Yes, I am saying yes."

And then Josiah helps Martin back up, and they're kissing and hugging, and I wish I had rice to throw, because this might not be a wedding, but it feels a little bit like I just watched two strangers get married right in front of me.

I've never seen a proposal before. It was the most amazing, scary thing I've ever experienced. And I was just standing there holding a mug of cold coffee.

Josiah heads back to the car. I sip at the mug, which is still full. Because this was never about finding coffee. Those last two cookies brought them here. They called out with magic, and Martin answered. He needed a chance to show Josiah how he felt, before it was too late.

Have I been doing the wrong thing—waiting and worrying and focusing on the bakeoff when I should be showing Harley exactly how I feel?

"Oh, shit," I say, wincing at the coffee *and* the fact that I just swore in front of an old person. "I forgot to get you a map."

"I think I can find my way home," he says, looking at Josiah's back as he sways his way into the car. Martin takes his rightful place in the car next to Josiah. Their car disappears around the corner, and I run inside to put down the coffee and grab my bag for the bakeout.

I should have left minutes ago. I check my phone to find the fastest route to the bakeout—and every single road is red with traffic.

"Not today, Austin!" I shout, shouldering my bag.

I've been trying to give Harley space, but the truth is that I need the city's cutest bike messenger right now—for more than one reason. So I send a text, hoping with all of my might that Harley hasn't already left for the bakeout.

Traffic problems. Stuck at home. Can I ride with you?

Wait. You mean. Bike?

Yes.

Yes!

It's the first exclamation point I've gotten from Harley in a week—and I honestly can't tell if it's for me or just biking in general.

I have ten to fifteen minutes before Harley gets here, and I go into a frenzy getting ready. There's not much time to pull off what I'm thinking about. I run around gathering what I need: recipe cards, pens, and some of my favorite food websites pulled up on my phone. Then I sit on the front steps and settle in.

Twelve minutes later, around the same corner that Martin and Josiah just turned, Harley comes rushing, standing up on the pedals and leaning into the curve—on the front seat of a tandem bike. Harley skids to a stop right in front of me, looking breathless.

"Hey." Harley's ever-present messenger bag is missing, but the pronoun pin is on the pocket of Harley's T-shirt: they.

Harley's cheeks are a deliciously flushed pink. I try not to feel too many feelings at once. And fail. I'm nervous and flustered and completely out of time and really, really happy to see them.

I'm also confused about this bike choice.

"Wait, what about Shadowfax?" I ask.

"How do you know that name?" Harley asks through a suspicious squint. They lift a bike helmet out of a large canvas bag hanging on their handlebars. It's silver and more or less my size. Harley hands it to me.

"I thought I was finally getting that handlebar ride you promised me," I say, strapping it on. I can't quite keep the flirting out of my voice.

Harley blushes all the way up to their hairline—or rather where their bright blue helmet cuts off their hairline. "Yeah. That."

We've never been *not* flirting.

But now I know that isn't enough.

"That works if we're just going a few blocks away, but not when we have to beat traffic and cross like four highways," Harley says. "This is how I taught my siblings to ride on the street. It's way more practical."

"I have never, never heard anyone describe a tandem bike as practical," I deadpan. It's just such a cute rom-com thing to do. Riding around Zilker Park on rental bikes with Harley was one thing, but not quite as ridiculously adorable as this. If we arrive at the bakeout together on this bike, and we're *not* dating, how do I explain that one to Marisol?

It sounds excruciating.

"Well, your other choice is renting from one of those scooter stands all over the city," Harley says.

"*Those scooters,*" I groan in utter agony. "Tandem bike it is."

Harley pulls out a silver pair of riding gloves that match my helmet—the kind with the exposed knuckles. "You knew I was going to love those," I say.

Harley shrugs. "I pay attention. Speaking of which, I like your shirt."

This morning, I threw on my *Cupcakes Have No Gender* tank top. It just felt right.

"All right," Harley says, nodding to the seat behind them. "Hop on."

"Wait. I have something to give you." There's no time, but I don't care. Or rather, I care way too much about trying to fix this, and I can't stop myself. I pull something out of the chest pocket of my shirt. It's not a ring, and I'm not down on one knee, but it's definitely how I show my feelings.

"A recipe?" Harley asks, turning the card over with this faint but sticking amusement on their face. "For turkey pot pie."

"Turkey and butter," I say.

"Our favorite flavors, together at last," Harley adds with a quick laugh.

"I really feel like I can improve on the generic, stodgy recipe, you know?" I sound breathless as I rush back to my comfort zone—talking about food. "Throw in some brighter flavors. Update the whole thing. Make it something truly special."

"Sounds pretty delicious," Harley says, but I can tell it isn't enough.

I can feel my heartbeat in my fingertips as I pull out another card. "Here's one more."

Harley flips this one over. "It just says 'Falling in Love.'"

They look up at me, straddling a bike in the street, waiting until I explain exactly how I feel.

"That's because . . . I don't know how it works. I don't have a recipe for this, for *us*. But I know I want to finish our fight, which is very new for me." My throat sticks, and I have to manually restart my voice. "Watching all of those people break up and get back together hasn't taught me how to make the perfect relationship. At all. The only thing I've figured out is that there are no standard timings and no obvious ingredients and . . . I don't want the same thing all over again. I liked W and I needed to feel safe with someone, and I don't regret that. But then with us? I feel *so* safe and *so* happy and also like my heart is completely at risk."

Harley's eyes go wide.

"Syd . . ."

My phone vibrates and dings with a message notification. I grab it from my pocket—and find a dozen different variations on "Where the hell are you?" from literally everyone I work with.

I need to get to the other side of this with Harley, but I can't let down the Proud Muffin, either.

"We are so late," I say, throwing myself onto the seat behind Harley. "But we're finishing this fight later, okay?"

"Okay, Syd," Harley says, and I swear there's a teaspoon of anticipation in their tone. "Just hold on and don't stop pedaling."

"Right," I say. "Pedaling." I've been so worried about telling Harley how I feel that I haven't had any time to worry about biking ten miles through heavy traffic. We lurch into motion, and my body pitches forward. I grab the tandem bike's secondary set of handlebars, my eyes fixed firmly on Harley's back.

I pedal as fast as my feet can possibly go.

The whirl of colors and the scream of cars all around me starts out intense—and stays intense. We tear across the city, pausing at stop signs and pushing through green lights, letting the scenery rush and settle: bike shops and coffee shops and trees in flower, restaurants and houses, bright paint and neon everywhere.

The rush never really stops, but I refuse to close my eyes. They water as the wind pushes against us, and I feel my way further into this sensation. And at some point, I start to like it. My body feels like part of a much bigger picture. My breath is no longer fighting the breeze. We stop at a red light, and Harley checks in with me.

"You okay back there?"

I shout, wordless and happy.

We go fast and then, when we hit a string of lucky green lights, faster and faster. I inhale the whole blurred, beautiful neighborhood. My legs spin so hard that they burn, my smile pins itself in place, my heart stretches wide with fear and love.

They feel like the same thing.

A Big Gay Bakeout

~~~ INGREDIENTS ~~~

1 big lawn, open field, or other outdoor space

12 ovens

1 big tent

2 hosts

2 bakers to act as judges

3 challenges chosen to produce the most subversively, creatively, flamboyantly, or otherwise queerly delicious bakes

50 or so handy phrases like "that's nice but the gay just isn't coming through" and "no soggy bottoms" (look, some things are already perfect)

1 local news crew, invited to spread the word and encourage donations from people at home

As many amateur bakers as you can find

As many LGBTQIAP+ people and allies as you can possibly invite

1 empty stomach

~ **DIRECTIONS** ~

Give yourself at least a week to plan, but not too much more time, because you'll realize how much work this actually is, and you'll stop yourself before you've truly started.

Invite every single person you know. Yes, that includes your sister and her college friends who live several states away. Yes, that includes your new crush. Yes, that includes your ex-girlfriend. Yes, that includes her grandma.

Put on your best outfit.

Make your way to the event space. Watch as your crew mills around, excited and terrified in equal measure, ready to raise an absurd amount of money and save the day.

Watch as the bakers arrive, lugging their mixers, muttering frosting recipes under their breath.

Watch as the crowds gather.

Wait for that moment when everyone is paying attention, and paying good money for their extremely cute, screen-printed *Love Comes in Every Flavor* T-shirts.

Ready?

Set?

Bake!

13

"But what *makes* it a bisexual babka?" is a sentence I
never thought I'd hear coming out of Marisol's mouth, and
yet here we are. The ovens are hot, the day is hotter, and the
bakeout is the hottest thing of all.

There are so many people on Rae and Jay's sprawling
property that I can barely keep track of my coworkers, though
it helps that most are wearing Gemma's screen-printed shirts.
Harley has been a bit elusive, but we're so busy with the bakeout itself that I'm trying to tell myself it's not a bad thing, just
a sign that the event is in full swing and we'll finish our conversation later.

Not that it keeps me from scanning the crowd every three
or four minutes just to see if I can glimpse their curls.

Right now, everything is centered on the bakers, who are

busy slicing, melting, whipping, kneading, laminating, blend-
ing, beating, heating, and decorating like they've been waiting
their whole lives for this chance.

Gemma, in a silver sequined three-piece suit with the
slacks shortened to hotpants, and D.C., in a floor-length silver
sequined ball gown, bounce from oven to oven, announcing
the bakes, interviewing the bakers, and updating everyone
with ravenous anticipation. We've already made our way
through Queer Up Your Comfort Foods and Holigay Favorites,
and we're just about to start on the final round, Over the
Rainbow, which is all about creating the most wild, unfettered
cakes that our bakers can imagine.

"But first, dance break!" D.C. shouts. Lex, who is on music
duty, cues up a song. We've been doing this during every
break, all day, which means this is the sixth time the crowd
has collectively exploded.

When we were planning, everyone felt strongly that for it
be a Big Gay Bakeout we needed to add some special touches.

Lex has pretty impressive DJ skills. Somehow she coaxes
the entire crowd of people from every stripe in the rainbow—
and everyone who showed up for us—to throw their bodies
into it.

I find myself jumping high enough to catch sight of people in the crowd. Like Araceli and Verónica, twirling until
they're both so dizzy that they cling to each other and laugh.
Like Kit and Aadi and a bunch of their school friends, bust-
ing self-conscious moves and taking videos of each other
on their phones. Like Josiah, owning the impromptu dance

floor, attracting spontaneous backup dancers half his age. And Martin, watching the whole thing with a loving glow. People are doing their own thing until the chorus pulls us back together, and we're jumping and landing in time, like a single pounding heartbeat. Everyone is sweating, everyone is screaming.

It feels good.

In fact, there's so much happening that it makes sense no one has stopped to notice my *Cupcakes Have No Gender* tank top. Besides Harley, of course.

I thought I was making a statement, choosing today to share this part of myself with everybody else. I don't think I could be much clearer without grabbing the megaphone from Gemma and D.C. in the middle of the festivities. I know that today is about the Proud Muffin, it's about all of us, and I'm not trying to make it just about me. But what if we don't raise enough money? What if I lose the bakery? What if I'm not around a group this big and loving for a long time? I thought wearing this today was better than waiting.

Now it feels like I've already waited too long.

Because nobody seems to see me in all of this. They just see a baker judging contestants with a keen tongue, a sharp eye, and encouraging words because I don't believe in helping people by being a dick.

It doesn't feel like I'm hiding. It feels like I'm shouting in a language that nobody else can understand. Which is frustrating, because being agender already feels like that a lot of the time.

I keep going around and testing the cakes, giving out helpful tips to the home bakers while Marisol judges each slice like her professional reputation rests on it. "This could really benefit from another egg, but I like the height you've achieved on your gay penguin wedding cake." I'm kind of glad she's taking it so seriously. I'm glad that everyone is taking it seriously *and* having fun.

We've taken up every inch of this space. We're fighting for more space. We *all* deserve a place like the Proud Muffin. There are people with signs, people running around with muffins all over their skin from the face-paint station, people dropping cash scrawled with notes of love and support in the jars we left in front of each baker. It feels like evidence that a fight doesn't have to be a grim and solemn thing.

We can make it a party.

We can make *anything* a party.

I only wish that I felt as perfect as this day does—instead of worried about Harley and slightly lonely in the middle of the best crowd in the world.

"Are you moping, Syd? In the middle of the bakeout?" Tess asks, hooking an arm around me. It's like a sibling sense, knowing exactly when to save me from my own worst tendencies. I still can't believe she drove all the way from Illinois to be here and brought a car full of hungry college freshmen with her. She says they all insisted after they tasted those cookies I sent. And besides, Tess always did love watching *The Great British Bake Off* with me. She freaked out whenever Mary Berry winked at someone. Every. Single. Time.

Maybe I shouldn't be *that* surprised.

"I'm not moping," I say. "I'm keeping an eye on things."

"You're keeping an eye out for that cute biker," she says, but her teasing has a soft texture. It's the marshmallow of sibling teasing.

Now that Tess mentioned Harley, I can't help checking the crowd one more time for their signature bounce-step. "That cute biker and I have unfinished business," I admit. And there's no better place to finish it than the bakeout.

Assuming it's good news, of course. Assuming that Harley believes what I said and still feels what I feel.

Assuming it's not already too late.

"Syd, the hopeless romantic." Tess grabs a rainbow ribbon from the stack that we brought to award really special bakes and slaps it on my shoulder, where it sticks.

"I thought you said I was a terminal romantic."

"Congratulations," she yells over the expanding noise of the crowd. "You've graduated."

"Something really good must have been put out for tasting," I say, in response to the flurry of noise. That's when I notice W over by a Disney on Ice cake with a really incredible Elsa constructed out of brown butter Rice Krispies treats. W leans close to someone as she takes a bite out of Elsa's flowing blue dress. It takes me a second to recognize the other person's long black hair and slightly folded posture.

Eve. From the improv theater.

It doesn't take me as long to notice that W is wearing her date-night boots.

I work my way over to them.

"I'm glad you could make it!" I shout over the dulcet tones of D.C. telling everyone that another Disney-themed cake— The Triumph of Ursula—will be available soon for anyone who missed out.

"Syd!" they both say. In two very different tones: Eve delighted, W much more wary.

"Do you know W?" Eve asks.

We look at each other, and it doesn't feel like a standoff.

That's progress, right?

"We've known each other a long time," I say. "And we used to date."

W nods slowly. It's the first time we've both acknowledged this in past tense.

"How do you know Eve?" she asks, kicking one heel like she always does when she's nervous.

I shrug. "I helped her break up with a velociraptor."

Eve laughs. Apparently, the memory doesn't touch her at all. It seems like she's moved on, completely, and I'm glad. "You two are exes? That's so random." It's not, exactly, but I don't think I can explain that part to her.

"Syd is why I'm here today!" Eve says after a bite of ice-rink cake. "Harley told me that you needed everyone to show up. Like, *everyone*."

"Yeah," W says. "We're all in this together, right?"

"Thanks for helping me with that pie order the other day," I tell her.

She gives me a half-hearted smile.

This isn't going to get easy for a while. But it's been over for a month, and things are starting to shift. For the first time ever, I can see us becoming friends on the other side of this breakup. Maybe not as seamlessly as Kit and Aadi, but in a year we could be catching up over iced green tea. Maybe someday I'll tell her that I shouldn't have acted like she broke up with me out of nowhere, when really we were both headed in that direction and I was just too stubborn to see it. Maybe someday I'll apologize for not even realizing my taxi light was on at the end of our relationship. But today, she deserves to have the same great time as everybody else, without her ex getting all sloppy and emotional.

"Have fun, okay?" I tell them. "Enjoy Elsa."

"Oh, we will," Eve says. When I walk away, I turn a corner around one of the tents and almost smack into Harley.

"Almost time for the final judging!" they say. "I checked in with Gemma and D.C. They said that we've raised seventy percent of what we need."

"That's good, right?" I say. Seventy percent is a lot and we still have our last big bake to make up the rest. But the same nagging certainty that tells me when an egg is bad or a cake is about to fall is currently telling me that we won't make it.

"Yep. Yep. Listen, I have to do something," Harley says. "I'll be right back. Just . . . don't let them start the afterparty without me, okay?"

Before I can respond, Harley is off, bouncing through the blank spaces in the crowd, toward their bike.

Wait—they're *leaving*?

I thought we agreed to finish our fight. I thought we were on the path to figuring this out and getting together. I thought, at the very least, they'd see the bakeout through to the end. I know they love the Proud Muffin as much as I do. Are they afraid to watch this whole last-ditch effort collapse?

Even if it does, I want to be holding Harley's hand. We've gotten through so much in the last two weeks, and I know we can face hard things together.

"Wait!" I shout after Harley. "Hey!"

I try to follow their path and end up face-to-face with Rae and Jay, who've given up on corralling their kids and are now chasing them from booth to booth in a free-for-all to see who can collect the most on their plates. One of the kids has gotten cake smeared into their eyebrows, which in all my time baking is a move I've never seen before.

"Syd!" Jay says, looking down at their plate piled high with cake. "Umm. Hosting privileges?" they add hopefully.

"We'll be bringing you cake for years to pay you back for this," I say. "Eat as much as you want."

"Those two will eat as much as they physically *can*," Rae says, smile-grimacing at the two kids spinning in tight circles around them, orbiting their parents. "Should we bring out the trampoline so they can bounce it off?"

"Not unless you want a bunch of sugared-up adults bouncing on it later, possibly with half of their clothes off."

Rae and Jay exchange a look. "I'll go get it," Rae says.

"So wise," Jay adds.

"Time for the final word on your last bakes of the day!" Gemma shouts. "Bakers, back to your stations!"

"Judges, get your taste buds out!" D.C. adds.

Marisol and I follow Gemma and D.C. from oven to oven. The crowd hangs on every word and watches every bite. Vin and Alec push to the front. Even though nobody stops the show, I can feel Marisol and Gemma and D.C. and Lex and all the other proud muffins focus on them.

We watch Vin's arm settle around Alec's shoulder when the final three are announced.

They watch us announce the winner.

We watch them kiss, and kiss, and kiss, nearly hidden by the wild celebration of the crowd.

It'll take us a few hours to count all the money, to see if we pulled in that last thirty percent of what we need to open up a new Proud Muffin, but we've done everything we can. Vin and Alec are back together. It looks like all the relationships that were shaken by my brownies are on stable ground. A heavy, tired satisfaction should be starting to settle through me. But I'm still buzzing with sugar and the sight of that kiss. I'm not willing to let go of any of this, not until I know it's really over.

I go and whisper to Gemma and D.C.

They light up like they weren't ready to pack it in, either.

"All right, now the judges are going to bake!" Gemma shouts, standing on a chair so everyone can see her wave. "Marisol v. Syd! Two of Austin's best bakers go head-to-head! No winners will be chosen! No cash prizes will be awarded!

Because competition isn't better than community, and capitalism in the worst!" There are cheers and boos from the audience, everybody seeming confused about how to respond but eager to stay involved. "Today you're baking for personal glory, friends!"

Marisol and I break through the crowd, pretending to square off.

"Ooooooooh," D.C. says, and the crowds pick it up.

Marisol and I choose our baking stations. Gemma follows Marisol, and Jessalee and Javi are right behind them. Javi has a copy of the third Ambrosia P. Jones novel under one arm and Jessalee is carrying Gemma's sparkly silver purse.

D.C. picks up the train of his dress and runs over to me, trailed by his partner Paola, who's carrying his purse. She stuffs bills into the donation jar set up in front of me. Marisol and I should be able to pull in some serious money, right?

"Let's check in with our youngest baker," D.C. shouts, "the ferocious and famed Syd the Kid!"

I look out into the crowd, knowing that I'll find my parents somewhere.

My dad shrugs, completely innocent.

My mom shrugs in a much more guilty way, and I know she's the one who coughed up my nickname.

But I don't mind.

I'll be Syd the Kid.

Because this is my family, wherever I'm baking is home, and I'm the same agender cupcake whether or not other people see it. At the end of the day, it's not about whether they understand. I don't really understand having a binary gender. But I still find some magical way to respect people who have one.

This is about saying who I am. In my favorite language.

On my own terms.

"What are we making today, Syd?" D.C. asks.

"Agender cupcakes," I announce as I start throwing sticks of butter into a bowl.

"Agender cupcakes!" he shouts in the megaphone, and the crowd goes wild.

Agender Cupcakes

～～～ INGREDIENTS ～～～

FOR THE CHOCOLATE CAKE

1 cup (2 sticks) butter, softened

2 cups packed dark brown sugar

½ cup granulated sugar

4 large eggs

2 cups buttermilk

2 tsp vanilla extract

3 cups all-purpose flour

1 ½ cups Dutch process cocoa

½ tsp baking soda

1 tsp baking powder

1 tsp salt

FOR THE RASPBERRY MASCARPONE FILLING

1 ½ cups raspberries

1 tsp granulated sugar

1 tbsp lemon juice

One 9-oz tub of mascarpone (it's a soft,
white Italian cheese you can usually find
hanging out with the cream cheese)

½ cup heavy cream

½ cup powdered sugar, sifted

FOR THE VEGAN CHOCOLATE GANACHE

8 oz bittersweet chocolate

⅔ cup coconut oil

⅔ cup coconut milk (can or carton—
just make sure it's smooth)

1 tsp vanilla extract

FOR THE DECORATIONS

Whatever feels right

~~~~~~~ **DIRECTIONS** ~~~~~~~

Preheat the oven to 325 degrees. Drop some cupcake
liners in your tins. This should make about 32 cupcakes. If
you're not baking for a big party or a Big Gay Bakeout, I
would recommend scaling this recipe down by half.

In a large mixing bowl, cream the butter and sugars with
a hand or stand mixer until light and fluffy. Beat in the
eggs, one at a time, then the buttermilk and vanilla. The
buttermilk is a big deal. It adds a tang that should never
be underestimated.

Sift the flour and cocoa over the mixing bowl, then add the baking soda, baking powder, and salt. Beat on the lowest speed until they're just mixed in. Measure out the batter into your cupcake tins and get them in the oven. Bake for about 25 minutes, or until a tester comes out clean.

While they're baking, make your filling and ganache.

Raspberry mascarpone is the secret heart of this recipe. It's bright and bursting with unexpected flavor. It's fun and playful. It's everything you can't see at first glance, but that doesn't mean it's not there.

Cook down the raspberries over medium heat in a small saucepan until they're reduced, about 5 minutes. Add the granulated sugar and lemon juice and cook for 1 more minute. Take the raspberry reduction off the heat and let rest while you get the mascarpone ready. Using the whipping attachment on your mixer, whip the mascarpone until smooth, then add the cream and keep whipping until soft peaks form. Add the raspberry reduction and powdered sugar and whip again until your peaks come back. Place the filling in the fridge while you make your ganache.

Don't be intimidated by the word *ganache*. Or the word *agender*! They might seem unapproachable, but they're not. Chop and melt your chocolate (microwave or stove, your call). Melt your coconut oil if it's not already liquid, add to the bowl with coconut milk and vanilla, and whisk everything until smooth.

If you can give the chocolate ganache time to cool, you can go at it with your whipping attachment for extra fluff and then load it into a piping bag for some really lovely swirls. But one of the best things about ganache is that it's pretty even if you slap it directly onto a cake.

Back to the oven. Take out the cupcakes and let cool slightly. Remove a scoop from the center of each. An apple corer or melon scoop works great here, a paring knife is perfectly fine. You can either pipe the raspberry mascarpone into the empty space or pat it in with a spoon. Top the cupcakes with ganache, so the raspberry mascarpone is fully covered.

Here's where we're going off the traditional cupcake script. Using whatever you have in grabbing distance, get into decoration mode. You're not going for a matching set here. Throw out the idea of every cupcake looking the same. *Definitely* throw out the idea of every agender person looking the same—or even one agender person looking the same from day to day. Adorn each cupcake, playing with the techniques you know or throwing them out the window.

Don't worry about impressing the judges.

Everyone thinks they have the right to judge when it comes to gender.

Guess what? There's no winning this game! The rules are made up!

You might as well have fun.

14

My cupcakes are ready. Marisol is still wildly working on a three-tier tres leches cake with elaborate sugarwork. People are gathered around her by the dozens, but she doesn't even seem to notice. I'm so proud that I get to bake next to her every day. I let myself imagine a kitchen that's ours—a kitchen where we work like this for years to come.

"All right, everyone, it's time to sample Syd's Agender Cupcakes!" D.C. shouts. "Step right up and taste the greatness of a cake that is not dairy-free or gluten-free but very much gender-free!"

I expect my family to charge up and grab cupcakes as a show of support, but they're mesmerized by Marisol. A few people flock over cautiously—mostly strangers. They're a mix of ages, a mix of presentations, a mix of pretty much everything. People start picking out whichever cupcakes call their name. They respond with grins at the ganache and shouts of surprise when they hit the mascarpone filling.

"Agender cupcakes!" cries a person in their mid-thirties, motioning over a friend.

"I feel seen," says a person with a small backpack and a long ponytail, who looks about my age.

I look over the crowd again. I take us in. Maybe we do all have something in common.

Jay gently works his way forward and grabs a cupcake with mile-high frosting and jaunty sprinkles.

"Hey," I say. I grab a cupcake and take a bite to fortify myself. That's when it hits me: I've been working all day and, besides a few strategic bites for judging purposes, I haven't eaten much of anything. I scarf down the rest of my cupcake right to the paper and then ask, "Are you . . . um . . . agender too?"

"Genderflux!" Jay belts over the music, swaying loosely with the beat. "Some moments are a little femme. Some are a little masc. Sometimes it's an agender paradise!"

I think about Jay's life, which is so beautiful. Jay's pronouns, which are so flexible. Jay's smile, which is *also* really beautiful and right now full of chocolate cake crumbs and little flecks of raspberry.

"Thank you," I say.

Jay waves the empty cupcake wrapper at me, like she can't even imagine why I'm thanking her.

I look down at the table that, two minutes ago, held thirty-two agender cupcakes. They're all gone. "These are my life," says the friend of that thirty-something who insisted they come over.

"I love your shirt!" shouts an old person with gray and purple hair.

"Y'all, have you *seen* Syd's shirt?" D.C. asks through the megaphone. "It's true! Cupcakes have no gender!"

A great big cheer goes up, but it's the little ring of thirty or so people around me who cheer so loud that it feels like the ears of everyone in Austin must be ringing. I thought I was finally doing something just for me—and it's the first time I've connected with this little community.

Looks like those two things aren't a binary.

Looks like nothing is.

The only thing I'm a little sad about is Harley missing this moment. They're the one who gave me the shirt. More than that—they're the one who gave me the confidence to really use my magic. We used it to bring people together, and I just did it again, but this time I was bringing people together in a whole new way.

Just because Harley isn't here, that doesn't mean my little triumph went unobserved, though. Marisol is staring at me from her station, where people are now digging into her cake. She's topped it with a crown made entirely of spun sugar. "Bow down to la reina!" Gemma shouts, and everyone does exactly that.

After reveling in her coronation, Marisol hooks her thumbs in the loops of her jeans and heads over to me. "Let's take a walk."

I look around, feeling certain that I've done something wrong. But I fall into step with Marisol anyway. We wander over to the dusty edge of the field, where the grasses and wildflowers grow as tall as our knees.

"Sit," she says.

There's a log, so I perch there, probably looking like I've been sent to the Big Gay Principal's office. Again.

"Alec told me about your brownies," she says.

"Really?" I ask, doing some frantic math. "You didn't eat one, did you?"

"No such luck," she says.

"What do you mean?"

"Oh, I've been seeing this girl for a while, she's okay." She gives the shrug of someone who's deeply uninterested in her own love life. I have no idea what that feels like.

"You think my brownies really broke people up?" I ask as she sits down next to me. "Alec believed it?"

"Alec and I have been wondering about you for a long time. If you're like us." She kicks back, letting her long brown legs glow in the last of the sun. Her cutoffs are surprisingly short and stringy. She's always in slacks at the bakery. She's always holding herself so carefully. She looks different here. More relaxed.

"Wait," I say, everything still catching up to me. "You and Alec are . . . like me? Why didn't you say anything?"

"Well, first of all, we weren't entirely sure, and that's not an easy thing to ask somebody. Second, you would have thought we were on equal footing in the kitchen, and I couldn't have that, could I?" She flashes me a grin that undercuts her point, so I know she's not *too* serious. She inspects her nails, one of the tips broken by her impromptu cake. "Also, I'm not your unpaid magical baking mentor. I have my own shit going on."

"That's beyond fair," I say.

Marisol nods.

"Can I ask you one question, though?"

A hundred clouds gather on her face.

"This new girl," I say. "You actually like her, don't you? Like, a lot."

The clouds on Marisol's face darken.

"Because you were *right next* to those brownies. I mean, if you had any reason to want out, you would have taken one . . ."

Marisol just shakes her head and smiles, which should be a contradiction, but it's exactly how I know I'm right. I catch her eyes flicking back to the crowd—to the new girl, Lex, with her amber curls and her unseasonable flannel and her unflappable calm.

"You're dating *Lex*?" For some reason I'm surprised. I didn't think Marisol would date anyone who works at the bakery—she never has before. It feels like another sign that maybe Lex is special.

Marisol sighs. "We went on a date . . ." Oh my god, the night I was at the gay bar! "And no, I did not eat those brownies you asked the counter staff to push the next day. I wanted to keep seeing her, but I tried to keep things chill . . . and it came off as cold I guess. Lex is a really warm person, right? So, I apologized." That was my cake! She stole my cake to help her apologize to the cute new barista! "And we've been hanging out ever since. I guess if the new bakery happens, we'll be hanging out a lot."

I bite down a smile.

Now I have one more reason that the bakeout needs to do its magic.

"Seriously, though, I promise I won't ask you too much about the magical baking stuff," I vow. "And I think I've figured some things out myself. Like, for a while I wondered why the magic doesn't show up at work all the time, or maybe it's just . . . quieter? But when I bake for myself, when I bake for people I know, that's got more of *me* in it." That's when I use my baking as a place to work through my own feelings and share them with people I care about.

Those brownies were the big exception. I couldn't hold back what I felt in that moment.

Marisol picks a flower, dismembers it prettily. "Sometimes we use work to hide, too. To not feel as much. Like it's easier to make cake for strangers and pretend it's just a job, like it's not your soul."

I swear that I'm going to limit myself to one question. "So, now that I know what I can do, what happens next?"

Marisol bats me on the shoulder with a wildflower. "Now you get *comfortable* with it. You learn how to work with your power and you can do pretty amazing things." She gestures around at everything we've done here today. The whole big bakeout, the crowds, the community. We found a way to bring everyone back together right when it seemed like we were breaking apart.

"I still can't believe that you *and* Alec . . ." I flash on the hazelnut cake. While I was eating it, I could feel secrets deep inside of me loosening up, coming free. I had Alec's magical bake in my hands and I didn't even know it.

"Syd, you have gotta stop thinking you're alone." Marisol stands up. "Speaking of which . . . I talked to the others. And we all agree that if you want in on running the new Proud Muffin, you can be our sixth." As if she can't offer me something so sweet without a little acid to balance it, she adds, "*When* you turn eighteen."

A week ago, I would have snapped that offer off the table and said yes as quickly as possible. Today, all I can think about is Alec, and how hard he's been beaming ever since he decided to go back to the kitchen. Plus, my brain is sending out warnings that running a bakery is going to be just as much organizing work as this bakeout—but every single day. I want to help the Proud Muffin however I can, but I have a lot to learn from people like Marisol and Gemma and D.C. before I'm in charge of anything, or anyone. "I think I'm going to just bake for now. Ask me again in a few years?"

Marisol looks over her sunglasses at me with no small amount of suspicion. "That's the most mature thing you've ever said."

We head back to the bakeout just as the afternoon melts

into evening. What used to be five hundred different bodies in direct sunlight is now one big silhouette, touched with yellow from all the string lights. Nobody seems to be leaving.

Nobody wants to walk away.

I wonder how much of the money Gemma and D.C. have tallied. I need to know if we're having a wild celebration tonight, or a wake.

"All right," Gemma shouts, as if she could hear my thoughts. "We have some good news. We've reached ninety percent of our fundraising goal, which is a shit ton of money that you gave to save the best bakery in Austin!"

Cheers rise up.

D.C.'s voice rises above them. "But ninety percent isn't one hundred percent. If people can dish out just a *little bit* more . . ."

I can feel the crowd deflate under the weight of this news.

We've given everything we have.

It's not happening.

And somehow, we're supposed to pick ourselves up and have an afterparty.

"Wait," I say, my voice rising to a shout. "Harley said not to start the afterparty until—"

"Where *is* Harley?" Marisol asks.

A light from the end of the driveway answers our questions. It's not a car—we've barricaded the driveway so nobody can park near the house, and back here there are only dirt paths.

I know what that light is. The flickering white headlamp of a bike.

Actually, it's more than one bike. Harley seems to be at the head of a small bike parade. I run halfway down the drive to meet them. As the headlamps pulls closer, I can see that Harley is on Shadowfax this time, flanked by two small people wearing pink helmets with Proud Muffin stickers on them. Dean and Verity wave at me. Bringing up the rear is a strawberry-blonde person with the same stubborn smile as Dean and the same curls as Harley.

Harley lets the bike fall right before reaching me. They've got their messenger bag back firmly around one shoulder. I didn't realize until just now how strange it looked to see them biking around without it.

"What's going on?" I ask. "Why did you leave right in the middle of . . . everything?"

"I couldn't carry this around with me all day," they say. "Besides, I wanted to surprise everyone."

"Okay, we are duly surprised," I say, looking back at my confused coworkers.

"Do you want to know what I've been doing all week?" Harley's smile outshines the string lights. They rock back on the heels of their worn-out sneakers. They dig into the messenger bag and give me a leather envelope. I unzip it, finding it thick with bills. There has to be at least a thousand dollars here.

Then they take the checks out of their pocket.

"Don't say that the tech gays never helped anyone," Harley says. "I've been in every high-rise in Austin this week. Everywhere we ever delivered an office party cake or muffins for a morning meeting. Actually, I've gone basically everywhere we've ever made a delivery and gave out some baked goods as bribes. People *really* like being given unexpected sweet things," they say, as if this is a wild new concept to them.

"Why didn't you ask me for help?" I cry.

"We weren't really talking," Harley says, taking off their bike helmet and roughing up their curls, trying to get them to bounce back to life. "I mean, we were texting, but not *talking* talking." I know what Harley's saying. We weren't really being us together. "And you were so busy planning the bakeout—"

"We helped!" Dean shouts, running over to me. "We baked things! We got more bags of chocolate chips!"

"Hi, Syd! Hi, Syd!" Verity chimes as she joins us.

"Wait," I say. "I thought you weren't coming back to the bakery, and you were doing all of this to save it?"

Harley tugs at their front curl. "Well, I might need to focus on school next year. I am *sort of* in college." I want to laugh—that used to be one of our jokes. "But I need the Proud Muffin to be right there when I get back, you know? I need it to be there for everyone. Especially . . . especially you."

The night is warm and my hands are nervously sweating and my heart is doing this very hopeful sort of rising.

I just hope it doesn't deflate.

"Is there any cake left?" Harley's mom asks.

Harley's mom is talking to me.

"Ummm, yeah."

"There's always cake near Syd," Harley says.

"So this is Syd," Harley's mom says, giving me the most excruciating once-over. "All of my children talk about you quite a bit. I think you've got them under some kind of spell." She smiles and holds out her hand.

"Mom," Harley says, cutting her off. "Cake?"

"Right, right."

Dean, Verity, and Harley's mom head down the driveway toward the tents, leaving us to run the envelope of money and the checks over to the Proud Muffin employees, who've flocked around Gemma and D.C. As soon as they see what Harley's pulled off, everyone is shouting and crying. Vin and Alec watch us from a safe distance, looking elated and exhausted in equal measure.

Gemma grabs the megaphone. "Austin, you did it! You brought the Proud Muffin back from the brink!"

D.C. swoops in next to her, letting out incoherent sounds of joy. He finally gets it together enough to add, "You made it work and now it's time to work the dance floor at our afterparty!"

Lex hurries over to get the music going, but it looks challenging with one of her hands fused to Marisol's.

As a beat spills through the air, Harley pulls me aside.

We wander away from everyone else, but it feels like we're wandering with purpose, and soon I realize exactly where

Harley's taking me. The clearing with the chandelier in the live oaks. The one we sat under the first time we were here together. It's lit up now, casting a warm buttery glow.

"Okay," Harley says, turning to me and shoving their hands deep in their pockets. "We're going to finish this."

"Okay. Yeah." I brace myself for an argument, pointed and intense.

"I still have two questions left," they say softly.

"From Truth or Pie?" I ask, feeling suddenly terrified. But I promised Harley—I promised both of us—that I would see this through.

Harley stands alone in the chandelier's light, and the afterparty in the tent feels a million miles away. I want to be celebrating, but I need to know exactly what I'm gaining and what I'm losing tonight. "I asked you if you were ever really in love with W," Harley says.

"And now I know that—"

Harley shakes their head, and I fall silent. "Really I should have asked: Do you think you could fall in love with me someday?"

"No," I say, with complete honestly. Just as Harley's face twists I rush to add, "I think I already am."

The smile sneaks back onto Harley's face. "Second question. Where do you want to go on this magical diner road trip?"

"Everywhere," I say, joining them under the light of the chandelier.

Harley's arms fall around my shoulders like that's where they go, like they belong there. Their fingers clasp lightly around my neck. "That's a very Syd answer."

"Well, you're the navigator. You pick where we go first. And then I'll pick the next stop. And then we'll pick the third one togeth—"

Harley leans forward, burning off every last one of my worries as our lips meet. There's a lightness I didn't expect, a giddy relief that our beginning isn't over, a whisper of sweetness as our lips brush and mingle and melt. Without breaking away from each other, we both smile, and Harley spins me under the chandelier. I bring one hand up to their face and tug that front curl for good measure.

"So this is what it's like," I say.

"What?" Harley asks.

"The best night."

I drop another kiss on Harley's shoulder, where their tank top cuts off. "You know, all of this biking makes you delectably salty."

Harley wrinkles their nose, suddenly shy.

They kiss me lightly, carefully.

Then boldly.

I kiss them again and again and again—every kiss I wish I'd given them over the last few weeks. When my lips are nearly numb and my smile is exhausted, we twine our fingers, line up our arms, and head toward the biggest tent, walking with our sides pressed together.

The night is getting darker. The music's getting louder.

We stop at the edge of the crowd and watch the other proud muffins making the most of their time together.

"Come on," I say. "Let's dance it out."

We step onto the dance floor and face each other, and on the same downbeat we start to move with zero abandon. Harley's shoulders pedal around in circles as I leap and punch the warm air like risen dough. All around us, people churn and shout. The city shifts and changes. I take a big breath of this night, this perfectly unplanned moment, Harley so close to me.

It tastes like a beginning.

Acknowledgments

Thank you to the baking friends, kitchen coworkers, Texas writers, and LGBTQIAP+ communities that have brought so much joy to my life.

A special thanks to Vanessa Lee for making my time in Austin sparkle.

Thank you to everyone who helped test a recipe for this book! That includes my entire family, who have been helping me hone my bakes for years, with an extra helping of thanks to my sisters Christine and Allyson, and a very sweet new generation of bakers: Samantha, Emily, and Walter. More recipe testing was provided by the amazing Ann Dávila Cardinal, Andrea Corbin, Annie Crane, Becky Wright, Christine Engels,

Ian McGullum, Jules Bertaut, Lisa Keegan, Lucas Sanders, and Liam Synnott.

A double batch of appreciation to my wonderful friend Jess Taylor, who helped plot, plan, test, and taste with me as I drafted and revised. If you love to bake and enjoyed this book, please check out Jess's store, Capital Kitchen, in Vermont, and say that I sent you!

As always, thanks to Sara Crowe, the most amazing agent, who also gifted me the best panettone I've ever tasted.

This book would not exist without my wonderful editor Miriam Newman, who sent revision cookies along with our very first editorial letter. Fourteen emails into a thread about frosting, I couldn't help saying "I think I might have a book for you." The entire Candlewick team has been incredible in their support.

All of my love to Maverick, who started cracking eggs at four years old and is now my favorite baking buddy. I can't wait to see what we make next.

And to the readers of my books—you make so much of the magic in my life. I wanted to thank you with the perfect proud muffin recipe, but after endless deliberation and a few delicious contenders I realized that it would feel wrong to pick a single one for everybody. Whatever muffin you love most *is* the proud muffin. But here's a tip: fill your muffin cups all the way to the top, set your oven twenty-five degrees higher for the first five to ten minutes of bake time, then turn it back down. You'll end up with a beautiful bakery-style muffin, standing tall and proud.